YOU, ME, AND THE GOLDFISH

Young adult romance

M T Straker

ISBN: 1548476331
ISBN 13: 9781548476335
Library of Congress Control Number: 2017910450
CreateSpace Independent Publishing Platform
North Charleston, South Carolina

CHAPTER ONE

I glanced at my mother as I took away yet another plate of uneaten sandwiches, which I had left at her bedside table this morning before I went to college, along with the cold cup of tea. I cried as I walked into the kitchen; she looked like a skeleton. I was terrified that she was dying. She wouldn't open the curtains and only made an effort to get dressed on a Sunday when her friend Samantha visited. Samantha had also noticed how underweight my mother was and decided that she was depressed. Mum rarely left the flat, spent most of her time in bed or cleaning, read the same book day after day, ate occasionally, and talked about being chased by dinosaurs and seeing her aunt Rosy, who had died after her twentieth suicide attempt many years ago, yet mysteriously Mum had seen her in her bedroom.

Wherever you read about depression on a website, you see a list of symptoms like suicidal thoughts, delusions, hallucinations, haunted feelings, and fear of dying. Samantha believed that my mother needed help, so she suggested going with her to see her regular doctor, Dr. Zabin, who referred her to Dr. Goatbell Vadel, who agreed that my mother was drowning in a cocktail of wool-ly clinical depression, that she needed medication, and that she should attend a twice-weekly group-therapy session.

I offered to go with her because I was worried she wouldn't go alone. Mum did not like to talk about stuff, but she agreed to my offer. The group therapy comprised a variety of victims at different stages of helplessness. Some were pointing at the wall, while others were shaking their hands as if they were having conversations with their invisible selves—symptoms of withdrawal.

The group therapy, essentially, was depressing as hell. It took place every Monday and Friday in a glass-walled building at the back of the hospital training wing. To get to the elevator or stairs, you had to walk past the mortuary. We all sat in the front row of what looked like cinema seats arranged in a half-moon circle. There was a projector in the ceiling.

I noticed this because Christine, the therapist and the only per-son over fifty in the room, talked about a doctor's presentation on avoiding relapses every freaking meeting. The presentation was all about withdrawing from treatment, recovery models, how to pre-vent suicidal thoughts, and whatever.

So here's how it went on how to combat depression: the twelve or fifteen of us listened with anticipation, gazing at the display of cupcakes, juices, and water; sat down in the room of hope; and listened to Christine describe for the hundred-millionth time her manic, miserable life story. She told us how her cat died; she had bipolar disorder; she shaved off all her hair; she cut her wrists, and they thought she was going to die, but she didn't die; and now she was a mature woman in a modern hospital building in the finest city in England—a spinster; addicted to baking cupcakes; scraping a living by utilising her catatonic past; slowly researching her family tree, which she hoped would improve her understanding of mania.

Then all of them introduced themselves: name, symptoms, and how long they'd lived with their experiences. "I'm Jessica," Mum said when it was her turn. "A trained nurse. Threatened and taken hostage by a gang of maniacs armed with guns in my workplace originally, but slowly lapsing into a state of panic, loss of appetite, weight falling off. And I'm blessed to have my supportive daughter, Alexia."

I didn't have anything to add. As it happened, I was the only person under eighteen and without a diagnosis. Once they got around to the last person, Christine always asked if anyone wanted a drink and a cupcake. And then they began sharing their feelings: everyone was talking about the voices, objects, smells, loss of ability to taste, perceptions, and delusions of being watched. To be fair to Christine, she didn't disturb or distract anyone; she let people talk about hallucinations, too. But most of them weren't on the verge of suicide. Most would succeed in leading a normal life, as Christine had.

Like, I realised that this was my mum's possibly only chance of living again. Reality kicked in, and you would start to contemplate the what-if and maybe…so you would look around and think, as any sensible person would, "My mum is going to prove these bastards that did this wrong."

Another of the group-therapy attendees was a lady named Sophia: round faced, six feet tall, slim, with straight silver hair hanging down to her shoulders. She had a huge pair of sunglasses over her eyes—like, her whole face was basically dominated by the sunglasses. You weren't sure if she was staring at you or not.

And her sunglasses were the problem. She had some incredible delirium about her face. One cheek was puffier than the other, she had applied so much makeup that her face looked orange, and she kept touching her cheek—like, her whole feature was mainly just one swollen cheek. From what I could gather, her granddaughter had been murdered, and she had had a breakdown. On the odd occasion when Sophia shared her experiences with the group, we would hear that the cause of her trauma was a sudden bereavement.

She carried a picture of her granddaughter wherever she went and would show it to a few people in the group.

Sophia and my mum communicated virtually through tapping fingers on their cheeks. Every time someone commented on having insight into their problems or how many times they had relapsed or whatever, Sophia would extend her neck, peep at Mum, and tap her finger gently. Mum would tip her head to one side, shake her head slightly, and tap her cheek in response.

So group therapy whizzed by, and after about five weeks, Mum appeared to start being nurtured. I grew to be rather fascinated by the whole affair. In fact, one Friday, Mum made the acquaintance of Todd Walker, who showed an interest in her, and she tried her best to discourage me from going to group therapy with her while we sat on the sofa together, watching the tenth series of past episodes of Absolutely Fabulous, which admittedly we had already seen, but nevertheless.

"You need to be with your friends," she said. "I'll be okay at group therapy."

"I don't want you to relapse and start seeing dinosaurs again," I said. "One of the symptoms of depression is denial."

"Why not invite your friend over? You can watch a movie. I'm okay, really."

"You will be lonely without me."

"Alexia, you're a teenager. You need to be with people your own age. You need friends. Wear makeup, play computer games, go shopping. You cannot be with me all the time. I need to be your mum, take control. You need to get out of the habit of attending group therapy with me and live your life."

"I will be a teenager once I'm sure you're back to being my mum. You need to continue attending group therapy, and I'm going with you."

"Alexia, teenagers your age don't want to be with their mum on a Friday evening."

"If you weren't depressed, you would be at work, and I would be spending the night at my friends', going out, faking my age to the bouncers to get into nightclubs, drinking shots, and smoking cannabis."

"You can't stand the smell of detergent, and drugs don't smell any better, so that's a nonstarter, missy."

"How would I know if I'm not given a chance to try?"

"Okay, you can come to group therapy for the last time."

"But..."

"Alexia, you ought to have a life."

That was it; we both knew the truth—that attending group therapy had its benefits to my mum's health and well-being, but for me, on the other hand, the only benefit was to see her get well. I missed normality, I missed my mum, and she didn't smile any more. I went to group therapy with her for the same reason that I'd allowed myself to believe that my dad would come back after he'd had enough of working in exotic places. I wanted us to be a normal, happy family. There are only two things on this planet: happiness and hopelessness. If that wasn't scary enough, according to research, one in four people in the world experiences depression in the course of his or her life.

The bus pulled into the stop opposite the hospital at 5:35 p.m. Mum pretended to be searching in her handbag while the other passengers got off. I kept looking at her, thinking the bus was going to move at any minute. The next stop was a twenty-minute walk away; we needed to get off.

"What are you looking for?"

"Just making sure I've not forgotten the flat keys," she said. She had used the keys to lock the door—how could she forget that? We got off the bus, but instead of walking into the front of the hospital, Mum wanted to take a scenic route.

"Where are we going?" I asked, following her.

"I want to show you something," she said, taking my hand as if I was a small child.

We walked by the side of the hospital, passed the library, and were about to step on the zebra crossing. I was wondering what she wanted to show me when we got distracted by a woman's voice: Sophia, calling through the rolled-down window of a black limousine that stopped just before the crossing, in a parking space that read Reserved for Doctors on Call. Mum and I crossed and walked over to the limousine.

A security man came rushing, waving a long finger in the air, saying that this parking space was not for public use. My mum gave him one of her questioning looks that stopped him in his tracks.

"Dawson, how are you?" asked Mum.

"Jessica, what a surprise. I'm okay, and you?" Dawson's lips curled into a smile. "Friends of yours?" he continued.

"Okay, yes, they're friends," said Mum.

Dawson nodded, turning to the driver of the limousine. "Five minutes, mate."

Dawson walked back to his little cabin. I wanted to ask Mum how she knew this man, but I was already distracted by Sophia.

"Jessica, Alexia, can I walk with you?" Sophia asked as the driver opened the door. She stepped out, followed by a young man.

"Sure," Mum said.

I found myself staring at this hot, well-groomed man with bronze hair that was swept back and neatly shaved behind his ears. He was long and lean, wearing a charcoal suit, light-green shirt, and a black tie. With enormous blue eyes flashing above sharp cheekbones. He rested one arm on Sophia's shoulders. He looked about early twenties, possibly older; I started to wonder if he was her son, friend, or whatever.

"That's my grandson, Justin," she said.

He extended his hand to shake Mum's and my hands.

"A pleasure to meet you, Jessica, Alexia," he said, smiling.

Oh my God, he had a sexy smile. Sophia was wearing a shocking-pink dress, her dark shades covered her eyes, and pearls dripped around her neck; she looked more like a celeb than someone who was attending group therapy.

"Shall we go? Nice to meet you, Justin," said Mum, pulling my arm.

"Yes, we should." Sophia kissed Justin on the cheeks and said, "Darling, send the car for me at seven thirty."

"Of course, Gran, see you then."

As we walked away, I wanted to look back, but that would have been too obvious, so I kept walking in between Mum and Sophia. We were heading for the elevator when Mum remembered what she wanted to show me and said that if it wasn't too dark, she would show me after group therapy. I grabbed a cupcake, poured some juice in a plastic cup, and looked around for free seats. There were two empty seats next to each other and one next to this guy who was gazing at my mum.

I'd never seen him before. He was tall and beefy and had broad shoulders. His legs were extended, and his arms rested on the arms of the cinema chair he was sitting on. His hair was black, curly, and short. He looked my mum's age—maybe a few years older. His posture was macho—regimental, like someone with a military background, and he wore combat trousers and a T-shirt advertising some computer game I'd never heard of. I looked away, swiftly conscious that Christine was glaring at me. I thought, Don't make a move on my mum, Mr. Whoever; she's here for hope—not to find a boyfriend. Mum was wearing an old maroon dress that had once fitted her frame but was now hanging off her shoulders, swinging on her body. Her hair, desperately in need of a cut, was pulled into a high ponytail, and she hadn't bothered to comb it. Furthermore, she had outrageously bony cheeks—a side effect of being extremely underweight. She was all skin and bones.

And yet she was also looking at him, and his eyes were still on her. She walked over and sat down next to Sophia, a few seats away from the guy. I was still standing and couldn't make up my mind where to sit—not that I had much choice; the only available seat was next to that guy. I didn't want to sit next to him. Christine was looking for a volunteer to practise on for today's session, and I took her up on the offer so I could sit in front of the group. I glanced again. He was still watching Mum.

Look, let's put this into perspective: I wanted my mum to be happy; he wasn't bad looking, but he wasn't as good looking as my dad. When a man who's not your dad stares at your mum persistently, it is at best embarrassing and at worst offensive. But how could I stop him?

I sat on the carpeted floor, crossing my legs on top of one another in meditation position on Christine's instructions. She pulled out an old cassette player, inserted a cassette, and initiated breathing exercises. "Breathe deeply through your nose, allowing your stomach to pull inward, then exhale, letting your stomach expand. In anxiety-provoking situations we breathe too quickly—learning to breathe slowly is more therapeutic." The man was still staring at my mum. I felt like walking over and poking a finger into his ribs but realised that wouldn't be wise.

This was a weird situation; I readjusted my legs, feeling a little uncomfortable. I was not used to sitting in that position, so I rested my feet on the floor and glanced at Mum. She was chatting to Sophia, not engaging in a staring contest with the guy. Christine pushed play on the cassette, and music that sounded like waves breaking on the shore played gently. She asked everyone to close their eyes and imagine that they were on a beautiful beach in some island paradise, safe and warm, relaxing, and free from depression. She went on about an effective strategy to use when experiencing anxiety or insomnia, and after a while it was time to open our eyes. I looked the guy over as Christine switched the cassette off, and he was on the edge of his chair having a staring competition with my mum. After a long while, he smiled and glanced at me.

Finally, pulling myself onto my feet and glaring at him, I flicked my eyebrows up as if to say, "Stay away from my mum."

He frowned. Christine carried on, and then at long last, it was time for the introductions. "Sophia, perhaps you'd like to be first. I know you're going through a difficult time."

"Yes, I'm Sophia. My granddaughter was murdered five months ago—she was only eighteen—but the strangest thing is that I keep seeing her everywhere. And my family doesn't believe me; they think that I'm losing my mind, that I'm mad. My cheeks have been puffy since; my doctor can't find anything wrong with me; that's the reason I'm here. Not to complain or anything, because I was a very shy person. Attending this group therapy has been a wonderful experience. I mean, I still see my granddaughter, but the anxiety of seeing her is not as stressful as before. The police haven't caught her murderer yet, but the investigation is ongoing. Losing someone in such tragic circumstances does suck when the culprit is still at large. My husband helps, though—and my grandson, Justin, the only member of my family who has always supported me." She touched her cheek. "So, yes," Sophia continued. She was looking at my mum, who had folded her hands into each other on her knee, as if she was praying. She placed a hand on Mum's arm. "Meeting friends like Jessica and her daughter, Alexia, who's given up her Friday evening with her friends to be here with her mum, help me to realise the importance of a family."

"We're here to encourage you, Sophia," Christine said. "Put your hands together, everyone, for Sophia."

And then we all clapped, chanting, "We're here to encourage you, Sophia."

Mum was next. "My name is Jessica. I'm a mother. Gun threat in the workplace, which causes continuous anxiety." To be fair, Mum had been struggling with anxiety since I was five, maybe longer. From what I can remember, she'd always been on medication. She'd managed to keep her job while looking after me. She was okay, or so she believed, popping another tablet into her mouth.

Dad was working away a lot, always somewhere I couldn't pronounce the name of. I pretty much grew up with Samantha, Mum's best pal and also my godmother. She didn't have children of her own, so she was happy to be my sort-of surrogate mum when Mum was on night shifts. Samantha had a niece called Mia, and she and I had been best friends since age five. Mia was now seventeen like me and attractive enough to be an object of desire in boys' eyes. She was good at sports and listening; she was my biggest supporter in a long battle with my mum's depression.

Mum talked about the day she found out that Dad was having an affair with some exotic woman and about how she'd wanted to protect me; how I used to pack my rucksack and sit by the window, waiting for my dad to come and pick me up, but he never arrived; and how she would console me by watching Disney movies together, which I had not previously known was her calming solution. She said, as she did the first time she attended group therapy, that she wanted to get stronger—beat her demons. I realised that yes, I needed my own life with people of my own age.

There were a few others before they got to the guy. He dropped his shoulders a little when it was his turn. His voice was calm, smoky, and dead smooth. "My name is Todd Walker," he said, "ex-army. I was shot in my balls over two years ago, but they managed to save me. I'm here today at medical request."

"And what are your symptoms?" asked Christine.

"Oh, well, the fucking nightmare, excuse my French." Todd Walker beamed with a corner of his mouth. "The same visions of war zones and dismembered body parts everywhere, the smell of gun residue. It's known in the medical profession as 'posttraumatic stress disorder.'"

When it was my turn, I said, "My name is Alexia. I'm seventeen. No diagnosis or symptoms. Here to support my mum, Jessica, who I love very much."

The hour moved along swiftly. As I looked around, it kept drumming in my brain that all these people in the room were adults—thirty plus. I was a teenager. I needed to find a place that supported young people like me who were living with a parent who was battling depression or other sorts of mental-health problems. I'd remembered reading an article in the local paper about a charity that provided support for what were called "young carers," or young people caring for ill parents. Although I wasn't exactly my mum's carer, my life involved making sure that she was okay, took her medication, ate, attended group therapy, and so on. That, plus my college work on top, but that was okay too. All I wanted was for her to get better.

Neither Todd Walker nor my mum spoke again until Christine said, "Todd, perhaps you'd like to share your experiences in the battlefield—prior to your injury—with the group?"

"My experiences?"

"Yes."

"At the beginning, I was a hero experiencing every boy's dream of going to war. I had my first pistol at the age of four."

Everyone glared at Todd. "A pistol at the age of four? Surely not." said Christine.

"Okay, it was a toy pistol filled with water. Dad and I chased each other in the garden." He laughed loudly. "My first army posting was in the Middle East, sampling black olives, mint tea. A fantastic experience fighting for your country, like doctors and nurses who're not afraid to save life. It's horrible when someone takes it all away."

"That's what we're trained for," Mum said, smiling.

"You're a nurse, I take it?" asked Todd, looking at my mum.

"Yes, that is my profession," said Mum. "I was about to finish my twelve-hour shift when a gang of armed hooligans stormed into accident and emergency, where I was working, threatening to end my life."

"How insensitive," Todd said. "You have my sympathy. That showed they had no respect or feeling for others."

Mum was laughing; it was the first time in a long time that I'd seen my mum laughing. It was amazing that a complete stranger had managed to make her laugh. They were staring at each other flirtatiously. A lump was growing in my throat, but before I could open my mouth, Christine interrupted with her hand in the air and said, "Todd, let's focus on your adventures in foreign locations. Some of us haven't set foot in London, let alone a foreign country. You said you ate black olives—what about the war itself?"

"That was good too," Todd answered. "Being a soldier was the best experience."

Christine looked at Todd, she seemed to be expecting him to expand on his experiences, but he had gone quiet. "Would anyone else like to share his or her experiences?"

I hadn't been out with a boy or kissed one in my seventeen years. Most teenage girls my age had a boyfriend, a weekend job; some worked in shops, others in pubs. Mia was my best friend. I spent my weekends with my mum, having the same conversation on the subject that my room needed cleaning again, even though I'd cleaned it last weekend. I was bored, fairly shy, and wouldn't say boo to a mouse. I preferred watching sports over participating because I wasn't good at any sport. I had never had a black olive—Mum didn't like things that were a bit foreign.

I decided that was probably my only chance to ask a question. I raised my hand, and Christine, her delight evident, instantaneously said, "Alexia!"

Being part of the group therapy was a big deal.

I glanced over at Sophia and Mum, and they both looked back at me. To my surprise Sophia took off her sunglasses. You could almost see through her eyes; they were ocean blue. Why did she wear those dark glasses? Presumably to hide her anxiety. "Excuse me, Mr. Walker, what does a black olive taste like? Is it like a black grape?"

"Alexia, no need to use mister—Todd will do. Olives taste really great. Not as sweet as grapes. In the Arab world, extra-virgin olive oil is used for salads. It is also very tasty with bread. The Italians use black olives to decorate pizzas. If it is okay with Christine, I'll bring a jar to the next group," he said, looking at Christine.

Christine smiled. "My friend is an Italian chef. He's got a restaurant not far from here—he would be happy for the group to sample pizza with a combination of toppings. Leave it with me; I will make the arrangements."

"Oh, thanks, Christine," I said. "Sorry, I've had pizzas before with my friend Mia, but with cheesy topping—I've never eaten black olives."

There was a slightly awkward pause, and then Christine said, "That's okay; you've been such a support to the group. Alexia, may I make a suggestion?"

"Yes, please."

"If Todd would bring a jar of black olives, I will arrange for you and your mum, or a friend, to have pizzas at my friend's restaurant."

"That's very generous of you, Christine and Todd, but you don't have to go to such expense for me."

"No, no, it is nothing to do with expense," insisted Christine.

"Thank you, Christine, Todd. Much appreciated."

After that there was a period of silence as I watched a smile spread across Sophia's face. Her dark glasses were still off, and her cheeks looked red even beneath all the makeup she had on. Sophia said quietly to my mum. "Alexia is a wonderful girl—she reminds me so much of my granddaughter. Jessica, you're very lucky."

Mum squeezed Sophia's arm and smiled, looking at me. "She's a good girl. We're very close."

I looked around. The group therapy had been a godsend for my mum and me. There was time before this when I didn't think we would survive the continuous anxiety of hallucinations. Mum slept with a pillow over her ears to block out the voices. There was a time when I wanted to run away—especially when she covered the TV with duvets because she thought that the voices were coming from it. Then one day I got home from college to find her collapsed on the bathroom floor after she cut her wrists. It was awful. I called Samantha. Mum was taken to hospital by ambulance. Sam went with her and came home later. I thought Mum was going to die. After that she promised me and Sam that she wouldn't cut herself again.

I was also conscious of the others in the room; they seemed reluctant to share their experiences with the group. Finally, a woman named Joanna raised her finger. Christine always encouraged the group—her joyful voice instantly said, "Joanna!"

"God is the power of all things; he knows what others don't," she said. "I was in love with a man I met through a dating agency. At first, I believed that he was in love with me, but I soon realised that he was a thief. When I couldn't find my gold necklace my mother gave me for my twenty-first birthday, I asked him if he'd seen it. His answer was 'I've pawned it to keep the drug dealer off my back.' That was the last time I saw him." Joanna struggled with tears dripping down her cheeks.

Christine walked over to her and put a hand on her shoulder. Todd was listening. "That's an awful experience, Joanna," he said. "I was fooled by a girlfriend when I was nineteen years old, but I soon realised that she was a cold, heartless person when she put my puppy in the bin. People like that worry me. I encourage you to forget it—you're here amongst friends."

It became obvious to me that all the people in the room had had some distressing experiences, and they were all in here searching for hope, normality, and a way to move on with their lives. I'd started reading the Bible some months ago in the hope of finding a solution to my mum's depression. I also found comfort in my secret best friend, Vanessa Helena Amadeo, the author of *Seeking Angels*. Vanessa Helena Amadeo was the only person who seemed to understand what it was like to live with someone who's depressed. Through my research I learned about her own suffering when her mother vanished.

There was another long silence. At the end, we all sat quietly and closed our eyes. Christine played another cassette, and we listened to calming music—whales chanting repeatedly, sounds of the ocean. Then Christine said, "I thank you all for today and every other day that you've made the effort to leave your home to attend group therapy. I understand how difficult it is, but we're here to encourage and support one another. Listening to soothing music helps us to relax—especially when we're disturbed by hallucinations. You're not alone; it's good to talk and share your feelings and experiences with the group. That's how we become stronger. Suppression is not the answer, and remember that we're fortunate to be free—to go out without asking permission. There are those who are detained, their freedom taken away, being watched while they are on the toilet, without any dignity. We pray for those who have lost the battle and now rest in peace."

I looked over at my mum. Her eyes were still closed; so were Sophia's. Christine was going on about a friend who refused to be admitted to a ward without her cats, which were her therapy. Christine had one of those unusual voices that would put anyone to sleep. She didn't stop talking when everybody had stopped listening to what she was saying, but then she also knew how to get everyone's attention.

When Christine had finished talking about cats, she reminded the group that she had recorded a relaxation tape for everyone and also that they shouldn't forget to take a cupcake on the way out. Two of the people I thought were snoring were first in line for cupcakes. Todd pushed himself out of his chair and walked over to my mum. I stepped in front of his massive frame; he towered over me and Mum, but he kept his distance. He was polite, to be honest. "What's your name?" he asked my mum.

"Jessica Collins."

"I'm going to go for a pizza; would you and your daughter like to join me?"

"Er," Mum said, "Sophia has already invited me and Alexia for pizza. Another time perhaps." He opened his mouth to say something else when Sophia grabbed my arm gently. "Is it okay with you, Alexia? My treat?" asked Sophia.

I nodded.

"Hold on," Todd said, running a hand over his head and turning to my mum. "I'll drive, as I understand we're going to the same pizza restaurant. It makes sense."

"That won't be necessary, Todd. My grandson is meeting us," said Sophia.

"Oh, okay. I'll leave you to it. See you there."

Suddenly, *bang, bang, bang.* The sounds took everyone by surprise. We all looked towards the back—that seemed to be where they were coming from—nothing. Christine was packing her bags. She stopped and walked between the seats to see if something had fallen. We all looked at her. She came back after a few moments without finding anything that could have caused the sounds. "That's very mysterious," she said.

Mum frowned. "How peculiar."

"Yes, it's strange. That was definitely a bang," said Todd.

While everyone was distracted, I looked towards the back of the room again. A young lady with pale skin and golden hair sat on a seat at the very back. "Oh my God," I said. "Look, there's a lady sitting at the back with golden hair."

Everyone looked together, but there wasn't anyone there. Where had she gone?

Sophia shook her head. "Sorry. No doubt that was my granddaughter. She comes and goes in a flash."

"Sophia, you mean that was a ghost?" I asked.

Sophia nodded slowly as she took the picture out of her handbag and showed it to me. Todd, who refused to move; Mum; me; and Christine, who had given up on packing, joined us in staring at the picture and then at the back of the room.

"Does the person in the picture look like what you saw, Alexia?" asked Sophia.

"Well there's some similarity, but it's difficult to say that she's the same person in the picture."

Sophia put a hand on my shoulder gently. I kept looking at the back in the hope of seeing her again. Oh my God, how cool was this, seeing my first ghost? But then I closed my eyes, imagining how painful it was to keep seeing someone who was dead—too painful to contemplate. We took the stairs—Todd and Christine followed behind, and Mum and Sophia chatted as they walked. Outside Justin was waiting by a flowerbed, talking on his mobile. He had ditched the suit for jeans and a polo top. I liked it.

Sophia was looking around as if she was expecting to see someone else. "Darling, is Granddad not with you?" she asked.

"He's meeting us at the restaurant with Mum and Dad."

Sophia nodded. He put his phone in his trouser pocket, reached for Sophia's arm, and gave her a kiss on her cheek. Justin leaned in, thinking we couldn't hear. "Shall we invite Jessica and her daughter for dinner, Gran?" I couldn't hear Sophia's reply, but Justin responded, "Fantastic." He looked at me. I couldn't help it but stare back; this was a hot guy. Todd said that he would see us at the restaurant. Sophia was back linking arms with my mum, leaving me to walk with Justin. He towered over me, walking slowly next to me behind Mum and Sophia.

"How was the group therapy, Alexia?" Justin asked quietly.

"Um, okay."

"Do you find it beneficial?"

"Oh, I don't go to group therapy for me. I go to support my mum."

Justin remained silent, studying the pavement. "You are still at college, from what I understand," he finally said.

"Yes, I am."

Dawson waved a hand as we passed by the ambulance entrance. "Jessica, it's great to see you getting back on your feet. Hope to see you at work soon."

Mum look at him, bewildered. "Me too, Dawson," she replied.

For the first time, I remembered Mum mentioning Dawson, the security guard who apparently too had helped her. A young gorgeous female walked past us. "Hi Justin, how are you?" she asked. He smiled and mumbled, "Hello, Beth. Good, thanks."

"She is a doctor who helped me and my family say good-bye to my sister," he explained.

"I'm sorry," I said, my voice lower than I expected it to be. He nodded, pointing to the black limousine waiting on the road by the hospital. For the first time, Mum glanced back to look at me. The driver held the back door; we slid onto the leather seat, and Mum looked around. We weren't used to such a lifestyle—bus and bike were more our sort of transport. Justin sat at the end of the seat, I squeezed at the far corner at the other end of the seat, and Mum sat beside Sophia. The car moved away, and I looked at Mum, who was chatting with Sophia. Oh God, they look so relaxed and normal—not two people who were suffering from depression. I peeked at Justin; he had a serious expression on his face. I wondered what he was thinking about. I wondered if he had also seen his sister's spirit. I watched Mum and thought about the way Todd looked at her. I couldn't bring myself to imagine what it would be like to see Mum with a boyfriend.

CHAPTER TWO

We stepped out of the limo, and I looked at the surroundings: busy street with cafés and restaurants, wine bars, people laughing and joking. I could smell booze and tobacco. Two teenagers about my age walked past in skinny jeans and T-shirts, their heels click-clicking on the pavement. There were bright lights overhead, and I could hear the distant sound of the metro. It was amazing; I couldn't remember the last time I was out on a Friday night, watching people enjoying themselves. Todd leaned against a wall, smoking a cigarette. I looked at Mum. She had stopped smoking when she started group therapy, just like she did not drink coffee anymore; nicotine and caffeine kept her awake, and sleeplessness caused her to think bad thoughts. She shouldn't go back.

Mum took my arm and looked at Sophia. "What is the name of the restaurant we are going to?" she asked.

"Tito's," said Sophia, pointing to a building with a huge circular window.

Mum looked around, noticing the big illuminated sign. "Oh yes, we'll see you inside. Need to visit a cash machine."

"There's one across the road," said Justin. "We'll wait for you."

Mum glanced at the cash machine and passing traffic. She was looking for a crossing—the road was pretty busy and the traffic light with pedestrian crossing was a good walk away from the restaurant. "No need to wait for us," she said. "It will take Alexia and I some time to get safely across the road. We'll see you inside."

"Look, wait a minute," Justin said. "I'm sure there's a cash machine on this side of the road. I'll see Gran into the restaurant—Granddad and my parents are there—then I'll come with you."

Mum shrugged, staring at Justin and Todd, who had joined us. "My daughter and I are quite capable of looking after ourselves, but as you are so polite, we'll appreciate your company if it's not too much trouble."

"No trouble at all—it is my pleasure," said Justin.

Todd was about to say something. Justin placed a hand on his shoulder. "I don't believe we've met—I'm Justin." He turned to Sophia. "That's my gran."

"Todd Walker, friend of Sophia and Jessica from the group, and it just happens that we are all fancy a pizza tonight." He laughed.

Justin nodded, looking at Todd with a smile at the corner of his mouth. "Nice T-shirt," he commented.

"Oh, I'm a total computer-game addict."

Mum and I waited while Justin walked Sophia to the door of the restaurant. Todd didn't move; he kept looking at Mum. Justin came back. "I've checked on my phone; there's a cash machine a few buildings away from the restaurant."

"Perfect," said Mum. "It is very generous of Sophia to invite Alexia and I to join you for dinner, but we've come out with very little cash."

Justin said, "I understood."

We walked in silence, me between Mum and Justin. I watched people walking past and wondered if they were going out for dinner like us and then back home to maybe watch a movie, or if they were going to bars and then nightclubs and dancing till late. A group of teenagers passed by, giggling. I peeped at Mum—she'd noticed me looking at them, and she reached and took my arm. She knew that I loved her more than anything in the world, but she also knew that I needed to get out of the habit of spending Friday and every other night with her.

Suddenly a man ran towards us, shouting abusively to another man running after him. He almost knocked Mum off her feet. She gripped my arm as the man lost his balance and stumbled onto the pavement. Justin paused. "You okay?" he asked Mum, looking concerned.

"Yes, thank you. That wasn't necessary," said Mum.

"Friday-night drinking. Sometimes they don't mean to frighten anyone; they just lose control when they're drunk," he explained.

The man was lying on the pavement where he'd tripped. Justin asked him if he was okay. The man mumbled something that sounded like "my brother." Another man who was running after the man who was now on the pavement stopped and looked at us and then the man on the pavement. It took him a few moments to speak.

"It's okay, mate—I'll take care of him," he said. "He's my brother, and he's just lost his job. He's a pussycat normally—never hurt a soul."

Justin nodded, and we carried on to the cash machine. Mum took some money out, and we went back to the restaurant. Sophia sat at a big round table by the window with a younger couple and a grey-haired man in a blue knitted jumper. They all stood up.

"This is my friend Jessica and her beautiful daughter, Alexia, who I told you about," said Sophia. "That is my husband, Gary, and Justin's parents—our son, Peter, and daughter-in-law, Rachel."

"Lovely to meet you," Mum said, shaking their hands. I smiled, not sure what to say.

"Jessica and Alexia: a pleasure to meet at last," said Gary. "My wife can't stop talking about you and how wonderful it has been to have met you both. You are a great comfort to her," said Gary.

"Yes, you've been great to my mum," added Peter.

"Well, thank you," Mum said. "We're all going through a challenging time, and we all need support and encouragement. And thank you, Sophia, for inviting my daughter and I to join you for dinner. We appreciate it—don't we, Alexia?" She looked at me for a response.

"Thank you, Sophia," I mumbled.

"You are welcome, angel," said Sophia.

Justin pulled out two chairs, Mum and I sat down next to each other, and then everyone sat down. Justin sat next to me. I noticed an empty chair next to mum and wondered if they were expecting someone else. I looked around the restaurant; it was small, with a high ceiling and old-fashioned lights hanging down, purple walls, and a picture of a canal with buildings on each side and men in gondolas. I knew that it was somewhere in Italy, but I couldn't remember where. Mum and I watched a film where James Bond was being chased by men on a canal that looked just like the one in the picture.

"Venice," Justin said quietly.

"Oh yes."

"Jessica, we've invited Todd to join us," said Sophia. "He was planning to have dinner on his own."

"Oh, I see," Mum replied.

A few minutes later, Todd walked in from outside and sat next to Mum. I wished Sophia hadn't encouraged him. The waiter came with menus and passed them around. While we read the menu, he asked what everyone would like to drink. He was young, short, and slim, with short black hair and the most amazing Italian accent. I looked at Mum; she ordered water and I a Diet Coke. Justin also ordered a Diet Coke. I noticed his granddad giving him a crooked smile. Justin shrugged. Todd ordered a beer.

"Shall we have a bottle of red?" asked Gary to his wife, son, and daughter-in-law.

The waiter handed him the wine list. Gary opened it and held it up so that Sophia could read the list too. It took a few moments.

Gary handed the list back to the waiter, looking at Sophia. "Any red in particular, my love?" he asked.

"I've not had a drink since…" Sophia stopped midsentence. Gary rubbed the back of her neck. She looked sad.

"Give us a moment, please," Gary said to the waiter. He then turned to Sophia. "We all miss her, love, and you're doing great. Going to group therapy has taken lots of courage—you've made friends and are going out again. It's all about us trying to reestablish some normality." He hugged his wife.

Sophia smiled. "You're right, my darling. One small glass of red wine wouldn't hurt; it would probably help me sleep." She looked wistful as she said this. "What about a bottle of Poggerissi Rosso, fruity and perfect with pizzas or pasta?"

Justin glanced at his gran, smiling. The waiter came back with the drinks and Gary ordered a bottle of Poggerissi Rosso, the name rolling off the tip of his tongue. I assumed it was an Italian wine. Rachel, Justin's mother, kept looking at me—it was hard to imagine what she was thinking about. Did she see the spirit of her daughter too, I wondered?

Todd leaned over the table, looking at Justin. "Have you got any preference in computer games?" he asked.

"Preference? My son is the master behind some of the most famous computer games out there," said Peter. "Tell Todd about the monsters that took a small army hostage in the Middle East."

"Oh, Dad, Gran is looking a little sad right now, and no doubt we'll see Todd again," said Justin. "We could talk about computer games on another occasion."

Peter shrugged. "You're right, son. First night out in months. Let's enjoy this moment with friends."

Todd rubbed his chin, still looking at Justin. He seemed confused. "Wait a minute—you are not Justin, as in Justin Hunter?" he asked.

Justin said. "Started designing computer games at uni."

"Goodness, when I left home today I didn't realise that I, Todd Walker, would be fortunate to make the acquaintance of an intellectual giant like yourself." He reached across the table to shake Justin's hand.

"Yeah, great to meet you too," Justin responded. He turned to me. "Alexia, what is your favourite topping?"

"Basic—cheese and tomatoes. And you?"

"Are you a vegetarian?" he asked.

"No, I just like it simple, without meat."

"Well, my all-time favourite toppings are pepperoni, onions, tomatoes, black olives, and herbs with lots of parmesan cheese on a thin pizza base."

"It sounds delicious. I've never had black olives."

"Really?"

I shrugged.

The waiter arrived with the bottle of red wine, poured four glasses, and got his little order book out his pocket. "Are you ready to order?" he asked.

Sophia was watching Justin and me whispering to each other. "Alexia, why don't you go first, as you are our special guest tonight," she said.

I didn't realise that I was her special guest. Anyway, I was hungry, so I ordered a small pizza with tomatoes, black olives, and cheese. Mum smiled at me. She ordered chicken, mixed peppers, and to my surprise, black olives. After everyone had placed their orders, Gary asked the waiter to bring a combination of olives and garlic bread.

Suddenly I remembered at college, all the kids were addicted to Justin's computer games, which were a main topic of conversation besides clothes, dad who's working away, dating, and their favourite books and films. I'd never played any of his games, and here I was sitting next to him. How cool was that?

"So what are you doing after pizza?" he asked quietly.

"Going home with my mum," I said.

He looked at me.

"What's wrong with that?" I asked.

"Nothing," he said.

"Why are you looking at me like that?"

Justin leaned closer to me and smiled. "Because you're gorgeous. I like looking at you—a gorgeous girl who prefers to stay in with her mum on a Friday night is very rare." A brief awkward silence followed. He was flirting of course. "I mean, there's nothing wrong, essentially, given that as you so delightfully pointed out, you have never tasted black olives before, so there's a first time for everything."

I kind of nervously laughed or sighed or exhaled in a way that suggested I did not want Mum or anyone to hear our conversation. I was aware that his mum and Sophia were watching us, and I said, "I'm not gorg—"

"Yes, you're like Polly Walsh. Perfect eyes, Polly Walsh."

"Never heard of her," I said.

"Really?" he asked. "Dark-haired beautiful girl, played netball for the county, never had time for friends. She was a rebellious sort and fell for a naughty boy she knew was a school dropout. It's a true story, so far as I can tell."

He was flirting. Honestly, he whispered so sweetly it turned me on. I didn't actually know that guys could be so romantic—not, like, in real life.

"Is this meant to be a compliment?"

He glanced at me with the biggest smile. "So can I see you again after tonight?" he asked.

"Oh, maybe. It all depends."

"On what?" he asked.

"What I find out about you. I hardly know you—you could be an ex-convict."

"Fair point, Alexia, fair point." He took a sip of his Diet Coke and sat up with his back straight as he gave me another glance.

He looked confident. I looked across the table—his mum was still watching; she smiled, and I couldn't help but smile too.

The waiter came back with a bowl of olives and a small jar of wooden toothpicks. Justin took a toothpick, picked up an olive, and handed it to me. I looked before putting it in my mouth. It was a black olive. Oh my God—it tasted of herbs, but good. They were all looking at me, waiting for my reaction.

"Well?" asked Justin.

"I like it."

Sophia smiled. "I'm glad."

There was a long silence while everyone ate their olives, and then the garlic bread arrived. I decided to pass on the garlic bread and save my appetite for my pizza. Mum took an olive and popped it into her mouth—that surprised me; she did not normally like anything like that. Todd was talking about his time in the army and his experiences with war zones and olives. Everyone was listening with interest.

I thought it was a good time to visit the loo. On the way, I glanced around and saw that a tall, curvy girl had a guy pinned against the bar of the restaurant, kissing him pretty aggressively. I was so close that I could hear the strange noises of their lips together, and I could hear her saying, "It's our secret" and him saying, "Our secret" in return.

There was a long queue for the toilet. I joined it and waited for my turn. Suddenly, standing in front of me, a girl whispered into her mobile phone; I could hear her saying, "They are at Tito's bar, and I've heard them say that it was their secret. Hunter and his family are also in the restaurant—do you think I should call the police?" There was a pause before I heard her say, "But they were suspects in the Hunter girl's murder. I bet you they've killed that girl, and that's what they mean by their secret."

The queue moved at a slow pace. From where I was standing, I could still see the bar and the couple. I watched the guy, who proceeded as if he were not in a public place. His hand reached for her bum over her dress and squeezed it, his palm slowly moved up her back then back to her bum. I wondered if they were literally murderers and thought they had gotten away with it. Didn't seem likely, but there was a possibility. I decided not to mention this to Mum or Justin when I got back to the table on the grounds that it would spoil their dinner. A person must be innocent until proven guilty and whatever.

The pizzas arrived. Mine looked like a miniature version of the garlic bread with extra toppings next to Justin's twenty-inch pizza. "Imagine eating the last supper before death row," I said quietly. "The last meal you'll ever have."

Without looking at me, Justin said, "You're a funny girl, Alexia. I almost lost my appetite a minute ago observing young love in its awkwardness."

"She seemed to be comfortable with his hand on her bum," I whispered.

"Yes, he's got a reputation for trying to arouse girls in public places. They were both arrested for my sister's murder but released without charge." Then Justin grabbed his knife and fork and proceeded to attack his pizza. He cut a big piece and then a smaller square with pepperoni and a black olive on top, and he popped it into his mouth. I glanced at him, enjoying the mouthful. Thinking of the conversation I'd just heard. I chewed my lip, looking at Justin, I knew it was not the right time or place, but I had to say this.

"I can see that you weren't serious, then," I said. "Pepperoni still tastes great? They didn't manage to ruin it?"

"Ruin what?" he asked, turning to me. He put his knife and fork by the side of his plate, picked up his napkin, and wiped the corner of his mouth.

"Your appetite and the thing where a boy who just met me—a girl who spends her Friday night having dinner with grown-ups and then goes home with her mum because she cares for her. It is also inappropriate to compare me with some sporty person I have never heard of and then pretend to like me, because it isn't cool, even though you're grieving for your sister. I'm not some sort of experimental computer game that you play and then drop because it isn't interesting enough."

I was not angry with Justin, I was angry with myself. I missed my dad—the only thing Justin had done wrong was compare me with some sporty girl I've never heard of. He looked at me with his mouth open and put the napkin on the table. I had so many unanswered questions inside my head: Why was my mum depressed? Why did Sophia keep seeing her dead granddaughter? Did the couple at the bar hold the secret to her murder? What was the conversation I heard in the toilet queue all about?

"I need fresh air before eating my food," I said, rising to my feet.

Everyone was looking at me. Mum asked, "Are you okay, Alexia? You've not touched your pizza. I'll come with you."

"I'm okay—just need some air," I reassured Mum and everybody else.

"No, I'll go," I heard Justin say as I walked away.

I couldn't explain the way I felt—it was a mix of disappointment, loss, and anger. I didn't quite know what it was. There was a huge sense of loss, and I wanted to slap someone. Justin grabbed my hand before I reached the door. I tried to pull my hand free, but before I could, he opened the door and wrapped his arm around my shoulders.

"I'm so sorry if I've said anything to hurt your feelings in any way, Alexia," he said, standing on the pavement outside. "That was not my intention, I assure you."

"It isn't you; it's me," I said. "It's difficult to explain sometimes—to think clearly when so much responsibility rests on your shoulders."

"Look, I understand. Believe me."

"I really wanted to enjoy the pizza, and I really like your gran."

"Oh, yes." He smiled a big, genuine smile. "She likes you too. She can't stop complimenting you, Alexia."

I turned and looked up at him. "Shall we go back to the pizza? I feel much better, thank you," I said.

He laughed. "Sure. Maybe we could have another Diet Coke afterwards."

I smiled. "Maybe."

CHAPTER THREE

Justin Hunter and I sat quietly in the back seat of the limo on the way to my flat. His dad and grandad were joking about sport and some big football game that they intended to watch over the coming weekend, and they kept asking Justin who was going to play against whatever. He kept naming footballers I'd never heard of. His mum, gran, and my mum were talking about Christine and her love for cats, her delightful cupcakes, and so on.

I counted the traffic lights every time the limo stopped and started. It was a smooth drive—not like on the bus, where there's a strange noise each time the driver hits the gas, and where the person in the seat next to you knocks into you without an apology for hurting your ribs. I admitted to myself that I was nervous sitting next to a strange guy, deeply aware that my life was so complicated, and living with a mum who was depressed and seeing dinosaurs. Since she'd watched *Jurassic Park*, Mum kept having the same nightmare with roaring T. rex noises, and she rarely slept with the light off. Astonishingly, Mum appeared more relaxed since she started group therapy; she had not mentioned the nightmares or dinosaurs.

We'd gone perhaps a few miles in silence before Justin said, "Fancy catching a movie?"

"Sorry, I can't leave my mum alone."

"I get it," he said.

"Alexia, go and enjoy yourself," Mum said. "I'll be perfectly fine."

I didn't realise that she was listening while talking. Mum used to do that a lot when I was younger. When she used to pick me up from school, she would be chatting to other mums on the playground but heard everything I was saying to my friends. I remembered once a friend invited me for a sleepover, and I said I couldn't because Mum would be alone. Mum insisted that I go. She had not done this since depression had taken over the caring Mum I once knew, but she seemed to be slowly recovering control.

"Are you sure?"

"Yes, sweetie. Go and enjoy yourself."

I smiled. "Well, I shouldn't be later than eleven," I said, looking at Justin.

"I'll make sure you're back by eleven," Justin said.

Mum kept, looking at him. "You better," she said.

Sophia and Rachel laughed. "He's a good boy, our Justin," Rachel said. "Alexia will be in perfect hands."

Suddenly the driver slammed on the brakes, thrusting me into the triangular embrace of the seat belt. My neck snapped backwards. Justin and everyone looked concerned. Mum was holding Sophia's arm, Rachel grabbed the edge of her seat, and everyone looked around in shock.

"You okay?" asked Justin.

"Yes," I said.

Justin reached behind his head, opening the small window to speak to the driver. "What happened?" he asked.

"Sorry, sir. Someone ran into the road unexpectedly. Is everyone okay?"

"Just about," said Gary. "Poor Alexia here almost suffered whiplash."

"Apologies, sir."

"He's just managed to pass his driving test—after failing nine times," Gary said with a serious look. The old guy had a great sense of humour. I really liked this family. Even though they were going through their own distress, Gary could crack a joke. "Granddad, stop joking," said Justin. "You've always told me that Frank passed his driving test the first time, and that he was the safest driver on the road, and that's why you and Dad employed him."

"That's correct, son," said Peter, looking at me. "Alexia, my dad is a joker. Frank has been with us for many years. We are in safe hands."

I nodded but didn't comment; I couldn't drive, so I couldn't agree or disagree. Riding in the back seat of a luxury limo was a big treat—just like when I first rode my bike without stabilisers and Mum had the biggest smile on her face, shouting how proud she was. The driver eased off the brake and the car moved away gently. I braced myself in case there was another Friday night wanderer with a death wish.

"So, Alexia, are you taking driving lessons?" asked Rachel.

"No, not yet," I said.

"How old are you?" she asked.

"Seventeen."

"You're still at college?"

"Yes, I'm at CRT." That was the local college.

"You were at St Margaret's before that, in the same year as Laura?"

I nodded, trying to understand why she was asking so many questions and how she knew Laura. Laura was a girl in year four whose mum lost her battle with depression and jumped off a bridge into the river on a winter's night. After that, she got lots of support and treats from teachers—little things children get when they lose a parent: free tickets to watch their football heroes, trips to the zoo, clothes coupons, and so on.

"You don't remember me, Alexia?" Rachel asked. "I was a volunteer in the after-school club. I read stories in the library. You were the most attentive little girl—always sat quietly, never misbehaved."

Oh my God, of course I remembered. "I'm sorry, Mrs. Hunter. I didn't mean to forget or anything."

Justin glanced at me and then his mum. "That's the girl you've talked about—the one who used to help you put the books away."

"Yes," she said, "a loving and caring girl." She sighed in a way that made me wonder if she was missing her own daughter. A kid was never supposed to die before his or her parent.

There are a number of ways to establish someone's interest in doing something they enjoyed—despite losing a child—without asking outright. I used the basic, "So are you still a volunteer?" Generally, parents who lose a child stay away from school because it's too painful to be around children.

"Yes," she said. "I've just gone back, one day a week, after taking some time off. Are you planning on going to university after college?"

I contemplated lying. No one would like to leave a mum with the likelihood of relapsing, after all. But then I told the truth. "No, I'm planning on getting a job and staying home for a while."

Mum glared at me. "When did you come up with that decision?" she asked, astonished. "We need to talk about this, Alexia."

I shrugged.

Justin shook his head. Sophia rubbed her cheek, which was puffier than usual. I was convinced that something was wrong with her eyes, it wasn't normal to wear sunglasses, inside, but she didn't put the sunglasses back on. Mum told everyone about the onset of her diagnosis after I was born premature, weighing four pound ten ounces. After ten days in an incubator in a special baby unit, where I was fed expressed milk, I went home with Dad and drank bottled milk. Meanwhile, she stayed in the mental-health unit for ten more days before she was allowed home. She didn't tell them that the health visitors used to visit four times a week, and that she wasn't allowed to be alone with me, her newborn baby, for two months. Like, "Congratulations, she's yours, but we're watching you." Mum said that I bonded with Dad immediately, but it took months before I stopped crying when she held me. Then she felt we had bonded.

On my first check-up, the doctor told my parents that I needed surgery called "realignment," which is about as scary as it sounds. Both my feet were turned inwards. They needed to break my feet and then straighten them. Dad was trying so hard not to weep. He did eventually and said he didn't want me to have the operation; Mum kept kissing my cheeks as she cried. The doctor told my parents that the success rates were good and my bones hadn't hardened yet, so it was a matter of bending my feet back straight. They agreed. My little legs were in plaster for about a year. Mum showed me pictures where she and Dad had drawn on the plaster on the first day it was put on and written the dates and the paediatric ward and Zola, the name of the Caribbean nurse who looked after me after the operations.

Dad went back to work at his exotic location after a spell on compassionate leave. Mum and I were alone. She was on some tablets that made her a complete zombie. She went back to the doctor, who suggested she stop taking the tablets and attend counselling instead. Mum told me that I used to sit on a rug in the sitting room of an old lady called June with my teddy; Mum sat on a vintage chair, talking to the lady. She didn't say very much but shook her head; after three sessions Mum stopped going—she got fed up with the same routine.

By the time I was six years old, my dad's presence in my life was virtually nonexistent. He would phone once a month, making promises to come and see me that never materialised. On my seventh birthday, I ran to the door when I head the doorbell, wishing that it was my dad. Mum got to it first to find the postman with a large parcel. He said I was a lucky girl as he handed Mum the package.

I was angry. I ran to my room and hid under the duvet on my bed thinking, "Why doesn't my dad come home every day like my friends' dads?" I remember Mum coming into my room, kneeling beside my bed, pulling the duvet off, and saying, "Your dad loves you sweet pea." I told her that he didn't, and my mum kept telling me that he did love me, but he needed to work to pay the bills. Her voice was not convincing—even for a seven-year-old. I kept telling her that I loved her so much in between sobs, and then I asked her the question that I'd heard some of the kids at school talk about. "Are you and Dad getting divorced?" Mum looked shocked as she pulled herself up, sat on the edge of my bed, pulled me onto her lap, and cuddled me. Then she looked at me as she wiped the tears from my cheeks with her thumb and said, "Who told you about that?" I told her that the kids at school talked about living with their mums and only seeing their dads on weekends and on holiday, and I remember my mum telling me that it was not going to happen to us, that we were okay, and that dad would come home soon. I remember wanting to ask her, "But why didn't he bring my birthday present himself?"

Mum kept holding me close to her for a long time without saying anything. Eventually, she said, "Don't you want to see what's in that big box?" and I told her that I didn't want to. That was a lie, and she knew it, and shortly after mum and I sat on the floor in the sitting room, ripping the wrapping off. Inside the big box were two smaller boxes. One contained a Minnie Mouse dress—a black and red skirt with white polka dots. The other box contained a rucksack with an image of the Little Mermaid, one of my favourite Disney characters, and a birthday card with a huge number seven on it. I remember crying and telling mum that I didn't want to read the card, and she told me that we would read it together, and then she ripped the envelope open. "Are you ready, my sweetie?" and I told her I would listen. She kept kissing my cheeks, and then she read the card:

My darling Alexia, I'm so, so very sorry that I couldn't be home for your birthday yet again. I promise to be home soon. I love you so much.

—Your Daddy x x

When she finished, she handed me the card and said, "Put it with the others." Mum looked away as I stood up to put the card on the windowsill with the other cards I got for my birthday, desperately trying to hide the tears dripping down her cheeks. Neither mum nor I mentioned Dad again for the rest of the day as we sat on the sofa, ate birthday cake, drank orange juice, and watched *Bambi* over and over.

I knew something was wrong between my parents, but Mum was trying her best to protect me. Three months later the big volcano erupted. I came home from school one day to find a For Sale sign outside our house. Dad was home. He opened the door when my friend's mum dropped me off at home from after-school club, and the atmosphere was crap. Dad said, "How about I take my favourite girl for a Big Mac?" I told him that I didn't like McDonalds. "Where would you like to go, my darling?" he asked.

I shrugged.

Then Mum came into the kitchen, started to peel potatoes with the sharpest knife she could find in the drawer, and cut her finger by accident. Dad kept telling her to stop, Mum started sobbing as she washed her hand, and I ran into the bathroom to look for a plaster. I came back to find Mum sitting on a chair at the kitchen table, still crying. She let me put the plaster on her wounded finger, and then I kissed it better. Mum couldn't help but laugh and said, "Sweetie, your dad and I have got something to tell you." I remember looking at my parents as they said the *D*-word. Dad kept telling me that I will always be his special girl, and then Mum said, "I think you should go; you've hurt her enough." I couldn't say anything—or cry for that matter—when Dad kissed me good-bye. But when Mum was telling Sophia and everyone else, she painted the rosiest picture imaginable, emphasising what a wonderful and caring dad he was.

Then the limo stopped at the side of the road next to my flat. I got out to see Mum into the flat, and Justin followed behind. Mum went in and waved as she closed the door. "A quiet neighbourhood for a quiet girl," he said, looking around. "That explains the glow of sophistication." He smirked at me. I pushed his upper arm jokingly. I could feel the muscle, all tense and wonderful.

We went back to the limo. After a couple of miles, the driver made a turn up a hill and drove down a road with ten-foot-high brick and wooden walls and huge metal gates. His house was the last one on the right—a big, modern bungalow. The car came to a halt in his driveway.

I followed him up a set of steps and through a wooden porch into the entry hall, where there was a big glass table with photographs, above which was an engraved plaque with the words "You will always be in our heart." The whole house turned out to be ornamented in a similar vein. "Not a day goes by without us thinking of you" read an artwork above the fireplace. "A life stolen from those who truly loved you" read a pair of cushions on the leather sofa in the sitting room. Justin saw me reading. "She was a promising artist with a place at the London School of Art—this is my parents' way of keeping her spirit alive," he explained.

His mum and dad walked through. His dad tapped him on the shoulder. We went into the kitchen, where a ceramic tile magnet on the fridge read in big letters "You're gone but not forgotten."

His mum pressed the socket on the wall and filled the kettle. His dad opened the cupboard and took out a tin and then pecked his wife on the cheek. Justin shook his head, smiling. They didn't seem to mind showing affection in front of us. The fact that Justin made me feel exceptional did not automatically imply that I was exceptional. Maybe he invited a different girl home every night of the week to ride in his limousine and watch films, and I just happened to be his Friday night.

"Alexia, do you like ginger nuts or chocolate chip cookies?" asked his dad, holding out the open tin. His dad was tall, like Justin, but a little rounder in the waist.

"Chocolate chip, please," I replied.

He passed me the tin, and I took a cookie. His mum was rummaging in the fridge, and then she asked, "Would you like some cheese, Alexia?"

"No, thank you," I said.

"What about you, Justin, can I make you something?" asked his mum.

"Mum, why don't you and Dad go and relax?" Justin said. "I'll make the tea and bring Dad a bowl of peanuts and you a plate of biscuits." His mum looked a little sad, but then Justin wrapped his arm around her shoulders and said, "I love you, Mum. It's about time you chilled and let me do the little things like make tea—or hot chocolate if you prefer." His mum rolled her eyes.

"Your sister would have been proud," said his dad.

His mum was petite with strawberry-blond hair and very pretty.

"Oh, I forgot to mention—you had a call from Joe about the launch in London next month," his dad said.

"Yeah, I spoke to him while waiting for Gran."

"So, Alexia, how was group therapy?" his mum asked.

I paused a moment, trying to think of my response. Should I say that I'd seen what Sophia believed to be the ghost of their dead daughter? That would hurt Justin and his parents.

"It is a very supportive group," I finally said.

"That's precisely what we found with medical staff when we were at the mercy of God after our daughter arrived at the hospital," his dad said. "Everybody was so sympathetic—concerned, too. In our moment of need, the nursing and doctors couldn't do enough for us."

"I guess you better take the dog for his walk tonight, Peter," said his wife.

"No problem. I can do with a walk."

"Have you got any pets?" Justin's mum asked me.

"No, pets are not allowed in our building—except for fish."

"Fish are cute too," Justin remarked.

"All animals are cute, but they need attention—lots and lots of it," I said. "I wouldn't want to be responsible for neglect."

Justin was about to say something else but stopped himself.

His dad filled the gap. "That's a very sensible way to look at it."

They talked to me for a while about how Justin and his sister, Emily, had inherited the dog as a puppy after it was thrown out of a passing vehicle into berry bushes. That was the first time they had mentioned their daughter by name. They talked about how they took the puppy to the vet, and it had to stay overnight for treatment for its broken leg; how the vet couldn't save its leg—too much trauma; and how they were so proud of Emily when she volunteered at the animal-rescue centre. They also asked what sort of work I was looking for. "She's not looking for anything until she's finished college," Justin said. I glanced at the dog and noticed that it only had three legs. Then they moved on to how we were expecting snow in November and that it was very picturesque to have a white Christmas. Last year we had a light dusting on the ground. The winter before that it brought the motorway to a standstill. They didn't even once ask me if I still saw my dad, which was strange, and then Justin asked, "Alexia, would you like popcorn while we watch the movie?"

"Yes, please. So what is the name of the film?"

"*Polly Walsh Under the Spotlight.*"

"You're not," said his dad.

"Alexia has never seen it."

"We'll take the back room. The front sitting-room TV is free," his dad said, beaming.

"I think we're going to watch it next door. It's a bigger screen."

His dad laughed. "It's got a bigger sofa too, clever tiger. The front room is more appropriate given that it is Alexia's first visit to our home?"

Justin glared at his dad and then went over to where he stood in the kitchen, and started arguing with his dad quietly, as if I couldn't hear. He was saying that just because he'd moved back into his old room after his sister's death, they couldn't tell him which room he's allowed in or what TV he could watch a film on. I giggled. I was thinking that his parents were more concerned about me, in case he tried to kiss me. But his dad wasn't backing down.

"But I want to show Alexia my pet iguana and my electric guitar," Justin said.

"You've got a pet iguana?" I asked.

"Yeah."

"Okay, show Alexia the iguana and your electric guitar," said his dad, "and come up. I'll switch on the TV in the front room."

He obviously wasn't happy, the way he was staring at his dad. Justin ripped the bag open, and popcorn flew into the air, scattering in every direction, giving the dog a fright. It ran out the back.

"Fine," he murmured.

His mum laughed. "You're such a spoil sport. Go on; I'll sort this and do some more popcorn."

"Thanks, Mum," he whispered.

I followed him out the back door, where another door opened into a huge bedroom-cum-sitting room. A glass wall reached halfway across the room, and there was a giant iguana enclosed in the glass case lying on a branch surrounded by green leaves. The other walls were decorated with pictures of Justin shaking hands with various officials and receiving prizes for computer games. There were hundreds of trophies—silver and gold cups—a huge poster of wildlife on the wall next to his bed. In the poster, there was tiger, lion, monkey, leopard, giraffe, cheetah, elephant, snake, rhino and so on, and a glass cabinet next to his dressing table with a display of miniature animals similar to those in the poster. There were also lots of signed artworks on the walls. As I took a closer look at the signature on the canvas, I recognised the name his parents mentioned earlier: Emily Hunter.

"Some of my earliest computer-game ventures," he explained.

"You must be good at this."

"I suppose. It is all I ever wanted to do. These are some of my sister's works; she was pretty good." He walked towards his guitar, turned it on, picked it up, threw the strap around his neck, and played a rock melody. My knees wobbled. Oh my God, he was so like a pop star. He smiled as he put it back down and then walked over to his enormous TV, where shelves reaching all the way to the ceiling were packed with DVDs and computer games arranged in alphabetical order. He reached up and grabbed *Polly Walsh.* "I did consider football, like most guys my age—my parents sent me for lessons—but it wasn't my calling. They were a bit disappointed when I packed it in. I was more of a hands-on kid, all about how electronics worked. Taking thing to pieces and putting them back together was more fun than kicking a ball into the net. I've designed a few computer games before, but it wasn't a triumph. Then I designed my first computer game that everybody wanted. All of a sudden, I was being invited to meet computer giants, shaking hands with some big guys, and having my picture taken. It seemed like the easiest thing I could possibly be doing, and I really enjoyed it.

"I got a Sunday job at the zoo and started observing animals. I saw snakes a bit like computer games; the difference was that snakes pretend to sleep in the same positions and how they do it over and over again for years. When they move, they're bigger than you expect, and I saw that learning computer games were basically just a slightly more technical version of the same processes, you don't sleep in the same positions, you keep trying different technology that took years to master. Anyway, for the first few years at uni, I just kept working out how to be better. I studied computer science. Some days I stayed up all night when I couldn't figure out the technical processes of a computer game. Then one day it all happened. Dad and I were playing this game I called lion and wildebeest I'd designed, and he was laughing. Mum was watching, sobbing with laughter. As I kept playing, I felt more and more like a three-year-old. And then for some reason I started to think about it as a job. Are you okay?"

I'd taken a seat on the sofa. I wasn't trying to be provocative or anything; I had had enough of standing and didn't want to pass out in his bedroom or whatever. I was also conscious of an odd smell in the room all of a sudden. No, it wasn't the iguana or him—it was more like the fragrance of roses. It felt nippy suddenly; I was looking around to see if there was an open window. I rubbed my hands over my arms. "I'm fine," I said. "Just listening. Computer games?"

"Yeah, computer games became my life. I kept experimenting with new designs, and they kept selling. I'm about to launch a new one; it is totally fascinating once you get the hang of it. The more I launch, the more people want. And I wonder if they ever think, you know, this would be the last game."

"By the way—not changing the subject or anything—does your iguana that appears to be a sleepy pet have a name?" I asked.

"Juke," he said.

"That's not a very original name for an iguana," I said.

"It's my pet; I can call it any name I like."

"I guess you've called your dog King, then."

He laughed. "No, we've called her Lucky, because when we found her, she was close to joining the other thousands of unlucky puppies in the unlucky world."

I liked Justin Hunter. I truly liked him. I liked the way he told a story and the way he played the guitar. I liked his natural love of animals. I liked the way he experimented with technology and made me feel that I had learnt something. And I liked that he could joke with his grandparents. I've always liked people who had both grandparents; I never knew mine. For me, it has always been a lonely world—the world of Alexia, with billions of unanswered questions.

"How did your sister die?" I asked.

"Huh?" he replied, seeming a little preoccupied.

"You said when we were at the restaurant that people were arrested."

"Oh, yeah, well. The police are still working on the case. No one has been formally charged yet. Ten people were arrested, but nothing happened. They kept visiting my parents and asking the same questions.

"What sort of questions?" I asked.

"Why Emily didn't take her mobile phone when she went to her friend's that day. No one can answer that. It's difficult for the family—especially Gran. Anyway, have you got siblings?"

"No."

"So what's going on in your life—your story?" he asked, sitting down on the sofa next to me but at a safe distance.

"Not much: college, exams, and spending time with my mum."

"College and your mum aside, what's your story? Likes and dislikes, hobbies, passions, sport, favourite games."

"Um." I exhaled sharply. I didn't have anything interesting to say.

"Don't tell me that you're in the young-carers category, taking so much responsibility. I know so many people in that situation. It's awful. With the lack of funding, young carers have become a growing concern, right? Kids caring for parents without any assistance. But surely that can't be legal; something needs to be done."

It seemed that perhaps I needed to take this matter seriously. I struggled, contemplating a pair of terrapins in a glass box, with an urge to caress, pondering how to answer Justin. In the silence that followed, it appeared to me that I wasn't curious enough. "I am planning to attend a Young Carers group."

"That would help in the short term. Think of you something you like. Anything come to mind?"

"Um. Reading?"

"What do you read?"

"Just about anything. From, like, the Holy Bible to romantic comedies to dark secrets of lost kings. Whatever."

There was a pause.

"Extraordinary," Justin said. "Alexia, you must be the only teenager in all England who reads the Holy Bible. That tells me a lot. You read a lot of funny books, right?"

I struggled.

"What's your greatest?"

"Um," I said.

My preferred book to cuddle under the duvet with was *Seeking Angels*, but I didn't tell anyone about it. The thing is you can read a book that gives you goose bumps and makes your hair stand on the back of your neck, and you become convinced that the only answer to your agony is to run into a dark room and never switch the light on; there are books like that. And then there are books like *Seeking Angels* that you cannot share with anyone—books so revolutionary and unique that they give you courage and hope like no other books.

It wasn't so much about the book—it was more about author Vanessa Helena Amadeo's journey. Strangely, our lives were so similar in the most puzzling ways. *Seeking Angels* provided words of comfort—words that I couldn't go and ask my mother. It gave me the affection that my mother wasn't able to provide. It was my book.

Justin was the first person I told. "My preferred book is, without a doubt, *Seeking Angels*," I replied.

"Is it about cheerleaders?" he asked.

"No," I said.

"Chasing fireballs in the golden atmosphere?"

I shook my head no. "It's not that sort of book."

He frowned. "I'm going to search for this secret book with the mysterious title that doesn't contain fireballs and read it," he declared, and I instantly thought please don't. I wished I hadn't told him about it. Justin stood up and walked to a bookshelf next to his bed. He knelt down and grabbed a hardback and then took his mobile from his pocket. As he noted the name of the book on his phone, he asked, "Would you be interested in a swap in which you read this outstanding book about my favourite creatures on the planet?" He held up the book, which was called *The Mind of Wizards*. I laughed and grabbed it. Our hands kind of tangled while he passed the book over, and then he was holding my fingers. "Small," he said, looking at my palm.

"The best things come in small packages," I said.

"I love the logical thinking," he said. He took both of my hands and pulled me up to him. He did not let go of my hand as he fed the iguana and terrapins green leaves. When Justin and I returned to the front sitting room, his mum was sitting on the sofa, waiting, with a bowl of popcorn and two Diet Cokes on the coffee table.

"Enjoy the movie," she said as she left.

We watched the film while sitting at each end on the sofa. I did this insecure-girl thing where I took a cushion and held it to my chest and wrapped my arms around it; he laughed. He picked the bowl off the table and put it on the sofa between us, and we ate popcorn while watching.

The film was about a hijacked plane and this famous hero guy who died valiantly for a netball heroine, Polly Walsh, who was beautiful and incredibly sporty. She had great legs, which did nothing for my skinny legs and once-broken and realigned feet.

We reached into the bowl at the same time, his hand on top of mine. I smiled, and he moved his hand and let me have the last bits of popcorn. As the movie ended, he said, "Courageous guy, wouldn't you say?"

"Courageous guy," I agreed, although to be honest, it was more of a boy film. I don't know why boys think that girls should like their sort of movie. They wouldn't be seen dead watching a girlie movie, would they?

"Would you like another Coke?" he asked.

"No, thank you, I should go home. Mum will be waiting," I said.

I walked to the kitchen with him and waited while he put the bowl in the sink and got his keys. His mum stood next to me and said, "That is my favourite. Her last one, dedicated to her brother." I think I had been looking at the huge frame on the wall—a painting of a white bear catching fish in a lake.

This is an ancient way of keeping memories alive—seeing something every day—and it prolongs agony. It is insanity and only causes sadness on a daily basis, but one cannot truly grieve when a killer is still at large. "It is a wonderful piece of art," I agreed.

Justin drove me home in his truck. I listened to the music he was playing—a boy band called the Wild. They were great musicians, but because I hadn't heard this music before, it wasn't as fascinating to me as it was to him. I kept peeking at his hands on the steering wheel. He had great hands. I tried to imagine him and his sister playing with the puppy. I'd always wanted a puppy—just like I wished I had a brother. I didn't want to ask more questions about his sister, but I did want to know more about him. He probably wanted to know more about me, a girl with a depressive mother.

Justin slowed down, stopped outside my building, and switched the engine off. The atmosphere changed. He glanced at me, and I pretended to look out into the darkness. He was perhaps thinking about kissing me, and I was seriously thinking about kissing him. I wanted to. I'd never kissed a boy before and was too shy to make the first move.

He pulled the key out of the ignition and I looked over at him. He truly was gorgeous. I had often heard people at college say that supposedly boys weren't supposed to be, but he was.

"Alexia, what is your family name?" he asked.

"Collins," I replied.

"Miss Collins," he said. My name had never sounded so perfect as from his lips. "It has been such a pleasure to meet you."

"Thank you, Mr. Hunter. You too," I said. I felt my cheeks getting really hot looking at him. He had the most amazing blue eyes.

"Would it be possible to see you again?" he asked. There was an appealing unsureness in his voice.

I beamed. "Sure."

"How about I pick you up, say, nine thirty in the morning? We could go for breakfast."

"Gosh, Speedy Gonzales," I said. "You don't want to seem to be overly keen."

"Well, that's the reason I said morning," he said. "I wanted to spend more time with you tonight. But I'm an understanding guy, and your mum is waiting for you. I can wait till tomorrow without fail." I rolled my eyes. "I'm serious," he said.

"You don't even know me," I said, opening the truck door.

"Wait, allow me," he said, swinging his door open. Too late, I stepped out.

I was clutching the book. "How about I call you sometime over the weekend?"

"But how would you get my number?" he asked.

"I've got your gran's phone number. I suspect she wouldn't mind giving me yours."

"I'll save her the trouble. Can I have your phone, please?"

I handed him my phone, and he programmed his number. "There." He smiled and passed my phone back. "I'm on speed dial."

CHAPTER FOUR

Jessica, three months earlier

It had been just another manic day at work. I was looking forward to going home at the end of my shift. Suddenly there was a great commotion, and a gang of hooligans with guns burst through the accident-and-emergency department, demanding treatment for one of the men with a knife wound to his leg. They pointed the guns at me as I was about to run into a cubicle. One of the men stepped forward, grabbed me by my hair, and threatened to shoot anyone that made any sudden move. I was terrified. Two of the men forced themselves into the cubicle after me with the wounded man, and demanded that I treat him.

I attempted to say that I was a nurse, not a doctor; they needed a doctor to remove the knife and stitch the wound safely, otherwise he could bleed to death. But it did not matter what I said. The two men kept pointing their guns to my head and yelling, in broken English, "You treat him, or I'll shoot you and everyone else out there!"

My hands were shaking as one of the men lay the wounded man onto the treatment bed. I was struggling to focus and quietly praying for police assistance. It was difficult to concentrate, all that was going through my mind was my Alexia without her mother if these bastards shot me. I grabbed the treatment trolley and put pressure on the wounded area beside the knife with two rolls of bandages, and as gently as I could master, I pulled the knife out. "Fuck!" he howled. I could not place the accent, but they were not British.

I could hear other men outside the cubicles, threatening my colleagues, demanding treatment supplies. As it was late in the day, staff were handing over to the night staff in another room, so there wasn't a doctor present. I cleaned the wound, grabbed the staple gun, and stabbed some stitches and then put on bandages, while he kept roaring "Fuck!" When he was ready to go, the two men with the guns shouted, "Put your hands up!" and pushed me between the wounded man and the two gunmen. As we emerged, the other men outside the cubicle joined in shrieking, "We will shoot anyone that tries to follow us!"

Outside a BMW was waiting with its engine running, the men threw me to the ground, squeezed into the back seat, and sped away. Dawson, the security guy, arrived a few seconds later and helped me back on my feet. The police arrived fifteen minutes later.

CHAPTER FIVE

Mum was still up when I got in. We had hot milk while I told her about Justin's animals. She laughed, said she was happy I had a good time, and then went to bed. I stayed up late that night reading *The Mind of Wizards*. The story begins with a fortress and lights that stretched down a narrow stairwell with a big metal door and tiny windows to spy on their enemies. *The Mind of Wizards* controlled a secret underground tunnel with a river and a robotic army. Zac, the mad scientist who lived on the edge of the wood, was the number-one enemy. It wasn't to compare with *Seeking Angels*, but the central character, Barratt Joshley, was interesting; he could see into the future. Killing and turning his enemies into four-legged creatures was the name of the game. A giant, fearless guy dressed in a jade cloak and brown boots—owner of five hundred acres of wood on reaching pages hundred and two of the book.

It was fairly late when I got up the next morning, a Saturday. Mum normally slept late most days; four in the afternoon wasn't unusual for her. My phone buzzed a few times before I picked it up and said hello without looking at the number. I was sort of confused when I heard Mum's voice.

"Have you seen my note?" she asked.

"What note?" I asked.

"I'm at the hairdresser; I left you a note at the end of your bed."

"Hang on." I picked up the A4 piece of paper and had a quick glance. "Oh yes, I've seen it. You never mentioned that you had an appointment to have your hair done."

"Well, I didn't till this morning. They had a cancellation when I phoned."

"Okay, are you coming home after, or would you like me to meet you?"

"I'm going food shopping after; you're welcome to meet me, or you can get on with your college work, and I'll see you later."

I pondered for a moment and then said, "I'll get on with my essay—that way we can spend some time together this afternoon." I didn't want to seem like a detective; if she could get herself to the hairdresser without me, she was getting better.

"Excellent, do you need anything from the shop?"

"A pack of chocolate, please."

"Cheeky. I'll see you later."

I laughed, glancing at my phone. It was eleven in the morning. Oh my God—I couldn't believe that my mother was out before midday. I wandered into the bathroom, feeling happy and frightened at the same time. I was frightened that she had gone out on her own after months of being down with anxiety and depression, spending her days in bed and not opening the curtains, and fearing that she was being watched. In my heart, though, I was happy that she was gaining some control and fighting her demons. That's extremely courageous.

I showered, dressed in jeans and a jumper, and pulled my hair into a high ponytail. I looked in the bathroom cabinet and counted mum's tablets—something I did every day to make sure she had not forgotten to take her medication. The tablets prevented relapse. I knew that it was stupid, but I wanted her to get better. She frightened me when she heard voices. I pulled a face in the mirror while thinking about it then wandered into the kitchen and opened the fridge. The only things left were a tiny drop of milk, a dollop of butter, and two slices of bread. That would have to do. I watched a cookery programme while I ate breakfast. *Saturday Kitchen*: chefs preparing delicious food. "Yummy," I said out loud. I finished eating my bread and butter and switched the TV off. I wouldn't get anything done if I kept surfing channels, although I was tempted.

I walked to the corner table to look at my goldfish; it was swimming round and round in its bowl. I was sure it was lonely and needed company. Mum and I had talked about getting another fish—I would suggest it again later. I fed it and watched its eyes open and close. I liked my fish, but it was not like a dog that you could take for a walk and chat to while it looks at you with big droopy eyes. I looked out the window; it was a murky day with an inky sky—a day for writing essays or reading. I went back to the bathroom, brushed my teeth, and then peeked in Mum's room. It was tidy—the bed was made and the curtains drawn. What a difference from a month ago, when the room was in total darkness.

As I sat on mum's bed, I could hear noises: women laughing and talking loudly and children having tantrums. I was curious. Normally it was quiet, and you never heard what went on through walls. If I could hear them, that meant they could hear us. I got up and put an ear against the wall. It was difficult to catch what they were saying, but as I listened carefully, I heard a voice say, "The crazy woman next door has gone out on her own this morning. She must be getting better."

"We can't let that happen," another voice said. I started to wonder if perhaps they were playing a trick on my mum, and the voices she kept hearing were theirs. Feeling a little self-conscious listening to the neighbours' conversation, I turned and walked out of Mum's room and into mine. I was furious and wanted to confront the neighbour straightaway. But I was also mindful that I was on my own, and didn't feel my mum could cope if they attacked me, after what she had been through with her own fear for her life after her ordeal. My mum's mental health was still very fragile; anything could tip her right back into the gloom of depression. I needed to be sensible, that wasn't easy. My mum was the most sensible person I knew, she'd never had a bad word to say about anyone. I wasn't going to allow what I had heard to spoil my day.

"Idiots!" I screamed into my hands. "Stupid, stupid, stupid. Whatever you're doing is not working. My mum is rising above your disgusting, nauseating taunts."

I switched my laptop on, carried it into bed, pushed the pillow up, pulled the duvet over me, and grabbed my phone from the bedside table. I WhatsApp'd Mia to see if she would like to do something later, and then I started writing. The essay was about the biology of living organisms—functions, growth, and the like—an interesting subject on any other day, but not today. It was increasingly difficult to concentrate and stay awake. Twenty minutes into the one-thousand-word essay, Mia WhatsApp'd back: "Just done my first gel-manicure experiment on my grandma. Waiting for it to dry under ultraviolet light. Be at your place at 1:30?" Mia, her mum, and her grandma spent every Saturday morning together having their hair done or going shopping. She never organised anything before one in the afternoon. I replied, "Great, I'm just finishing my essay. I'll be ready."

Mum arrived back while I was on my last sentence. I quickly tapped the keyboard, pushed save, and got out from underneath the comfy duvet before she got to my room. She appeared at my door, smiling.

"Oh," I said, looking at her hair, cut shoulder length.

"What do you think?" she asked.

"It suits you, but what have you done with my real mum?"

She laughed. "It was long overdue. Do you like it?"

"Yes!"

"Have you done your college work?" she asked, pulling the duvet over my bed and putting the pillow down. She then reached at the corner of the bed, grabbed the brown stuffed rabbit, and put it on the pillow, making my bed in her attempt at being my mum. She had not done that since…I couldn't remember the last time. She couldn't stop smiling.

"Yes, all done, but I'm still sleepy. I was up late reading."

She took my hand. "It must have been a good story," she said. As we sat on the edge of my bed, Mum did not let go of my hand. She was looking at all the stuffed animals on the sofa bed in the corner of my room. I had a stuffed animal for every birthday and day out. My favourite was the tiger, which I called Parker, because my parents bought it on my first day out to the zoo. I was about eighteen months and had just started wobbling on my feet.

Mum squeezed my hand gently and reminded me that I should be getting on with my life, not staying at home with her. "Did Justin give it to you?" she asked, looking at my bedside table. "I think he likes you, Alexia. I've got a good feeling about this boy."

"Mum, yes, he gave me the book, but not because he likes me. He probably feels sorry for me."

"Nonsense. I saw the way he was looking at you last night. He likes you, and you like him. I can tell."

I pursed my lips and shrugged, looking at mum. She looked like a completely different person. It wasn't just the new hairdo; she was more relaxed. "I love you so much, Mum. Promise me that you won't stop taking your medication again," I said, leaning on her shoulder.

"Stop worrying; I won't. I promise—cross my heart," she said quietly, kissing the top of my head.

"Have you heard from Mia?" she asked.

"Yes, she is coming over later."

We pulled to our feet. Mum and I walked to the kitchen, still holding hands. I helped her put the shopping away. She had bought lots of vegetables and meat. It looked like she was planning to cook. She handed me a box of chocolates and said that it was for tonight. It was a quarter to one.

"You didn't come home on the bus with two big bags full of shopping, did you?" I asked.

"No, I got a taxi."

I watched Mum make ham, cheese, and cucumber sandwiches, which we ate at the kitchen table while we talked about her morning. She said that she felt like doing something different when she got up, if only to gain confidence at being out on her own again. She said that she was horrified when she walked to the bus stop, but once she was on the bus, she started to relax. She had been up half the night budgeting—it was her last month on full pay. She had an appointment with the doctor on Monday to review her mental health, and then she had a meeting with her manager. She said that she wanted to get back to work part time.

It was wonderful to listen to Mum's plans, although I thought that she wasn't ready to go back to work yet. Shortage of staff on a busy hospital ward could cause her to relapse. But after what I'd heard the neighbours saying in her bedroom earlier, I thought it would be a good idea for her to be out doing something to distract her.

"Would you be all right if I went out with Mia? I've been in all morning. I need a little air. I'll only be a couple of hours."

"Of course. Go and enjoy yourself. I'm going to sort out my wardrobe."

I was about to say don't spend too long in your room, but then I would have had to explain, and I wasn't ready. I needed more evidence to prove what I'd heard had foundation.

"Mum, yesterday when we were going to group therapy, you said that you wanted to show me something. What was it?"

"Oh, nothing that can't wait for next time we're passing."

I nodded. I suspected it wasn't anything that was about to change our lives, or she would have told me. I counted the months she had been off work with depression. Six already, and she was just starting to get back on her feet. I offered to wash up, but mum insisted that she would do it. She tapped me on the shoulder as she got up and took the plates away.

"I dropped by Sam's after the hairdresser; we just managed to finish our cup of tea before her first customer walked through the door. She's coming over tomorrow. Then I met up with Clare." Samantha was a professional florist, and Saturday was her busiest day. Clare was Mum's psychiatry caseworker and a pretty amazing one at getting Mum to think more positively. They got on well. Mum listened to her.

At 1:25 p.m. exactly, the intercom buzzed. I picked it up to hear Mia's voice. I pushed the button to let her in and then opened and stood at the door. Mia ran up the stairs. She never ever took the elevator; she got stuck in one when she was eight, and the fire brigade had to rescue her. She arrived on the landing of our second floor flat without puffing out of breath. She air-kissed me at the door, flashed her newly manicured gel nails at me, and walked in.

She wore black skinny jeans that fitted perfectly and an anorak over a knitted jumper. Mum hugged her before going into her room.

"Your mum looks fabulous," she said. "I just love her new hairstyle. Has she just had it done?"

Mia was the queen of style. She was known within our close circle of friends as "Lady V." She just happened to be an incredibly glamorous seventeen-year-old who looked like she belonged on the front cover of a magazine. She had been approached by various top agencies for modelling, but her parents wouldn't hear of it. She kept reminding me often enough, and to be fair, she had the most perfect body in the North East. Everyone admired her.

"She had it cut and styled today. Great nails, by the way."

"Thanks. How is she doing?" she whispered.

"More good days than bad. She went out on her own for the first time today, and she's talking about going back to work."

"Positive. Getting out is better for your mum's health than being stuck inside. That's so bad for your mental health. I read that in one of those medical articles. Like exercises and endorphins. How do you feel?"

"She is my mum and I love her. All I want is for her to get better. How are you? Is the gel manicure a new thing?"

"Mum did a course," she said, smiling. "It's her new thing. She wanted to learn about nails and beauty, and she got a certificate. She is teaching me and practised on Grandma. She can do yours if you like." I nodded and handed her a 7UP. She took a sip.

"Something really, really sad happened last night," she said.

"You broke up with Brad?"

"Oh, no, we are okay. He's watching some big match, Newcastle versus Man-U, with the boys. It's Chloe and Osman—they have broken up after like three years."

"No, you're joking. How did you find out? I thought you weren't friends after last week's episode in the library."

"We're okay; she did apologise for pushing me into the wall and grabbing the last philosophy book." She continued to name seven people, friends on Facebook who go to our college, but I couldn't recall any of them. They were more her friends than mine. I didn't belong.

"That is sad," I said. Although it wasn't really; people broke up all the time, but for Mia, things like that were a tragedy.

"Yes, I know. They were a perfect couple. Like, together forever," she said.

"Well, that shows nothing lasts forever," I said.

I thought of telling her that I was seeing a boy—a graduate who's a bit more grown-up than college boys—and that I'd been to his house and met his pet iguana and three-legged dog. I knew that she would be stunned and wouldn't believe that someone who didn't socialise, restricted after-college activity, never went to the arcade on Friday night, and was as plain as me could win a boy's affections. But I didn't tell her; I decided to let it be my secret for now. I tried changing the subject instead and told her about the next-door neighbours' conversation that I'd heard through the wall in Mum's bedroom. But she did not hear; she was still banging on about her social life.

"Brad and I are going skydiving tomorrow, his birthday present from his parents, but I don't think he'll do it. He's such a scaredycat. You can come and watch if you like, but it might be awkward, you know, with lots of couples as is always the case, but you would be with us," she said, meaning her and Brad.

"I've got plans for tomorrow."

"I know you might be spending time with your mum, but I thought I'd ask you anyway. How is your pet fish?"

"Lonely," I said.

"Have you finished writing your essay?"

"Yeah, have you?"

"No, I always leave it to the last minute. What about the neighbours?" she asked suddenly.

"Oh, it doesn't matter. I was just being silly. Shall we go?" I thought that it wasn't wise to resurrect the neighbours' conversation. She would say that we should contact the police. That would only aggravate my mum's depression.

We walked to the metro while she told me that her mum and grandma were visiting her grandad, who died six months ago after he lost his battle with a brain tumour. He was buried in one of those woodland burial sites that doesn't allow crosses or flowers, but her mum and grandma went and talked to him every Saturday. Mia found visiting the dead spooky.

The metro arrived two minutes after we got there, and four stops later we went into this pet shop in the arcade. As we were shopping, Mia kept picking out all the dog beds, saying, "Isn't that adorable? I want a puppy," which reminded me of Justin's dog hopping about on three legs. I wondered if they made prosthetic legs for dogs. When I pointed out a dog coat and diamanté lead to match, she was like, "Oh my God, oh my God, that is just so, so cute." Then she said in a funny voice, "Dogs are the most intelligent animals on the planet. I want one."

She sounded more like a spoilt child than a seventeen-year-old. "Mia, I'm sure your parents would buy you a freaking dog if you asked," I said. "I'm going home if you don't get away from the world of doggy fashions."

"Dad wouldn't," she said. "I've asked for a puppy every Christmas."

An elderly lady who had been listening close by put a hand on Mia's shoulder and said, "Honey, if I were you, I would buy the full set and take it home, and that would be a big hint to your parents that you really wanted a dog."

"You think so?" Mia asked, sniffling.

"That's how I got my hamster when I was your age, but remember: a pet needs love and affection."

She gasped, threw her arms around her new best friend's neck, and said, "Thank you, thank you."

"You're welcome. It was a pleasure," she responded.

"You're something else," I mumbled.

She didn't comment. I left her by the dogs' world, walked over to the fish tanks, and looked at the variety of fish. There were just so many cuties: blue, yellow, green, black, and many more colours. A girl about my age came over and said, "They are just amazing creatures, but my favourite is the blue one."

I smiled. "I'll take a blue one, please."

She grabbed a little green net with plastic handle, fished out the blue fish, and put it in a plastic bag of water.

"I'll put your fish behind the counter while you continue shopping. I'm Carmel. Let me know if you need any other assistance with anything. Pets World is like a gold mine."

I thank her and I went in search of Mia. I found her still in the pooch world, holding a bright pink basket with a lead and coat to match—hardly surprising.

"Where have you been? I was looking for you," she said.

"In fishy heaven—and I bought one."

"Oh, what colour?"

"Blue."

"Okay, what do you think of these?" she asked, holding up the basket, lead, and coat.

"They'll look good on a puppy. I don't think your parents could resist when they see those."

She laughed and said, "Me neither."

Mia and I walked around and stopped at the rabbit corner, looking at the variety of rabbits in their hutches. They were cute—some were huge. Mia had three rabbits, a ferret, and a guinea pig—her own furry zoo—yet she wanted a puppy. We circled past the birdcages without stopping and ended up at the fish tanks. "Don't you just love these? Every colour in the ocean," she commented.

I tried to make an intelligent comment about fish, she bought the doggy things, I bought my fish, and as we left she said, "We should do this more often."

"I must head home," I said. It had started to snow. "Are you catching the metro or the bus?"

"Actually, the bus is more reliable. The metro might be delayed with the snow," she said.

"Sure, of course," I said. "The bus is much better." We walked to the bus stop, chatting about our pets. I looked at my fish happily swimming in its bag of water. A woman with a dog in an orange coat walked past, which set Mia off talking about her puppy.

Mia's bus arrived before mine. Number fifty-eight was always more punctual than sixty-two, my bus. She kissed me on both cheeks and lined up behind the waiting passengers to get on. It looked like other people had had the same idea of choosing buses over metro on a snowy afternoon.

She waved as the bus pulled away, sitting in one of the back seats. With all the passengers, she was lucky to have gotten a seat. It took number sixty-two a few minutes to reach the bus stop. It was really fun going shopping with Mia, something I had not done for a long time, but I needed a little time to myself before going home. I liked my mum, but her depression had taken over our life, and the idea of her going back to work made me feel strangely nervous. And I liked Mia, too. She was very supportive, really. But she had a social life, whereas I didn't. At times, I felt extremely lonely. Mum needed my support more than my friends—that was okay. I felt a certain comfort in Mia; she'd never given up being there for me. I thought my college friends wanted to help me better understand my mum's depression, but they eventually found out that they couldn't for one reason: depression isn't like a wound that you could see.

So it was best for me not to insist on going to any of the after-college activities—as I often had over the months—on the grounds that I had to be home to make sure that my mum had eaten and taken her medication. Mia often asked about my mum's condition, but my other friends didn't. In truth, it always hurt. It always hurt to be socially isolated and not do the things that normal teenagers did, like going out on a Friday evening and socialising with friends. I missed my dad. I wrote a letter every day—even if it was just a few lines—telling him how I felt, but the urge to go through with posting them overcame me. So he never got them.

The bus arrived and I got on. The driver said, "That is a very pretty fish," as I was paying my fare. I smiled. I had to stand because it was packed, and every time it stopped and started, I smacked into the person in front and the person behind stumbled into my back. But that wasn't the worst—a guy had his smelly armpit in my face. I wished I had a nose clip. After the fifth stop, I got to sit down next to a woman with a little girl on her lap. The little girl said, "Is your fish alive?"

And I said, "Um, yes, I think so." I glanced at the fish. It had flopped to the bottom of the bag. I gave it a little shake, and it started swimming again.

Her mother pulled her into her chest and said, "Natalia," with a frown.

I said, "She is only curious—it's okay," because she hadn't asked an impossible question.

Natalia asked, "Did you get it from Pets World?"

"Yes, I did." I said.

She smiled and cuddled up to her mother. "That's my favourite place in the whole world. Mum bought my ferret there, but I left the cage door open by mistake and it escaped, and it took Mum, like, all day to get it back."

"I'm glad you got it back," I said.

"I like your fish," she said, looking at her mum. "Why can't we have a fish like this one, Mum?"

"Next time we are passing Pets World, I will buy you one if you promise to stop being cheeky," her mum said.

"I do like this blue fish, and I'm not cheeky," she replied.

"I like fish too—any colour," I said. She smiled and put a finger in her mouth. Natalia had adorable big brown eyes, dark skin, and curly hair.

"Natalia," her mother said, "take that finger out of your mouth." Natalia whipped it out so quickly that she dribbled down her flowery yellow dress.

"Excuse me, please; this is our stop coming up," said her mum.

I stood up to let them pass. Natalia waved as they got off. I concentrated on looking around the bus. There were about ten people left on it. I looked out of the window, wishing I had my book with me. Even though my life wasn't amazing, seeing my mum getting back on her feet was. I kept thinking about all the little children who had lost their mums. How lonely and sad.

The other thing about Mia, I guess, was that we were both only children. She knew what it was like to be in that category. But her social interactions were way above mine. I was shy—for me, socialising took effort. I was amazed that I had managed to speak and spend time with Justin without my face turning bright red. I had always felt awkward and self-conscious around people; that was partly the reason boys found me unattractive. I was fine with kids—especially little ones like Natalia, who didn't know anything about me.

Honestly, watching my mum alone in a dark bedroom for months was depressing. I was praying that she would continue getting out of bed and opening the curtains from now on.

CHAPTER SIX

Music was playing softly in the background. A delicious smell came from the kitchen as I walked into the flat. I wanted to show Mum our new pet before putting it into the fish bowl with the other. I quickly glanced into the kitchen; the table was beautifully set for two with a white tablecloth, napkins, candles, and wild flowers in a small metal vase in the middle. There was a dish in the oven, but I couldn't see mum. She'd never, ever go to that much effort just for us. She must be expecting a visitor.

I thought she said that Sam wasn't coming till tomorrow. Oh no, I thought, I hope she hasn't invited Todd Walker. She wouldn't—not yet, anyway. I was about to walk into the sitting room when I heard her calling me. "Alexia, I'm in my bedroom. I've got something to show you." She sounded cheerful, so I didn't panic but rushed down the narrow corridor still holding the plastic bag with the fish in water. When I reached her room, Mum stood by the window, her dressing table pulled away from the wall, curtains open, the light on.

"What happened? Are you okay?" I asked, looking around the room. It was a mess, like we had been burgled. There were mountains of clothes on the bed, bags, shoes—some still in boxes, photo albums, and broken picture frames thrown on the floor. She looked annoyed.

"Yes, I'm fine, but something has been bothering me for some time, and I couldn't figure out what it was. I thought it was the plumbing, but while I was clearing my wardrobe earlier, I heard it again. At first, I thought someone or something was trying to knock the wall down, but then it got louder. *Boom, Boom.* I stopped what I was doing, looked around, pulled furniture away from the wall, and that's when I found this." She pointed, and I looked in the direction of her finger and noticed a big hole in the wall.

"Oh my God. Who did that?"

She paused and looked at me. It started to make sense. I knew I should have told her about what I had heard that morning. "The people next door, would you believe, neighbours from hell, thought they would frighten me by playing funny chomping noises after they smashed my wall," she said furiously. "I'm aware that I've not been well, Alexia, but there's no excuse for this sort of humming noise, which has contributed to this freaking depression. I thought I was going mad; it was them all along!"

"We need to get this wall repaired immediately," I said.

"I've already contacted the builder, Mr. Hills. He'll be around later. I then contacted the police. This is sabotage, and they're not going to get away with it. Normally it takes hours to get a police visit, as with every department that's short of staff. I was stunned when they turned up fifteen minutes after the call. A policeman and a community support officer—both extremely helpful. They came here and then went next door. According to the officers, they are renting the flat. The police will contact the owner; apparently the place was cluttered. That must be the reason my room smells no matter how hard I clean."

"You're moving into my room, Mum. This is crazy. They are mad, not you."

"I'm not abandoning my room," she said. "I can see you've bought another fish. Let's put it in the bowl with the other one."

We headed out the door together; Mum was fighting fit. "That was the most evil thing to do. You won't win, loser!" she screamed.

Oh my God—where was that coming from? I'd never heard Mum yell like that before. I was so excited that she was taking control of her life—I'd often wondered if she ever would—and now I was more hopeful. I was so proud I felt like jumping up and down. She was not allowing the people next door to take advantage of her. It all happened when she was in a vulnerable state of depression. They must have made a terrific noise making such a hole in that wall; it looked like they had blasted a hammer through. That's why it had taken some time to find. Mum was right—I did notice strange smells in her room and in the bathroom. I thought there was a problem with the drainage.

Mum helped me open the bag. I gently took the fish out with both hands and dropped it into the bowl, and then Mum and I bent at the waist to watch its reaction. The goldfish swam more vigorously, round and round in the water, while the blue one flopped about more gently. It took a few minutes for the gold one to stop this behaviour and swim up to the blue one. They put their mouths close together, like they were kissing. We laughed.

"That is just such a heart-warming affair; there is so much beauty in every creature," Mum said. "I believe they will get on, but they need a bigger home. This bowl is too small."

I nodded. "Who's coming to dinner?" I asked.

"Sorry to disappoint; it's only me and you, sweetie—no one else," she said, patting my shoulder.

"But you've gone to a lot of trouble for just me and you."

"Alexia, today is a new day—a new beginning. You've been such a supportive daughter through what has been like *Alice in Wonderland* for us both." Her face suddenly dropped. "I missed you. I missed normality." She paused. "Thank you, darling, for being there in these challenging times."

"You don't have to thank me, Mum. I love you so, so very much; all I want is for you to get well. Yes, you're right—it has been like the white rabbit in a deep hole without a tea party for Alice to enjoy after she fell in, but let's look forward to the future." I hugged her.

She squeezed my hand as the intercom rang. "It must be the builder," she mumbled, and she rushed to let the caller in. She lifted the receiver and said hello to be sure before pushing the button to open the door. I was still hovering by the fish. I heard her say, "Oh, come on in."

"Who is it?" I asked.

"It's Justin," she responded.

"Ooh, I wasn't expecting him," I whispered.

Mum was already holding the door open. I was still wearing my anorak. I hurried into my room, took off the anorak, combed my hair, changed my jumper—damp from my shopping trip, and rushed back to find Mum and Justin standing in the sitting room and talking. He smiled when he saw me walk in.

"Oh goodness, this is such a coincidence, but the flat next door belongs to my granddad's brother. Uncle Rupert, who is in a residential home for the elderly. He was diagnosed with Alzheimer's about eighteen months ago and deteriorated to the point where he wasn't safe in his own home. We're his only family left, so Gran got an agent to rent the flat. We never had any problems with the previous tenants. This lot has only been there four months, and they're causing mayhem and unnecessary stress to you both, Mrs. Collins. Gran sends her apologies; Dad is in touch with the agent. We're so sorry for the damage to your property," he explained.

"So your family is responsible for those hooligans—the evil lot next door?" Mum scowled at him angrily. "Follow me." She yelled, "I'll show you what sort of damage they've done."

Justin followed Mum out of the sitting room. I walked behind. There was another buzz from the intercom before we got to Mum's room. Justin walked with confidence; he was just amazing.

"I'll get it," I said.

"Thank you, darling," Mum said.

This time it was the builder, Mr. Hills. I pushed the buzzer to let him in. As I waited for him at the open door and listened to the elevator rattle to the second floor, two white men came out of a door on the landing. They were about early thirties, tall, and slim. They had shaved heads and were carrying shopping bags. A young brunette followed in a pair of towering heels; how could anyone walk in those? I wondered. She was holding a little boy's hand and pulling a red suitcase with the other. It looked like they were going on holiday. They glared at me, and I stared back. They didn't wait for the elevator; they took the stairs. Like Mum, I had never met the neighbours. I wondered if that was them maybe, running away.

Finally a short, shaggy-bearded man with a massive belly and hardly any neck walked through. He was carrying a piece of wood and a huge square black and yellow box. It looked heavy; it must have been full of tools.

"I understand that you've had a bit of trouble that needs my help," he said by way of introduction.

"Yes, thank you for coming," I said. "It's in my mum's room; I'll show you. It's a big hole in the wall." I stepped aside, watched him waddle through the door, closed it, and led the way into Mum's room.

When we got to the room, Mum was putting clothes on hangers and hanging them back in the wardrobe. Justin was down on one knee, peering through the hole. I leaned against the doorframe, looking at him.

Mr. Hills shook his head. "That's a big job," he said. "I'll patch it with wood for today, but I'll need to come back next week to brick it off."

"Totally agree," said Mum. "It will need decorating after."

Justin got to his feet. "My apologies again. We'll pay for the repairs, as it's our tenants that caused the damage. Send the bill to this address." He produced a business card and handed it to Mr. Hills.

He took it and said, "I would need to go next door to do a proper job. Can I call you to gain access?"

"Yes, please do," said Justin.

"I've not contacted the insurance company yet, but if your family wished to pay for the damage, that would save me a call," Mum said.

"Of course," Justin said.

Mr. Hills turned to look at Mum. "Mad neighbours you got," he said. "It must have taken some force to cause that much damage. Have you had a disagreement?"

"We've never met," Mum said.

"Sorry?" barked Mr. Hills, turning to stare at Justin, who was looking confused. "Yeh're Hunter's boy—computer-games whiz kid. Your granddad and I go back—played footy with his brother Rupert, who owns next door. Is that his handiwork? Last time I did some work for Rupert, he didn't look too good; he was kind of losing his marbles." He stopped himself. He exhaled, rubbing his hands together. "We're in for some bad weather; you need all the heat you can get to keep warm."

Mr. Hills got down on his knee and then sat on the floor next to the hole, inspecting it. He shook his head a couple of times and then pulled the piece of wood from under his arm and started to measure for size. He cut a big square, and with his electric drill he blasted some screws into it. "That should do yeh until next week. I'll get some bricks for the job. My missus is cooking a hot pot for our tea; it would be murder if I'm not home soon." He licked his lips.

I was staring at his belly brushing against the floor as he stumbled back onto his feet. "Do yeh need any help to put the furniture back?" he asked, looking at Mum.

"No, thank you. My daughter and I will manage. I will see you out," said Mum.

After Mum and Mr. Hills left the room, Justin asked if he could help tidy the room. I said no thanks, Mum and I will sort it. The truth was that I didn't want him to see the pictures of me when I was little that were in the album on the floor.

"Have you started reading the book yet?" he asked.

"Yeah, interesting. I like it, but it's big—like three books in one. It will take some time to read. Did you watch the football match?" I asked.

"Yes, fantastic game. Did you?"

"No, I went shopping with my friend Mia. I've bought another fish; would you like to see it?" I asked.

"Sure, lead the way," he said.

We walked side by side along the corridor into the sitting room. The fish looked contented swimming with each other in their bowl.

"What are their names?" Justin asked.

"I've not named them yet."

"Pets with no names. I like it; maybe someday we can choose the names together," he suggested.

I smiled. "Er, maybe," I said.

Mum and Justin's dad, Peter, walked into the sitting room. Peter kept apologising to Mum and me for the damage, distress, and inconvenience that their tenants had caused. Peter said that the flat was in a terrible mess and there were about ten people living in a three-bedroom flat with a young child. Two men, a woman, and the child had left, and they have given the tenants notice to vacate the property in four weeks. Mum kept nodding.

"Dad, why four weeks?" asked Justin.

"Son, you need to give tenants four weeks' notice; that is in the contract. But I will contact our solicitor on Monday. The contract didn't say anything about vandalising the property and smashing the wall or causing distress to the neighbours," he explained.

Justin shook his head, looking from Mum to me. "I'm sorry. I know it's not satisfactory, but hopefully they won't make any more noise to disturb you," he said.

"Well if they torment you any more, they will be out on the street, contract or not," Peter said.

Mum looked out of the window and then turned to our guests and said, "Let's hope that we've seen the end of their madness. I wouldn't wish homelessness on my worst enemy in this snowy weather—even if they are heartless."

Justin and his dad shook their heads but didn't comment as they walked towards the door. Mum said bye and went into the kitchen.

Peter glanced at his son and said that he would wait for him in the car.

Justin nodded. "Do you fancy walking the dog in the morning, even if it is still snowing?" he asked, making a funny face.

I laughed, "Let's see how much snow is on the ground in the morning. If we're able to go out, then the answer would be yes."

He beamed as I walked with him to the elevator but changed his mind. He chose to take the stairs. He took my hands and said, "Alexia, call me if there is any problem or you just need to talk. I'm a good listener."

I watched him run down the stairs. When he reached the last step, he turned, still beaming, and waved. I waved back, grinning.

CHAPTER SEVEN

B loody people. What happened to nice, decent neighbours, children playing together, and parents inviting each other over for a cup of tea and a chat? When did the world become so cruel and full of lunatics? Mum was really, really trying her best; I hoped that it wouldn't tip her into relapse again. I suddenly felt downhearted. I glanced at the landing and the door where I'd seen the people come out earlier. They are so pathetic. My mum had gone to so much effort today: going out on her own, cooking—that took some courage. I was outraged that they thought they would blemish all her hard work. I felt like knocking on the door and yelling at them, but I would be wasting my energy on losers, so I went back inside. Mum was still in the kitchen, chopping cucumber, lettuce, and tomatoes on a chopping board and dropping the veggies into a bowl.

"What are you doing?" I asked.

"Making a salad to garnish our meal," she said cheerfully.

"Can I help?" I asked, happy that she wasn't talking to herself.

"No need. I've done it." Mum looked at me, smiling. "Has Justin gone?" she asked.

"Yes."

"That boy is really something else; I thought of asking him for dinner, but I didn't want to prolong his visit. I should imagine the family was waiting for news and to eat together like a normal family."

I smiled. "It looks like we are having dinner as a normal family too," I reminded Mum.

"Of course, sweetie. I made your favourite: shepherd's pie."

"Oh, Mum, thank you." Shepherd's pie was like the best meal ever—like chicken soup with lots and lots of vegetables that Mum used to make when I was small and not well, which used to happen a lot.

"It wouldn't have been acceptable to invite Justin without inviting his dad to dinner as well. Maybe one day we'll invite him and his family, and yes, he's nice." I sighed.

Mum laughed. "Would you mind helping me to tidy my room? The food needs to cool; it's far too hot. I've switched the oven off but left the dish in."

"Of course." I knew that she wouldn't rest until her room was spotless. I kept looking at her while she finished hanging her clothes. She didn't seem to be experiencing any anxiety; her breathing was steady. She often breathed too fast when something bad happened. Mum looked calm and relaxed. I picked up the broken picture frames and glasses, and Mum handed me an empty shoebox to put them in. I then pulled Harry, our black and green vacuum cleaner, to clean the carpet and make sure all the tiny splinters of glass were picked up. Mum walked barefoot.

I looked at the picture from the broken frame: Mum and Dad standing in a beautiful garden. Mum was pregnant. They were holding hands, looking into each other's eyes, and smiling. The picture had obviously triggered a memory of happier times with my dad. She wouldn't have broken it otherwise; she loved pictures.

I shut my eyes to stop the tears running down my cheeks. I really missed him, and I think mum missed him too—even if she'd never say. They were in love once. I didn't want Mum to see me cry; it would have ruined what was already fragile. Once we pushed all the furniture back, we sat on the bed, looking at albums of my baby pictures. There was one of me with chocolate all over my face. Mum said that was her favourite. We laughed and then closed the curtain and went back into the sitting room. We stood by the window next to each other, watching the snow lashing down in the darkness. After a while we closed the curtains and went into the kitchen. I lit the candle while Mum served dinner.

Mum said grace before we ate: "Lord, we thank you for the food that you have given us today and for giving me the courage to go out. Amen."

We ate shepherd's pie—perfect British winter cuisine. After dinner, I did the washing up and Mum cleared the table.

"Fetch your laptop. We'll search for fish tanks," Mum said afterwards.

"Are you sure?" I asked.

"Yes. They can't stay in that tiny bowl; they need more space and water."

"I agree, but maybe we can wait a while."

"Alexia, stop worrying. That reminds me—why did you say to Justin's mum that you aren't going to university?"

Oh, I wished she'd forgotten that conversation, I really didn't want to talk about it right now. "I've been in education since I was, like, five. After college, I should get a job before I continue. I'll be eighteen in three months, and some eighteen-year-olds take a gap year, work, save some money, and go travelling. We could go on holiday."

Mum looked at me. "Once I'm back at work, we will have holidays. You shouldn't put your future on hold. I've relied on you far too much."

I noticed the sadness in her voice and said, "What about eBay? I'm sure there will be lots of fish tanks on the site."

Mum watched while I went eBaying; there were so many tanks to choose from, and cheap too. We settled on a tall, rounded tank with greenery. To our surprise, the seller was Mum's old school friend who lived two streets away. After we paid, Mum sent her an e-mail. She e-mailed back straightaway and offered to bring it to our flat in the morning.

"That was a bonus," Mum said. "Let's have a treat."

"Chocolates, maybe?" I suggested, laughing.

We had two chocolates each to celebrate our investment.

Mum went to the bathroom; I waited for her to finish, peeping through the sitting-room curtain. The ground was covered in a white blanket. Suddenly, a woman in a long white coat leapt over a rosemary bush, streaking across the snow in a blur and striding down the road without leaving any footprints. I shut the curtain quickly, feeling a chill at the back of my neck.

"Mum!" I yelled. She came running.

"What is it?" she asked, looking at me, horrified.

"I was looking out the window at a strange woman walking in the snow without leaving a single footprint," I said.

Mum screwed up her mouth and blinked twice.

"You shouldn't look out at night—you never know who's out there," she said. "It could have been a ghost."

She cuddled me and kissed my cheeks and then went into her room, and I went into the bathroom. The vision still haunted me as I brushed my teeth. I checked the cabinet to make sure Mum had taken her medication. She had. I never asked her—I didn't want her to feel like I was policing her, but I had to be sure for her well-being. Then a thought went through my mind: perhaps it was the spirit of Justin's sister wandering in the snow.

We both went to bed early that night. I changed into my flannel onesie before creeping under the duvet of my bed, which was single size, pillow topped, and one of my heavenly places of peacefulness. I then began reading *Seeking Angels*. Although I'd read it hundreds of times, I kept discovering new stuff.

Seeking Angels is about this girl named Kelly and her six-fingered mother, who is a professional dog walker besotted with lighthouses. They are typical, hard-working people in the port city of Newcastle. One day her mother vanishes, and Kelly gets an unusual personality disorder.

But it's not a personality-disorder book—"the symptoms of personality disorders" is terrifying. In the story, it described the person with the symptoms who starts a foundation to raise awareness in order to help others with the same or similar experiences, and the foundation was to establish a logical, safe environment where sufferers can express his or her feelings, hopes, despair, fears, in therapeutic surroundings and make the person feel precious and appreciated because there was no cure to the disorder. However, the treasurer, who was a handbags and shoes addict, had other ideas on how to spend the funds. But, in *Seeking Angels*, Kelly becomes so determined to make living worthwhile for people with personality disorders—and she wants to do more creditable and well-meaning things for herself and others—that she starts an organisation called The Kelly Institution for Personality Disorder Sufferers Who Seriously Want to Overcome Their Conditions.

Kelly doesn't doubt herself; she is honest and transparent in a way that allows people to trust her. Throughout the book, she describes openness as the way forward. People with personality disorders use words to contrast what is going on in their head in their attempt to distinguish between what is real and what is not, as being haunted by dinosaur. As the story unfolds, Kelly gets increasingly paranoid, jerking her head in every direction and searching for elephants racing after her. And then she finds out that her Mum is alive and has fallen in love with this control-freak lighthouse inspector Kelly called the Lighthouse Freak Man. The Lighthouse Freak Man had inherited a fortune and a country estate dating back to Victorian times from a peculiar aunt who heard voices. His idea is to turn the estate into a home where personality-disorder victims can express themselves freely, but Kelly thinks the guy might be a serial killer who possibly murdered his aunt and claimed her estate as his. She thinks he keeps the bodies in a massive freezer in the lighthouse. Just as the lighthouse guy and her mother are about to get engaged, and Kelly is about to start an insane experiment that involves green vegetable smoothies and sleeping in a dark room for a week, the book ends with a big question mark.

I knew that it's a strange choice of story and everything, and perhaps that's why I was so fascinated with the book, but there is something to ascertain from a story that end snappily. This story was like looking at a photograph of a house with a door and no windows, and you are kept guessing what lies within. One should at best continue on a journey of discovery like the adventures of Zac, the mad scientist, character in *The Mind of Wizards*, in his quest to find a cure for the symptoms of personality disorders. I understood the story ends because Kelly becomes too paranoid, or she is taken into an asylum against her wishes and too withdrawn to write, whatever—but then one starts to wonder what happens to the rest of characters in the story. I've sent hundreds of e-mails to the e-mail address on the back cover of the book—to Vanessa Helena Amadeo—requesting that she please provide some logical answers as to what happens after the end of the story. So much is left unresolved: whether the Lighthouse Freak Man was a murderer, why Kelly's mother went off with him, what happened to Kelly's parrot who bit her mum's finger, whether Kelly's older sister married the guy she met at the fairground—all these questions. But sadly, she never replied to any of my e-mails.

Vanessa Helena Amadeo didn't write another book after *Seeking Angels,* and all that the searches seemed to say about her was that she had relocated from London to somewhere in the Lake District. I imagined her running a tearoom overlooking a lake, searching for new ideas—like Beatrix Potter. Maybe Kelly's mum and the Lighthouse Freak Man ended up living happily together. But, unlike Beatrix, who continued to invent new characters, Vanessa Helena Amadeo had not published any other books after twenty-five years. She had an e-mail address and a website but didn't update it. I would have more luck searching for a lost planet than reading a new story from her.

I checked the time on my phone; it was only ten thirty, and I couldn't sleep. I picked up *The Mind of Wizards* and read a few pages. Zac and Barratt Joshley come head to head in the woods, and Barratt tries to run Zac off his land with his horse. But Zac has a secret weapon: he throws a bottle containing fox specimens on the ground, and even the robotic army cannot stand the pong. The horse makes a funny sound before it gallops away out of control, with Barratt ducking between trees and branches that smack him in the face. For a man like Barratt, that is deflating, but the mad scientist laughs all the way home. I laughed too, closed the book, put it back on my bedside table, and got out of bed. I glanced out of my bedroom door towards Mum's room; the light was off. The whole thing must have worn her out. Thank heaven they didn't actually come into her room—well, I hope they didn't manage to.

I dived back under my duvet, imagining Justin Hunter feeding his pets and working on a new computer-game venture. I wondered if he would mind me calling him. He did say earlier that he'd like me to walk his dog with him in the morning. He probably wouldn't mind me calling him; on the other hand, I didn't want him to get the idea that I was keen, although I was.

I put my hands over my eyes in an attempt to avoid looking at a picture of my dad in which he looks very handsome—tall and trim, with sharp cheek bones—and is digging the pond in the back garden of our four-bedroom house. I'm on Mum's lap, watching him. That was before we moved into this crap flat. Dad loved fish, but he didn't like them in a tank. He used to say that the pond was much more like the ocean, with space and freedom for the fish, but we couldn't take the pond or fish with us. They went to Mrs. Pear, who bought our house.

I kept having the same dream of our next-door neighbour at our old house, Mrs. Dusty. After we'd moved, I used to spend lots of time with her and Sam after school, when Mum was at work, at Mrs. Dusty's pipe-tobacco-smelling house. On the other hand, Sam's kitchen always smelled of baking—chocolate cake mostly. While the cake cooled, she would take me to the park, holding my hand, and we would walk by the duck pond on a Sunday afternoon. It was her favourite place. She almost squealed with delight as we walked around the birds' sanctuary and passed the ice-cream van, where children had tantrums because they didn't get their favourite ice cream.

One day we walked along the path to the far end of the park, where there was a bat cave. At the entrance, a nice lady smiled and gave us a leaflet. She then pointed to the huge sign, which read, "please respect the species by being quiet." Samantha took the leaflet, smiled back, and kept holding my hand as we walked down a tunnel. It was cold and dark in there, with just enough light on the floor to see your way. Behind a glass screen were the bats. I had never seen bats before; it was bizarre watching them with their long wings—creatures of darkness hanging upside down with their beady eyes. Samantha kept whispering to me—as if the bats could hear her—that they were fruit bats and had very sharp teeth to spear the skin of the fruit. She also said they had extremely long tongues that unfolded when they were eating, and once they stopped, the tongue folded back inside the ribcage rather than in the mouth. I just nodded.

An hour later, the toilet next door flushed twice. I was still wide awake, staring at the dark ceiling. "This is stupid," I moaned. I grabbed my phone from my dressing table, found Justin's number, and sent him a text.

"It's all quiet so far; when I glanced outside two hours ago, it was still snowy. But I'm up for a walk or maybe building a snowman with a carrot for a nose in the morning."

He responded before I could put my phone back on the dressing table.

"Text is so impersonal; I prefer to call—that's what we agreed earlier: if there was any disruption or you'd like to talk, just call. I'm a good listener." Justin reminded me.

So I called.

"Alexia," he said cheerfully as he answered. "So would you like to build a snowman?"

"Yes, that's what people do with the white stuff." I said.

"I agree, but how about we do something different?" he said.

"Oh, different as what?" I insisted.

"A unicorn or maybe a family of ice creatures?" Justin said.

I laughed and then joked, "Intrigued, mister full of great ideas, a unicorn it is."

"I'm glad you like it," he said. "Have you read any more since I last saw you?"

"Yes, a few more pages. It's a long book, but I do like Zac's weird scientific experiments. He does keep Barratt on his toes."

He laughed. "I've finished reading the one you suggested. It was quite short. Not sure about the ending though."

"I totally agree about the ending. However, I shouldn't have mentioned the book; I have to admit that I'm feeling a little embarrassed that you've taken the trouble to search for *Seeking Angels*."

"Don't be; I enjoyed it and suggested it to my mum. She's reading it as we speak. So what is your conclusion? Is the lighthouse guy wicked? I'm a bit suspicious about him."

"I reserve judgment, but I've seen something weird tonight. My mum thought that it might have been a ghost."

"Oh no, you shouldn't believe in that. My gran kept seeing this young girl who she thought was my sister. It was creepy. But to be honest, something is setting Lucky off at night—she has been acting strange lately, running to the window and barking every few minutes."

"Er, dogs have got six senses, and to be honest, I don't believe in ghosts either. But in view of *Seeking Angels*, if the lighthouse man is not a perfectly amicable nobleman, I'm going to chop his toe into pieces." He laughed. "A bit drastic! I better behave. We're still up for the morning, right?"

"Certainly. I hope your mum enjoys *Seeking Angels*."

"I will let you know her verdict in the morning. I better hang up and let you sleep—otherwise you won't want to come out."

"Well, yes," I said, and the line went dead.

I bit my lip. Flirting was like a new chapter in my life. I giggled. I liked it.

My head was spinning as I opened my bedroom curtain the next morning. There were five or six inches of snow and not a single footprint in sight. It was early, and mum was still in bed. I tiptoed to the cupboard in search of my sledge; I wanted to be out before anyone spoilt my fun. Then I remembered that I'd promised Justin that we would build a snow unicorn or whatever. Well, that would be more fun than doing it on my own like Billy no-mates. I couldn't find my sledge. I shut the door and was about to go back to my room when mum appeared.

"You're up early?"

"Yes. Have you seen my sledge, Mum?"

"It's in the cupboard in the spare room. You're not going out there on your own this early?" Her voice sounded a little sharp.

I put my hands on my cheeks and laughed. A few months ago, she had no idea what time of day it was or where I was. Now I needed to ask her permission to go out. Actually, I preferred my more curious mum to the way she had been. "It's so pretty out there, Mum. It's like a perfect Christmas day."

"I know—let's make a wish," she said, taking my hands.

"What shall we wish for?"

"A white Christmas." She grinned.

"Silly me. Of course."

She smiled, kissed my forehead, and walked to the bathroom. While I just stood there looking at her, I noticed that she looked so chill. Sleep fights depression. I waited for her to close the bathroom door, and I went into the spare room. Just as mum had said, my old pink plastic sledge was tucked into the corner of the cupboard. I decided to leave it for a while, went back to my room, and concentrated on what to wear; it was a day for jeans, jumpers, and Wellingtons. My phone buzzed suddenly. I grabbed it to hear Justin's voice.

"I'll be at your house in an hour. Lucky is excited about her snowy outing."

"Okay, see you both in an hour." The line clicked, ending the call without another word.

Mum came out of the bathroom, and I went in, showered, and brushed my teeth. By the time I'd gotten dressed, Mum had made a cup of tea and gone back to bed. I went into her room and sat at the end of the bed. I reminded her about the woman who was bringing the fish tank.

"I've not forgotten. You look lovely." I was wearing black jeans pulled over a jumper; Mum said that I looked like her aunt Yvonne—small frame, long brown hair pulled into a high ponytail, and not one for designers. I didn't have any siblings, so I never had to compare or compete with anyone. It was weird to be compared to someone I'd never met.

"I take it you've got plans for today?" she asked.

"Yes, Justin has invited me out dog walking. Will you be okay?"

"Of course. I'll be fine. I've got to prepare Sunday lunch—Samantha is coming."

I nodded. "What sort of food are you planning for this winter Sunday?"

"Roast beef and Yorkshire pudding. Sam is bringing dessert. Have fun on your outing. Does it involve sledging?" she asked, smiling.

I shrugged. "Perhaps."

CHAPTER EIGHT

Sophia, a year ago

I had invited my family for dinner at my house. It was a beautiful sunny evening; the food was ready. It was my granddaughter's—Emily's—last weekend before she went off to London School of Art. She had gone on a bike ride with her friend Jade, promising that she would be back in time for dinner. My two grandchildren were moving on with their lives. I was proud of them both. My grandson, Justin, a successful computer-game designer, had moved out of his parents' home into his own apartment closer to the centre of Newcastle a few months ago. But we were all here to celebrate his sister's last weekend at home.

We were in the garden enjoying a predinner drink while waiting for Emily. When it got to 7:40 p.m. and Emily hadn't come back, we started to be concerned. Justin rang his sister's phone, but it went straight to voice message. I knew my granddaughter had always kept her word and was never one to be late without calling, and young people these days never go out without their phone. My heart was pounding against my rib cage, fearing that something had happened to her. Everyone looked at each other, concerned. Justin hadn't had a drink so he went looking for her in his truck.

It was a nightmare waiting for news, I couldn't focus on anything. My family and I were just staring at each other. My son Peter kept calling his son, even though Justin had barely left.

When my son's phone rang, we all looked at him. His face turned white, his lips twitching. Then, he said that it was Justin, who'd just managed a few words, too distressed to talk. Another voice came on saying that they were in the ambulance with Emily, and she had been injured, to meet at the hospital. I wept, we all did. My husband was calling a taxi when two policemen rang the doorbell.

The police told us that they received a call from a dog walker who had found two girls lying on the pavement, bleeding. When they arrived at the scene, the two girls were unconscious, but it was evident that they'd both been stabbed. They found two bikes, but could not find mobile phones or any other items. Then a young man arrived telling the police he was Justin Hunter, looking for his sister who was late home. Justin identified the wounded girls as his sister, Emily, and her friend Jade. Then he went in the ambulance with his sister. The police gave us a lift to the hospital, but we were too late; Emily died on the way, with her brother holding her hand.

He wrote a poem about the magical arts that he read at his sister's funeral. But, despite our best efforts to come to terms with her death, I keep seeing her spirit, and Justin continues to be haunted by the fact that he could not save his beloved sister.

A few weeks later, he moved back in with his parents. My once-happy family was left distraught and fighting for justice for our Emily's murder.

CHAPTER NINE

I pulled two pairs of socks on—my feet always get cold—and checked my phone. It was 9:45 a.m. Although it was a dark morning, it wasn't as early as we'd previously thought. Mum was dressed when the door buzzed.

"I'll get it," I said.

"Okay," she replied.

I did not answer the door straightaway. I went to the sitting room, opened the curtains, and looked out the window. Justin's truck was parked by the side of the road, so I rushed to answer the buzzer.

"I'll be down in two minutes," I said.

"Okay. I've got the carrot," he said.

"What carrot?" I asked, surprised.

"It was your suggestion, Alexia, or have you forgotten?"

"Oh, sorry, of course…" I felt stupid. It was my idea; he'd remembered, and I had forgotten all about it. "Yes, a carrot for our snow creatures," I said, feeling childish.

I heard him laugh. "Okay, see you soon," he said.

Suddenly, I felt a pain in my stomach, and it rumbled loudly. I'd been thinking a lot about my mum last night. I felt bad leaving her alone—especially after what had happened yesterday. I shouldn't leave her alone, I kept saying to myself—what would happen if the neighbour kicked the door down? She couldn't defend herself. I put the receiver back down and stared at the door. I could hear footsteps along the corridor. She would be furious if I told her that I'd heard the neighbours' conversations before she found the hole in the wall. Then I remembered that she was on her own yesterday when she found the hole, and she had called the police and the builder. She was getting stronger.

"Who is it?" she asked.

"It's Justin, but I don't think I should go out in this weather," I mumbled.

She looked at me curiously. "A moment ago, you were searching for your sledge and ready to go out there. What has changed, Alexia?"

"Nothing, I just don't think you should be on your own again. Justin would understand. I'll go and explain and come right back."

"No, you won't. That boy has invited you out, and he's waiting, I'll be perfectly fine. Anyhow, I'm not lonely—I've got two lion fish to protect me."

We both laughed. "Are you sure, Mum?"

"Go and enjoy yourself. You'll need your gloves and coat. I've got plenty to do, and I need to wait for our new fish tank."

I grabbed my coat and checked the pockets for my gloves. Mum watched me pull my Wellingtons on. I hugged her, and she kissed my cheeks. I took the stairs. Oh my God, she looked so much better. She was fighting back—a single mum who had always put her daughter first until depression struck. I loved my mum so, so much; we'd stuck together even in those dark and lonely days. Sometimes, in the dead of the night, I'd watch her sleep to make sure she was alive. I couldn't survive without her. Samantha had been a rock to my mum and me—she was such a crucial element to their friendship, and she had never given up on us. Nerves shot through my stomach as I got to bottom of the stairs. I should have had breakfast.

Justin was making snowballs and throwing them back into the snow. He turned when he heard the door shut.

"Hi. You look amazing," he said with a goofy smile. "Are you okay?"

I nodded. "I'm fine." I looked around for the dog.

He noticed me looking and said, "She's in the truck."

He waited for me while I zipped up my coat. A breeze ruffled my ponytail, and my cheeks felt cold. It was a dark, inky-sky morning as we walked side by side to his truck. A neighbour was screaming at a child: "Up! Get up! Now! Your father is waiting." I realised that there were a few one-parent families in our building; Mum and I weren't unique by any means. A little boy came running past with his rucksack dragging in the snow, still in his pyjamas, and his trainer laces undone. A man who was waiting by the kerb behind Justin's truck hugged and kissed the boy and opened a car door. I presumed he must be his dad. The little boy dived into the back seat. The man shut the door and drove off in his black Audi SUV. He reminded me of my dad, whom I hadn't seen for over ten years. I rubbed my neck, feeling chilly.

"You okay?" Justin murmured.

I nodded. "Yes, I'm fine."

The dog was jumping up against the window of the truck, excited to see its owner. He opened the door, and I got in the front seat. As we turned the corner away from my flat, he glanced at me and smiled.

"What's that smile for?" I asked.

"Mum loved the book, but we both agreed there are missing pages; a book doesn't end like that."

"Sorry to disappoint, but I guess we will never know if they lived happily ever after or whatever," I said.

"My guess is Kelly turned into a vegetable in closed institutions, so that would make sense of the ending. Pity to be punished that way."

I changed the subject. "How are the rest of your pets?"

"Okay. So what are you studying at the moment in college? Any homework for the weekend?"

"Er, I spent yesterday morning writing essays in preparation for Monday."

"What's the subject?"

"Biology."

"Interesting subject. Have you been to the aquarium?" he asked.

"No, I've never really had time to visit places."

Justin didn't seem surprised or even particularly bothered. "Would you like to visit the aquarium after we've walked Lucky?" he asked.

I exhaled sharply. "I'd like that."

We stopped at a park with trees covered with snow. It looked so pretty, like something off a postcard. Justin switched the engine off, opened his door, and rushed around to open mine. I leaned against the truck, watching him while he grabbed the lead in the glove compartment and opened the back door to let Lucky out. She had the most gorgeous green doggy coat on with a little hood. We walked on the path underneath the trees, with him holding the lead and me walking beside him. We were close, but our hands weren't touching. I was so impressed with Lucky; she was a well-behaved dog and didn't woof—even when we passed other dog walkers and their dogs tried to snuffle her.

"What sort of breed is Lucky?" I asked.

"She is a beagle. That's a smaller breed of hound—mostly used as a hunting dog."

"Oh, fascinating. Your very own hunting dog," I joked.

"And a very lucky one, for that matter!"

My stomach rumbled loudly again—enough that he could hear, and I felt embarrassed. "Sorry. Didn't have time to eat breakfast."

"Me neither. Are you okay for a short walk, or we could head back?"

"I'm okay."

I suddenly felt he was a caring guy. He didn't seem to think it was strange and, more importantly, didn't question me even though it was past ten o'clock. I took a deep breath and pulled my sleeves over my hands. Winter was here. He let Lucky off her lead and threw a ball into the air. Lucky ran, leapt, and caught it. A very sporty three-legged dog.

"Clever girl!" he shouted as she brought the ball back.

Lucky was brown and white with fluffy ears and a short tail. She was a pretty dog in my eyes and incredibly well mannered.

After a while, he drove us back and stopped at my building. Justin turned off the engine, opened the back window a little to leave Lucky in the truck, and said, "Shall we do this?"

"Do what?"

"Hang out in the snow?"

"Oh yes." I laughed.

We both moved in front of the building, knelt on the snow, and started scraping the white stuff into a huge pile, looking at each other as we built our first snow sculpture together. Justin carefully shaped the snow into a perfectly formed unicorn with his gloved hands, and then he made a fish and a snowman. I could see he was a talented guy. Perhaps that is why he was so good at creating computer games. "That is so cool," I said.

"Not bad," he responded.

When he got back onto his feet, he took his gloves off, shook ice off them, and said that he would be right back. I stared innocently at him; he smiled and rushed towards his truck. I watched him open the door, take something out from the glove compartment, and hide it behind his back. He shut the door and sped back.

When he got back to me and the snow creatures, he said, "Close your eyes," with a big grin on his face.

"Why?" I asked.

"It a surprise," he mumbled.

I decided not to challenge him and closed my eyes, since I knew it had something to do with the snow family.

After a few seconds, he said, "You can open your eyes." We were both roaring with laughter, looking at our masterpieces. He'd put the finishing touch to the unicorn—a carrot horn and marbles for eyes on the fish, unicorn, and snowman.

"What shall we call them?"

I glanced at him. "What about 'the Ice Pearls'?"

"Yeah, I like it," he said. "That deserves a memorable picture, don't you agree?"

"Certainly!"

He pulled his phone out from his jeans pocket, we knelt beside the Ice Pearls, and he took a selfie of us—our first photo together with our snow masterpiece. It was just amazing. I didn't realise that Mum and the neighbours were watching until we heard clapping. Justin took my hands and helped me to my feet; he kept hold of my hand as we looked behind us.

Mum stood by the entrance with the neighbours. "What a tremendous imagination, you two!" she shouted.

Justin and I looked at each other, smiling.

"Fun and cheap," one of the neighbours said.

A couple, with a boy about ten or maybe older, came out the building and walked across the snow to us, smiling. My brain was all mushy and woozy next to Justin. None of them had ever taken any notice of me and my mum before; we had never met any of the neighbours. I kept looking at Mum; she was smiling with pride. Justin didn't let go of my hand.

"Would you mind if our son had his picture with your gorgeous snow creations?" asked the boy's dad. "He could never play in the snow."

"He's diagnosed with Raynaud's," added his mother, pulling off the boy's woolly gloves to show us his hands.

My heart was pounding as I looked at the boy's hands; his fingers were like a skeleton's. He kept looking at Justin and me without saying anything.

"He's got learning difficulties as well," said his dad. "He doesn't mean to stare."

Justin nodded. "Would you like me to take a family picture?" he asked.

"Yes, please," said the father, handing Justin a camera. They stood, smiling, with the boy in the middle and behind the Ice Pearls. His mother put his woolly gloves back on.

For a moment, I felt brave and glad that something like snowfall had brought the neighbours together. I glanced over to Mum; she was chatting to people confidently. It was amazing. The couple thanked Justin and took their son back inside.

"These three are gonna be famous someday," he whispered.

"They're already famous," I groaned, my stomach rumbling for the third time.

"Yeah," Justin said, looking at the Ice Pearls. "Would you like to go somewhere for something to eat?"

"Um, okay. Would you like to come up to my flat first? We bought a tank for the fish last night on eBay. It was due to be delivered this morning; I just wanted to make sure it's all okay."

"Sure."

He glanced at Lucky in the back of the truck as I opened the door; she had her head to one side and was looking out the window. I was tempted to take her with us, but I knew that pets weren't allowed—fish were an exception. Mum followed us inside. I was so proud of my mum when we got in; she had filled the tank, turned the light on, and got the water bubbling. The fish were swimming through greenery.

"Mum, it looks amazing, thank you," I said, kissing her cheeks.

"They look happy," Justin commented, his eyes on me.

After a second admiring the fishes, I said, "I'm going for something to eat with Justin."

"You two go and enjoy; don't hurry back," Mum said.

I changed out of my Wellingtons and tucked my jeans into a pair of boots. Justin and I said bye to Mum, who seemed happy to see the back of us. I was a bit concerned for Lucky; Justin wouldn't want her staying in the truck alone for long. When we pulled into the driveway to his bungalow, his parents and gran were there. His mum rushed to open the door when she saw us through the window.

"Alexia, how lovely to see you," she said. "I totally enjoyed that book; sad though—poor Kelly, after all her hard work…"

I nodded. "Yes, a sad ending."

Justin carried Lucky in, changed from his dog-walking anorak into a woollen coat that was hanging in the hallway, and said, "Alexia and I are going out for some food. See you later."

"How is your mum?" asked his gran.

"She is okay," I said.

"Drive carefully," his grandad said.

"I'm a careful driver, Grandad."

CHAPTER TEN

Justin closed the door for me and walked around to the driver's side. We drove over to the Aquarium, where we ate cheese sandwiches and drank water in the café, and then walked through a glass tunnel, watching fishes swimming around us. It was a kind of tropical heaven being under the ocean, surrounded by huge sharks and different varieties and colours of fishes. It was incredible.

When we got out of the aquarium, Justin asked, "Did you like it?"

"Oh yes, fantastic. It certainly doesn't compare with my new tank and two little fish."

He laughed. "I love this place. My sister and I used to come here often. I've not been here since she passed away. She used to research the species of goldfish too; her favourite was Shubunkin. It has a fancy tail with a pattern known as calico. Originally from China." Justin ran a hand through his hair.

I noticed the sadness in his voice. It had stopped snowing when we got outside, but it was cloudy. Typical Newcastle: the kind of weather that takes effort to go out and enjoy. We walked across to the arcade. Inside was a group of young people handing out leaflets. A woman was blowing long balloons and twisting them to form animals; it was amazing. Right in the middle of the walkway, a man was blasting into a microphone about a charity called Young Carers Association, which he said provided support for young people caring for adults. Justin and I stopped.

"That sounds interesting," he said.

Justin took a leaflet and passed me one, and we looked at the leaflet while we listened to the commentary. I noticed the name on the leaflet: Mr. Silver. Oh my God, that's so crazy. I looked up between the groups of people, and yes, it was the same Mr. Silver who taught me Religious Education (RE) in primary school. His wife apparently killed their baby daughter by holding her head underwater in the bath. She was six months old, and the story goes that his wife was suffering from postnatal depression. He stopped teaching after that.

A chill ran through me. I had not seen him since the death.

"He used to be a teacher," I said.

"Yes, I remember. His wife was friends with my mum, and according to rumours, he's haunted by the spirit of his dead daughter."

I looked at Justin and saw him lower his brow in bewilderment. I wondered if he had been haunted by his sister's spirit.

"Welcome to the tortured world of snowy freaking Sunday," Justin said. "What would you like to do? We could go to the cinema or go and check this place out."

The Young Carers Association meetings were being held every Sunday afternoon in the church hall—a five-minute walk from the arcade.

"Let's check the place out," I said.

"Okay."

I knew about Young Carers Association, but I couldn't face going on my own; besides, Mum needed me. I felt Justin was being supportive by offering to go with me. Although he wasn't in my position, he might learn something from it, as I'd learned so much from going with Mum to group therapy. We walked up the path between tombstones and graves covered by the snow. The huge oak door was open when we got there; looking through, I saw that the church hall was completely deserted. Inside was a big circle of black plastic chairs, one chair in front, and a long table at the back. How bizarre. Then, suddenly, we heard an almighty sobbing coming from the other end of the hall.

"Don't move," Justin said.

"Be careful," I said. Whoever it was, he or she was howling like a wounded animal.

Justin turned before pushing the door open at the far end of the hall. He pressed his lips and shouted, "Can I help you?"

The wailing continued and grew louder. He pushed the door and disappeared behind it. I got goose bumps and followed after him.

"Shhh!" hissed a man in a long brown robe in the foyer. "You'll wake the dead. You've come seeking my help, so I'm trying to help you."

"I didn't mean to," said a voice.

Justin stopped, looking down at two elderly men sitting on the floor in the foyer. The man in the robe had a shaggy face and was wiping the foot of the other wrinkly man. "He has injured his toe," said the man in the robe without looking up. "Are you here for the meeting? Mrs. Bell won't be long; she's fetching the refreshments."

Justin bent down on one knee. "Uncle Rupert, what are you doing here?" he asked.

The man in the robe turned his attention to Justin.

"You know this person?"

"Yes, that's my Uncle Rupert. He's a resident at Hilltop Manor. How did he get here?"

Hilltop Manor was an exclusive home for the elderly, with extensive grounds. They were famous for their caring manner; for the bronze statues of Lord Frederick with his dragons, looking over the lake of the land and home he once owned; and for their scones, strawberry jam, and cream-tea parties. If you could drive in a straight line, it would only take like ten minutes to get from the church to Hilltop Manor—but you can't drive in a straight line because Oakdale Shopping Centre is in between.

Even though it was an environmental inconvenience, I liked Oakdale Shopping Centre. When I was younger, I would sit in the trolley going round with my mum, and there was always this magical moment when she would say, "If you could choose a toy, which one would be your favourite?" She would lift me out of the trolley, I would look at her smiling down at me, and I would look around the toy department. She would watch me reach out for a Barbie doll, and then we would both take the elevator to the café, me keeping hold of the doll while Mum ordered hot chocolate with marshmallow for me and a cappuccino for her. Then, we would sit by the massive window looking out at a duck pond, and it would be our precious moment. We made pinkie promises that she would always be there for me, and I said, "Mummy, I love you so much."

"I'm Father Leonard," said the guy in the robe. "I'm in charge of this parish. I've been asking the same question of how Rupert got to the church. I've met Rupert on occasions when I'd visited the home—a quiet soul. I'm unsure how he got here. Mrs. Bell has contacted the home. The manager was shocked to hear that he had left without staff noticing that he wasn't in his room. They are sending someone for him. But he did say something peculiar."

"Oh, what's that?" asked Justin.

"Rupert mumbled something about how he was following his niece, Emily, and she had led him here!" Leonard exclaimed.

"Impossible," said Justin dismissively. "Emily was my sister. She is dead."

Leonard opened his mouth, changed his mind, swallowed, and then said, "I guess there's a reasonable explanation, of course. But the matter remains how Rupert managed to walk all that way in this weather without getting frostbite. The only injury, as far as I can tell, is that he caught his toe on the lion statue outside."

Justin eyed Leonard strangely. "How could you tell he did not have frostbite just by looking at his feet?"

"I volunteered with the paramedics for many years. I've seen frostbite that would scare you. Rupert hasn't got any. Yes, his feet are red and painful. Understandable—he's walked all this way in socks and slippers."

"I knew you won't believe me, because you all think I'm mad," said Rupert. "That's why I've been thrown into a home against my wishes and have to survive on mashed-up food and a million tablets three times a day. There's nothing wrong with me; I forgot to switch the gas off once or twice and that was enough to condemn me. I know what I saw was Emily, and that's not the first time." He stood and glanced up at the statue of Saint George and the dragon.

Rupert stood tall and slim, his square glasses resting on the bridge of his nose. He looked like Justin but older. He put a hand on Justin's arm and nodded. "Oh well, I guess I have to go back, having inconvenienced everyone," he said.

"You're not an inconvenience, and you know if you could be at home with us you would, but I think it's wise for me to take you to accident and emergency (A&E) for a medical opinion," replied Justin.

Rupert looked at Justin curiously, taking out a large blue handkerchief and blowing his nose. "You've heard Father Leonard say that there's nothing wrong with me. I'm not going to waste anybody else's time. Can we have a private word?"

"Sure," Justin replied. He then glanced at me, as if asking my permission.

I nodded my head. "It's okay," I whispered before turning towards the front of the church. I was fascinated by the stained-glass windows behind statues of God and the Virgin Mary. Rupert leaned into his nephew and whispered, "Can you trust this girl with what I'm about to tell you?" as if I couldn't hear.

"I would trust Alexia with my life," said Justin.

"She's a pretty girl. Have you been dating long?" asked Rupert.

"That doesn't matter. Alexia is a caring and sensible girl, Uncle, and you were saying?"

"Justin, I know and understand that mentioning your sister is hurtful, but I've seen her, and it's astonishing—as if she is trying to tell me something. She was my niece. You can't take that away."

Justin shook his head. "It's a mystery. What was that?"

A roaring sound had broken the silence around us. It grew steadily louder as we looked at the back of the church for some sign of what was happening. Justin reached and grabbed my hand. We all ran to the open door. The sound increased into a scary flash of lightning and boom of a thunderstorm. Everyone looked up into the stormy sky, and a massive vintage car appeared on the street outside the church.

It scared the crap out of me. Rupert got onto his hands and knees while Father Leonard pulled rosary beads out of his pocket and started praying. Justin and I jumped.

The car has gull wind door that flung open upward. The car was huge and long; it was impressive, but not as extraordinary as the woman who stepped out of it. She was taller than any woman I had ever seen. She looked too tall to be normal, and so slender. She had long ringlets of black hair down to her waist, cheeks like a skeleton, glazed eyes, and hands the size of dinner plates. Her feet, in their knee-high green suede boots, were like baby sheep. Between her twig-like fingers, she was holding a bright-red object.

"Octovia," said Leonard, sounding surprised. "Where have you been? And where did you get that car?"

"On loan, dear Cousin—the only one available," said the titan, shutting the car door and limping up the path between the burial chambers as she spoke. "I had to get away in a hurry; these were the only keys I could put my hands on. I shot him twice—maybe six or seven times. I lost count."

"Keep quiet, Octovia. Who is he?"

"No idea, Leonard. He almost destroyed our family and certainly took me hostage before I could escape. I bought my time as he swanned around. He fell asleep in the doorway—family heirlooms all gone. That's all I could find." She handed him a picture with a red frame: the two of them as children playing in a tree house. He looked at it and blinked furiously.

Rupert got to his feet, and Leonard stepped aside. Justin and I looked on in disbelief. She looked like a walking, living, dead apparition with her fingernails bent inwards and her cheeks deeply hollowed. She wore a long black coat that was falling to bits, like that of a witch. We noticed a curiously shaped cut, like a stab wound, on her chin.

"Is that what he—?" whispered Leonard.

"Yes, that's just one of many," said Octovia." I'll have to live with those scars for the remainder of my days."

"I'm so very sorry," said Leonard. "We all tried. I almost got arrested outside the Tower of London. Have you driven all this way?" He patted Octovia gently on the arm.

"Yes," she said, stepping into the foyer and burying her face in Leonard's shoulder; he hugged her in his arms tenderly. For a full minute, the three of us stood looking at the strange woman without exchanging a single word. Rupert shook his head, Justin looked at me, and I stared back at him. Lightning forked furiously, cutting through trees. This seemed a most unusual Sunday.

"Well," said Leonard finally, "that car cannot stay out there. We need to do something about it."

"I agree. It's so unusual it would arouse suspicions," said Octovia. "Have you got a garage large enough to conceal the monster?"

"Yes," said Leonard, "at the back of the church." He glanced at the three of us and said, "Mrs. Bell would be in the hall, I expect. You can join her—no need to wait. And Rupert, it was my pleasure to see you again. Take care. Next time you fancy an adventure, call me."

Rupert nodded.

Octovia turned and walked back down the path. She flung the door open, swung into the driver seat, kicked the engine into life, and with a thundering roar the car flew down the street and round the corner into the secret garage.

In the hall were about six young people around my age—seventeen, maybe older—sitting on the chairs, talking to each other. Mrs. Bell glanced at us in the doorway and asked if we were there for the group. I nodded.

Justin held back with Uncle Rupert.

Mrs. Bell walked towards us and said, "Mr. Barker, the weekend manager from Hilltop, is waiting by the door to take Rupert back. He's brought transport."

"I'll be right back," Justin murmured.

I followed Mrs. Bell in, and sat down next to a girl with dark skin and massive, fabulous dreadlocks. She had the most amazing smile. Mrs. Bell went around introducing everyone. A girl with a long face wearing a Pooh Bear woolly hat was first. "I'm Chelsea. My mum is wheelchair bound, and I've been her carer for four years. I've missed school a lot, and it's difficult to make friends."

Next was the girl with dreadlocks. "My name is Phoenix. My dad has cancer; I've been his carer for three years, and it gets lonely at times. This place helps."

Mrs. Bell looked around. "Nice to see so many of you today. Thank you for making the effort. The Lord be with you. We are here to help you get through those difficult moments."

Goodness—everyone was telling his or her story, which was extraordinary. There was a boy called Gino, who was caring for his alcoholic dad. So many children were unpaid young carers and missing out on their youth. When it was my turn, I said, "Alexia. I'm seventeen—eighteen soon. My mum suffers with depression. I've been her carer for six-plus months, but she's getting better."

"We welcome Alexia into our Young Carers Association group," said Mrs. Bell. "We're here to support you, listen to your concerns, and provide a place for you to share your feelings, hopes, and dreams with others in similar circumstances."

After a while, Justin popped his head in and knocked at the door. Mrs. Bell and everyone turned and stared at him, as if to say, "You don't have to knock." He looked embarrassed. Mrs. Bell waved him in, and he sat opposite me.

"Would you like to share your experiences with the group?" asked Mrs. Bell, looking at Justin.

"I'm Justin Hunter and here to support Alexia," he said with a smile.

"Yes, we all need one another," said Mrs. Bell. Father Leonard came in with a plate of sandwiches and passed it around. They were ham and cucumber. Mrs. Bell served refreshments—orange juice in plastic cups. I suddenly felt as though everywhere I went, people felt the need to feed me: Justin's gran with pizza and his parents with popcorn at their house that same night. Do they think I'm too skinny? Justin moved from his seat and sat next to me. Everyone was talking about their experiences with being young carers, but the church hall was not about that; it was a place where you could be normal, listen to music, read, or just chat to each other. No pressure.

CHAPTER ELEVEN

By the time Justin and I arrived back at the truck, it was three in the afternoon and starting to get dark. We sat in the front seat of his truck for a while, talking. He kept mentioning his uncle Rupert and his sister in the same sentences. I was kind of scared to ask if his uncle had done that before or whether the weekend manager had said anything. Listening to someone talk about two people he obviously loved dearly was sad. It was quiet outside the arcade, except for a few cars in the car park opposite the supermarket. The snow, lightning, and thunder had stopped. I glanced at him. He looked distracted, staring straight through the windscreen.

Suddenly he said, "Alexia, isn't that Todd Walker wrestling with a car?"

I looked in the direction of his pointing finger and saw a man struggling to push a car. He kept falling, getting back up, and kicking the tyres. "Oh my God, it looks like Todd from group therapy!" I exclaimed. "He could never move that car in this much snow."

"I agree. I'll go and help him before he freezes to death," Justin said.

"I'm coming with you," I said.

He gave me a questioning glance. "Okay—as an observer, not a participant."

"Whatever."

He took my hand in his as we walked towards Todd, who tried once again to push the car and fell face down on the ice. He lifted his head and howled like a bear with a toothache. Justin shook his head slowly. "That is the sound of a desperate guy," he mumbled.

The sound drifted off, but Todd didn't get back to his feet.

It seemed that the only sounds I'd heard that day had been people shrieking in grief; that was not the way I was planning to spend my first Sunday with Justin. Sledging down a hill would have been more fun.

But this guy needed help.

"Todd Walker," Justin said on approaching, reaching out a hand to help him up.

He looked up at us, confused at first, and then said, "Justin, Alexia, from group therapy. What a surprise." Todd's expression shifted. "Oh, I just happened to run out of cigarettes, and my car decided to give up on me when you just happened to be driving past."

"Yeah, mate. Has it got gas in?" asked Justin.

"Tank is half full." Todd stood up and leaned against his car. "It must be this weather—even cars suffer psychosis in snowstorms." He beamed and stepped forward. "I'll push if you don't mind getting behind the wheel, please."

Justin glanced at me and back to Todd. "You must be exhausted—how about I push?" he suggested.

"Only if you're sure," said Todd.

"Absolutely," Justin responded.

Justin spread his fingers on the boot of the old black Volvo and ground his boots deep into the snow behind. Todd switched the engine on, and it made a horrible noise. Justin pushed and walked and then started taking big steps. After the fifth try, the car fired and sped forward.

Todd shouted through the rolled-down window: "I better head home. Thank you, mate."

"No worries. Happy to be of assistance," said Justin.

We stood side by side and watched Todd disappear. All of a sudden, Justin said, "Alexia, would you be disappointed if we dropped by my uncle's? Or I could drive you home first."

"Of course not. I'd be delighted to go with you."

He smiled at the corner of his mouth. "Thank you."

Justin pulled into the driveway of Hilltop Manor. The place was gigantic—huge grounds with statues of lions, dragons, and dinosaurs in the front. We walked up to the door. Justin rang the bell and knocked the brass lion head twice. A short, stocky man answered.

"Justin," he said. "You wanted to make sure he's settled."

"Yes, how is he, Mr. Barker?" asked Justin.

"Russell," he said. "He had a nap, and now he's having a game with his friend."

Justin nodded. "This is Alexia. Is it okay for her to come in?"

"Sure. He and Wynn are in the back lounge. You know the way."

"Of course," said Justin. He led us down a long corridor with a huge framed picture of a man standing with his arm on the back of a dragon. I suspect the gentleman with the medals on his fine clothes was Lord Frederick, the previous owner of Hilltop Manor. There were also pictures of elephants, deer, tigers, and lots of other wild animals hanging on the high walls. We stopped at a door with a brass plate that said Entertainment Lounge. We heard a sound of howling as we stood by the closed door. Oh no, not again.

"I guess someone is discontented, or Uncle Rupert's feet are giving him some trouble for the abuse they received," Justin joked.

I shook my head. "Oh no. There's only one way to figure it out," I said.

The door was shut but not locked. Justin and I peeped through. Rupert and Wynn were sitting on comfy chairs with their feet up, staring at a gigantic television. The screen was divided between Wynn's on the right and Rupert's on the left. They were in combat, fighting a robotic army out of the woods. Justin and I smiled, acknowledging the scene from *The Mind of Wizards*. We stood at the door for a while, watching. There was nothing abnormal—just two elderly guys sitting in their comfort zone, heartily immersed in a fantasy world, killing their enemies.

It was only when we stood opposite them that I noticed Wynn's neck. It was scratched as if he'd been in a fight with a wild animal. The wound was long and raw and weeping blood in a continual flow, his neck tense as if in agony. Rupert stared at the screen, not even greeting us, and yelled—all the while hammering at his controller. "Justin, you didn't have to come," he said. "I'm perfectly in control."

"Alexia and I were worried," Justin said. "Hi, Wynn, how is it going?" There was no recognition—not even the smallest head nod that he knew we were present. He just sobbed and wiped the tears with the back of his hand as red liquid poured down his neck and onto his brown pyjama top.

Rupert glanced away from the screen momentarily. "You don't have to stay. This is no place to bring your girlfriend," he said.

I stood next to Justin, our shoulders against the wall, looking at the action on TV. He glanced at me, smiling at his uncle's comment. Why is it that uncles think a girl is only allowed out with a boy if she is his girlfriend? What happened to normal friendship? I like to think that a woman should be free to make a choice to go with a boy to visit an elderly man who's walked four miles in freezing weather following a ghost—a boy who cares tremendously for his uncle's well-being—goodness gracious, there is nothing wrong with that. I'm going with him, even though he's not asked me on an actual date yet. So in reality, I'm not really his girlfriend—yet.

And yet, I thought, Wynn, who knew and liked Justin but had never met me before, won't glance at us. Too engrossed with fighting illusions, I suppose.

"That is the result of living with dementia," Justin said. "Victims scratch their body and experience hallucinations, like seeing and following ghosts. A complicated subject. Wynn and my uncle have been friends since the war. They've always kept in touch. A few months after my grandparents chose this place for Uncle Rupert, Wynn's wife died of lung cancer. They didn't have children, so he moved in here, and the friendship continued."

"Have you seen Wynn's neck?" I whispered.

"Yeah, he always has some sort of injury on him, I've asked my uncle about it often. He says that Wynn sees and fights dragons."

"Fair enough. I think he needs a doctor, then, not *The Mind of Wizards*," I said.

"It's their favourite game."

"Wynn, I feel that we're being hunted," said Rupert. "On the bridge on your left. If you agree, we'll fire." Wynn slid his hand by the side of his comfy chair while Rupert reached under his, and they both pointed machine guns at the imaginary bridge and fired steadily in a series of vigorous blasts, wheeling them from side to side.

"That's a regular pastime," Justin whispered to me. "It keeps their minds occupied and doesn't disturb the other residents. My uncle and I used to play war games when I was younger. He would say that in the 1940s war, the army embraced nine-millimetre submachine guns."

"Oh, how interesting. I was under the impression that Wynn was in pain," I said as a blast of bullets from Wynn killed a baby dragon that had flown out of a cave and across the metal bridge. A big black one followed, shot a big ball of fire into the air, and dived into the woods.

"Oh my God, that is crazy," I said.

Rupert nodded at the screen. "It was asking for that after the pain it caused you, my friend," he said, quoting Zac's favourite line from *The Mind of Wizards.*

"Hmm, that was not a bad shot, but the big one is still at large," said Wynn. "She'll be back for revenge."

Seconds later both men were lying on their stomachs on the carpeted floor, roaring bullets zipping randomly in every direction. "She's not getting away again, Wynn," Rupert said. "I don't mean to be disloyal in your moment of agony, but you have to allow me this blast or she will kill us brutally. We have a duty to protect the other residents from the sort of wound that damned dragon inflicted on you." Wynn rolled onto his knees and pulled his chair behind Rupert, weapon pointing straight ahead.

"You need extra force in that situation," said Justin, kicking into position on the floor next to his uncle—a skill learned from *The Mind of Wizards.* This was not a traditional game. It was a virtual-reality game that Wynn and Rupert enjoy to pass their time.

"What on earth?" Wynn groaned, shaking his head. Justin and Rupert jerked their heads. "What is it?" they both asked.

"Look, sorry—sadly that little monster is still alive, and there are five of them, all heading for us," said Wynn. "Take my gun, Justin; damn, I'm going to use my secret weapon." He pulled a bow and arrows from under his chair.

"Gladly, my friend," Justin said, his voice husky. "That was a magnificent shot. We'll finish those freaking creatures so we can all sleep in peace."

I had a feeling that Justin would prefer the bow and arrows. I smiled. Boys will be boys, no matter their ages. "You better," I said. "Getting eaten alive by dragons wasn't part of the plan."

Justin looked at me and smiled. "I'll protect you—just hang in there." He glanced at his uncle, who turned away from the screen and flashed him a questioning grin, shaking his head.

"Now let's kill some fictional dragons," said Rupert.

Together, they crawled on their elbows to the window, firing and ducking to avoid the whizzing and roaring balls of flame that were coming at them from overhead. They squatted behind the curtains, listening to the massive swoosh of the wings that flew past. Once it stopped, Wynn peeked out, and three of the creatures had landed on the other side of the wall, close enough that he could see their huge horns. Without any sudden moves, he nodded to his mates, and they clashed one by one.

"Is it done? Are we safe?" I asked.

"We'll live to fight again," Justin answered.

Rupert leapt to the controller, crashed the buttons, and rapidly increased the volume. Sweat streamed down his forehead. Wynn scanned through the curtain before he stumbled back to his chair and concealed his bow and arrows beneath it. Justin stared at me with a big smile. "They were no match for us. Mission accomplished, comrades," he said, shaking hands with Wynn and his uncle.

"Whoa—what now?" I said. "There were more than three—it's not over yet."

Justin looked over at me, gun still in his hand, and half smiled. "I was thinking the same."

Suddenly there was a bang that shook the whole building, followed by a rumble that radiated into my ears like thunder. Justin rolled onto his back, slid his gun towards Wynn, and grabbed Wynn's bow and arrows. As he moved between the curtains, he shot the arrows continuously into the creature's eyes. It rolled onto the lawn outside knocking them over and slamming into statues until it disappeared from view.

"Liberation! Liberation!" Rupert shouted as the screen turned black. Suddenly there was a knock on the door. Wynn threw his blanket over the weapon in a flash, for a man in agony, he was fast—faster than the dragon's balls of fire. Justin quickly pushed his weapon behind Rupert's chair.

Wynn looked away in disappointment. "He needs a shot up his ass for disturbing us at such a significant moment," he grumbled.

Russell, the weekend manager, walked in. "Oh, killing dragons I take it, again." He frowned.

"You're next on Scientist Zac's list, and if that bastard Barratt had any brain he'd stay well clear," Wynn said as he jumped on to his feet.

Russell glared at him; he was carrying a narrow tray with two small cream pots and a jug of water. "It's time for your medication, and the doctor is here to check that wound on your neck, Wynn," he said.

"I don't need a bloody doctor to tell me what I already know," said Wynn. "This place had been haunted—spooked by ghosts and dragons from the previous owner. What you call wounds are dragons attacking people while they sleep, and that always happens when you're on duty. Why is that?"

"Wynn is right," said Rupert, looking at Justin. "That's what I've been trying to tell you. These damn tablets that he keeps throwing down our throats are to keep us quiet. I've refused them. I refuse to be bullied."

"Uncle Rupert, the medications assist with your mental well-being and stop you from deteriorating," Justin said.

"Deterioration my foot. There's nothing wrong with me. How could you say that, after what you've seen with your own eyes? You've finally killed those predators that are continually attacking us and the others in this establishment." He pointed a long finger at Russell. "His mission is to destroy us with his poisons, not to save us from these murderers."

Wynn, who had been staring at Russell, rushed frantically to the window, grabbed the curtains, and tugged at them so hard that the whole lot—plus plaster that had been part of the wall for centuries—tumbled atop him. He got to his feet in a flash; Wynn, refusing to be beaten, reached for the handle and pushed the window open. "Out there beneath the bridge is where they lived. We've seen and killed them tonight," he said in a rage.

"It's just an illusion," Russell pointed out.

"No illusion. Rupert and I fought in the war side by side; we have been exposed to dismembered bodies and rivers of blood but never been at the mercy of flying monsters."

Russell handed me the tray. I took it and glanced into the pots. There were countless tablets in various colours inside. Justin shot me a look. I shook my head.

Russell shrugged as if he didn't believe what he was hearing, but to Wynn and Rupert, it was real. Rupert was shouting and slapping his face continuously. Wynn rolled onto the floor like a ball, holding his knees. A small coffee-skinned man pushed past us. He had a syringe in his right hand. When he reached Wynn, he bent at the waist, pulled Wynn's pyjama sleeve up, and shot him once with the needle in the upper arm. Wynn didn't protest.

I imagined he was the doctor. Then he and Russell moved on to Rupert, but before he could inject Rupert's arm, Rupert knocked him to the floor with a punch and kicked him in the nuts. It took everyone by surprise as Rupert continued kicking the crap out of the guy, who was still holding the needle in the air. Rupert grabbed the needle and stabbed Russell in the stomach with it. "Oh my God," said Justin as he tried to grab his uncle's arms but missed. Rupert chased after the doctor, who had managed to stumble to his feet, and kneed him in the balls. He fell back onto the floor, howling.

"I don't know what's the worse shit out here: Russell or the damn drugs you're killing us with," said Rupert, kicking the guy again as he tried to escape from the room. He was trapped.

All of a sudden, the door flew open and two elderly ladies came charging in with pillows and started smashing them against the doctor. They stepped over the lifeless body of Wynn and whacked the massive TV off its stand. It went *boom* on the floor, and sparks flew everywhere.

"Mission accomplished," Rupert shouted, looking at Wynn, who had drifted onto his back on the floor.

Justin looked over to me, his mouth wide, and half smiled. "I never, ever want to be old, but when my time comes, I want to be like my uncle."

"He's certainly very strong," I said, glancing at Rupert, who had collapsed back into his chair. I looked around. The two elderly ladies had vanished, leaving behind a cloud of smoke from the wrecked TV. Hair stood on the back of my neck. Russell and the doctor stumbled to their feet, and Wynn was snoring. I stood a few feet away from Justin, who was looking from his uncle and back to me, nodding his head as he witnessed the madness.

The doctor who had come to treat the wounded was now a victim with a few broken ribs. Russell had a broken nose but was otherwise functioning. A once-desirable lounge now resembled a battlefield, with pieces of TV, dismounted curtains and pole, and feathers flying around the room. Justin asked Russell if he needed any assistance. Russell shook his head. "*No, thank you. I have seen enough!*" he responded.

Justin stepped towards his uncle and tapped him gently on the shoulder. "Sleep well—and no more wandering," he said.

"I've never felt so accomplished in all my life," Rupert mumbled.

Russell's mobile made a sound like a tornado; he rushed out of the room, followed by the doctor.

"That's the thing with medical people—they have no idea of the pain they inflict until they feel it," Rupert said. He glanced at me. "We're freed, thanks to my brave nephew. Take care of this girl."

CHAPTER TWELVE

I did not see or speak to Justin again for over a week. I did call him on the night of the dragon fights to report that our snow creatures had vanished, which was very odd, given that it was below zero and still snowing. So it was his turn to call, but he didn't. It wasn't like I was watching my phone, hoping for it to ring in my jeans pocket, or staying awake and staring at the ceiling, impulsively waiting for his charming voice to transform my world; I carried on with my life.

On Friday, when I got to college, there was a huge notice saying "Closed due to adverse weather conditions." Okay, none of us had been notified. Mia was hanging around with her cool-dude-but-not-as-hot-as-Justin boyfriend. She invited me for lunch one day. I contemplated the offer, along with my obligation to attend group therapy with my mum and my new once-a-week Young Carers support group on Sunday and being there for my mum. I sat down and chatted to Mum while she prepared dinner.

Mum was getting stronger each day. That night she wanted to surprise me again with her cooking; we had roast cod and cornflower bake. We were seated facing each other at our little round table in the small kitchen when my phone started buzzing; but we never, ever check or answer a call when we're having our meal. That was the rule.

So I ate small bits while Mum talked about a phone conversation she had had with my dad the day before. As far as I was aware, my parents hadn't spoken for about ten or maybe twelve years. Though I texted Dad while Mum was in hospital after her attack, he had never, ever replied, visited, called, or written. Samantha was all we had for support. I was surprised to hear of Mum's call to Dad; whatever had happened during that phone call had not caused Mum any distress, or she was hiding her feelings. I looked at her. Mum wasn't good at concealing her feelings—especially if something terrible had occurred. It was like, all of a sudden, she was not scared but fully in control—the Mum I'd longed for: brave, young, optimistic, self-sufficient, and hardly changed, like normal people who were free from mental-health problems, and glowing with so much enthusiasm that she didn't even glance across at me as I pushed my food around my plate. I breathed deeply. Her confidence made me worry that something was wrong—that she was relapsing. I banished the thought as best I could. It was two weeks before my eighteenth birthday; she and Dad could be planning a huge birthday bash. If something was wrong, like Dad was dying or something, she would have told me. I picked up my fork and ate a little more. The food was delicious. Nothing to be achieved by worrying. Mum had gone to group therapy without me today; she was slowly gaining her independence.

And yet I worried. Mum had a mental-health review scheduled for Wednesday. I was hoping her consultant would say that she was better and could go back to work. That was what mum wanted. Dad getting back in touch could disrupt it all.

Finally mum said, "Your dad is in the North East. He's coming around tonight; is that okay?"

I looked at mum, "Yes, but why now, after all these years? Are you okay with it?"

"He is still your dad, sweetie," she said, standing up and picking the dishes from the table.

"Mum, you've cooked. I'll do the dishes," I said.

"No, no, I'm sure you want to answer the caller," she said, smiling.

I paused, watching her load the dishwasher. I sensed that she wanted to be alone—maybe to gather her thoughts before Dad arrived. I grabbed my phone from my bag on the chair next to me and checked the last call. Justin Hunter.

"Mum, please, call me when Dad is here," I said.

"Of course," said Mum, loading the dishwasher. I went into my bedroom and shut the door. I sat on the sofa bed, shoved the stuffed animals to one side, and crossed my legs into a meditation pose. I cuddled a stuffed bunny rabbit and called him.

"Alexia," he said.

"Hi," I said, "How are you?"

"Okay," he said. "I have been wanting to call you every day, but we have been involved with another police arrest in my sister's murder—someone who sounds like he's guilty on the basis that they found pictures of my sister on his computer, and they found her iPad in his room when the police searched his flat. But they wouldn't tell us his name at this stage. Understandable, although that caused suspicions that it might be someone we knew or maybe the same guy they arrested and let go last time. It has been difficult; I couldn't form a rational view of the matter. It was hurtful and painful for me and my family. I've hardly slept. I've read *Seeking Angels* again and again in search of comfort." He sounded lost. He really did.

"I'm so sorry," I said.

"No need for apologies. As I was reading, I felt something oddly familiar. I kept feeling as if it was telling me something."

"Something?" I asked. "Like what?"

"Like you are meant to be my girlfriend, and we are meant to go searching for the author of that book. She might tell us what happened to that girl in the story," he said, his voice more cheerful.

"Oh," I said softly.

"Are you up for it?" he asked.

"Maybe after my exams and birthday, but I can't be away for more than a day," I said.

"I understand. What if I invited you to the Lakes on a first date? Just for the day, or we could maybe spend the night. Your choice."

"Deal," I said.

"Right, so in your previous text, you mentioned that our snowy friends had vanished?"

"Yes, they're gone," I said.

"That is odd, given that it is still freezing. It's impossible for them to just melt away."

"Correct."

"The probability is they just disappeared beneath falling snow," Justin suggested.

"Absolutely. Possibly," I said.

"Oh, flipping marvellous, I was planning to drive my gran over to see them. She has been a bit down lately; she was looking forward to it too. What am I supposed to say?"

"You'll figure something; I feel that life is full of surprises. As it happens, I've got a surprise of my own. I'm expecting my dad any minute; given that I've not seen him for well over ten years, it should be quite a reunion."

"Truthfully?" he asked.

"Truthfully," I replied.

"What the hell happened? He just deserted you and your mum, just like that? Has he been in a war or something?"

"Frankly, I have no idea. All I know was that my dad worked on oil rigs in the Arabian Gulf. I'm worried that something is wrong

with him. My mum wouldn't say why he was in England or the reason he was coming tonight apart from that he wanted to see me."

"It would be interesting to hear his explanation—his reason
why he never visited you all these years. Oil rigs in the Arabian
Gulf could be lonely—not that I've any experience," Justin said.

"I'm not sure that he was lonely. According to my mum, he left
her for another woman."

"Oh, no, is that what caused your mum's anxiety?" he asked.

"It has definitely played a part, but wasn't the whole reason.
Mum was depressed long before dad left; she told me so. I thought
mums and dads were meant to be together forever, but I was wrong
in my case." I heard the intercom rang. "He's here. I've got to go.
Keep reading."

"Okay, can I call you later?"

"How about I call you back?"

"I'll be waiting," said Justin.

I spent ten to fifteen minutes in my room, allowing my parents
time alone. I wanted to see Dad, but I was also angry with him for
leaving us. Mum's reactions earlier told me that there wasn't any
chance of forgive and forget. I'd had enough of waiting. It seemed
I was getting angrier, so I grabbed the shoebox from the back of
my wardrobe. It contained all the letters I had written Dad but
never had the courage to post. I flung the door open and raced
down the narrow corridor like an athlete. I stopped short, stood
at the door of our small sitting room, and saw an old, rugged,
unshaven man on the settee. Oh my God, who is this? That can't
be my dad. No, he is not my dad. I glanced over to Mum; she was
feeding the fish. She looked at me and nodded her head slightly.
Oh sugar, yes, he is my dad. There wasn't any conversation. On
my approach, Mum had turned the lights on in the fish tank. It
looked magnificent. What had happened to my clean-shaven dad,
the Dad I remembered? The man in the room was a shabby old
skinny guy I hardly recognised.

He rose to his feet and walked over to me, wrapping his arms around me. Alarmed that something was really, really wrong with him, I was overwhelmed by the fear that I might have to go through what I went through with Mum with her depression. Trying to force away the thought, I wanted to say, "Hi, Dad," but the words refused to come out. I began to quiver, dropping the shoebox. It landed open, and all the letters scattered on the floor. I tried to push away from him so I could pick up the letters, but he wouldn't let go of the bear hug.

"Please, I need to pick up the letters," I said quietly.

He wouldn't let go. "I've missed you, and I knew you would be angry. You have every right. I've missed so much of your life, Alexia. I'm so, so sorry." His words were coming quick and fast. Suddenly his arms dropped to his side; I was free. He stood there, looking at me and then the floor. I stared back into his big brown eyes and realised that his eyes were just like mine. We had the same features: a pointy nose and small lips. After a while he bent to one knee, picking up the box and the letters all addressed to him.

Mr. Thomas Collins

Oil Rigs Offices

PO Box 12

Abu Dhabi

He ripped a letter open, read it, looked up at me, shook his head, and looked sad, but there weren't any tears. Typical British male—intellectuals and professionals never show emotions. Mum stopped feeding the fish, thank God—they were at risk of being overfed. She walked over to me, took my hands, and kissed me on the cheek.

"When did you write all these, and where have you been hiding them?" she asked, looking at the letters. Dad took the shoebox once he had finished tidying the letters and sat back down on the settee. Looking at Mum and me, he nodded.

I wanted to hug him and tell him how much I'd missed him—tell him that I loved him, but I couldn't. I didn't know if I would see him again after tonight, or if it would take another eighteen years before his next visit. By then I might have kissed a boy.

I couldn't contain my fury. I exploded. I didn't think; I just said what I was feeling. "Why did you never come to see me? You never sent me a birthday or Christmas card, and you've never replied to my texts. What are you doing here, and for how long are you staying?" I asked.

Dad rubbed his left arm, which pulled his sleeve up a little, and I noticed it immediately, "Oh my God, when did this happen?" He looked in agony.

"Three years ago, I was airlifted from the rigs to the hospital after a helicopter smashed onto the rig and burst into flames. I suffered first-degree burns. Everyone thought I wouldn't survive; I was on the verge of death. The first year was touch and go. In the Abu Dhabi burns unit, I was fed by a tube through my navel and wasn't able to open my eyes. My friends read me William Shakespeare's poem 'The Battle for Survival.' I couldn't speak. I had the same recurring dream about walking in grassy meadows with a little girl in my arms, watching wild ponies racing past.

"Twenty months later, I opened my eyes for the first time since it happened, wrapped in linen like an ancient Egyptian mummy and immersed in pain. I couldn't remember where I was or my identity. Mick, a close friend, in his attempt to help, located a picture of you as a four-year-old that was pinned on the wall in my room. He handed the photo to me. I recognised my little girl instantly. It was an emotional time, but my medical team were hopeful. I was moved to the recovery unit, and Mick kept visiting on his days off, reading the Elizabeth Barrett Browning poem about the mysterious wife who pushed her husband away from his beautiful daughter. I felt extremely vulnerable."

It took me a moment to make sense of what he was saying—including the joke about the poem. Mum was still holding my arm. Dad stood and took off his shirt, exposing the extent of his burns: his left arm, chest, and the back of his neck were totally scarred. It looked scary. I glanced at Mum in anguish. Dad buttoned his shirt and sat back down; he exhaled and looked at us both.

"Jessica, you have done a wonderful job raising our daughter. I'm not walking away again. I understand that at the time of the decision you were unwell and confused, and I didn't wish to cause you more distress—I agreed to live and stay away, but it has been torture. Alexia will be eighteen in a couple of weeks; she deserves the truth. Apart from the time in hospital, every year I sent Alexia's birthday and Christmas present and cards. It sounds like she's not received them."

Mum frowned. "Alexia is our daughter, yes, but you're right: I've raised her. You weren't around when she needed you. I've kept her cards and presents. I didn't want her to build her hope," Mum said.

He looked at Mum, running a hand over his shabby face. He was furious at her, but he also knew that she wasn't well. He said calmly, "You drove me away. No more pretence, Jessica. Alexia must and should know the truth about why I missed out on her upbringing."

Mum glared at him. It was evident that Mum was trying her best to hide something. I wasn't having it. I needed to know the truth; honesty is best—even if it hurts.

"One or both of you are keeping something from me," I said. "Please, as my parents, can you explain what is going on? I ought to know."

Mum hesitated for a moment. I looked at her. She exhaled sharply and said, "It's best we sit down, Alexia." Without letting go of my arm, she walked me to the sofa and sat down opposite Dad. "I love you very much, Alexia, but carrying and having you was probably the most difficult experience in my life. You left the hospital with your dad, and I had to stay behind without you. By the time I was allowed home, you had bonded with your dad, and I felt empty and tormented. I couldn't bear, think about, or make sense of life. The delusion of your dad taking you away from me got worse; I became overly protective. Eventually I asked your dad to leave and stay away from you—from us. For years he refused to agree to what I was asking of him, and I made various trips to medical professionals and solicitors. Then my psychiatrist decided that I was okay to care for you. Thomas reluctantly agreed to leave on the condition that when you turned eighteen, he would tell you the truth."

My mouth dropped open. Oh my God. I shut my eyes to stop the tears. After she had lied and lied to me for years—letting me believe that my dad didn't want to be part of my life, that he left her for another woman—she dropped that sort of bomb on me now. I was angry with both; I stood up and sat back down. I wondered if Mum's secrecy was part of her delusion—obviously her decision was a result of her mental illness. I was disappointed, but I was also relieved. Having watched my mum hallucinate about dinosaurs, worried that she would die next time she self-harmed, had helped me make sense between what was real and what was fictitious. The magnificent advantage of *Seeking Angels* was that everything Vanessa Helena Amadeo wrote in her book was right. But there was something I needed to know that my parents weren't willing to express: whether they were still married or divorced.

"Okay, I should be so frantic with you two right now, but I can't—the reason being that I've witnessed Mum at her lowest and prayed that she'd get out of the darkness and into the light. It was frightening when I went with her to group therapy and watched people talking to walls. I've seen ghosts and given up hanging out with my friends—including Friday evenings—to enjoy adult company since Mum's attack. That's okay too. I'm not complaining. But could you answer a sensible question?"

"Of course. What is the question?" Dad asked.

"Did you actually get divorced?"

Mum gave Dad a questioning gaze, and a smile curled at the corner of his mouth, as if I'd asked a funny question, but they weren't in a hurry to reply.

"Take your time," I said. "I'm just curious, and you can't blame me for that, after years of desperately hoping that my dad would walk through the door and take the responsibility of caring for Mum, making sure she took her medication, ate, and stayed safe. I have joined a Young Carers group recently—a group of young people in the similar situation of caring for adult parents with illnesses. I just thought you'd like to know what it's like to be in my world. Here you are, my dad, mysteriously dedicated, appearing two weeks before my eighteenth birthday, wounded and vulnerable."

"I'm so sorry, Alexia. Nothing was planned, but I take full responsibility for your loneliness. The answer to your question: I never signed the divorce papers. Again, it was something your mother wanted, but I recognised that she wasn't in the right frame of mind at the time she made that decision. I have never stopped loving my wife. Seeing you and your mother again was all that kept me going in that damn unit."

Mum tipped her head to one side and glanced at Dad, like the way she and Sophia communicated at group therapy. Dad smiled a little crookedly. "You are still my wife, Jessica. I'm terribly sorry for the pain you have suffered, and for our Alexia taking that much responsibility at her age."

Mum shrugged, but she didn't agree or disagree, and they didn't question me about the Young Carers group either.

CHAPTER THIRTEEN

I left my parents alone and called Justin back, and we stayed up into the early hours, talking about *Seeking Angels*. He told me that through his research on Google Earth, he had found what he believed was the home of Vanessa Helena Amadeo located in a quiet village on the edge of the Lake District. He said he had e-mailed her through her e-mail address on her website and that he knew the place well, having been there on scout camping trips. I told him about my dad and his wounds and that I loved my dad but I couldn't tell him. Justin said that I was an affectionate and caring girl and that he was sure that my dad loved me too. Then he told me that he'd visited his uncle Rupert with his gran Sophia, and Uncle Rupert was reading *The Mind of Wizards*, page 395, where Zac finds the remains of a body buried in the woods that he believes to be Barratt Joshley's mother, who disappeared twenty years ago. I remembered reading that part. Then he told me that he would like to read me something, but I must promise not to laugh. I said that I promised.

"On a rainy, misty day, a perfect kiss warms your heart and soul—a kiss that feels like a summer day."

"Wow, interesting," I said. "Is it a poem from a famous poet?"

"Oh no, I wrote it. Experimenting with words. I believe Barratt Joshley wouldn't approve; he preferred killing, and Zac is too wrapped in madness to appreciate such words of passion."

"Yes, ducking and diving within the woods, no doubt. Damn, Zac ducks and dives nonstop in the book. He's certainly got to if he wants to survive against Barratt's robotic army and those dragons." I giggled.

After a short pause, Justin asked, "When did you last have a perfect kiss?"

I pondered on his question. Like everything in my life, I dreamt about kissing, but it never happened. Boys weren't keen to ask an unsociable girl who ran home to her mum after college on dates, and that's when the kissing thing was likely to happen. Besides, I was very shy and didn't think that I was pretty or desirable, so I lied. "A long time ago," I said eventually. "What about you?"

"I had some perfect kisses with a few ex-girlfriends. Last time was my ex Olympia Valentino. Over twelve months ago."

"What happened?"

"My family needed my support after my sister."

"So what happened with you and Olympia?"

"Oh, she couldn't deal with emotions, and there were loads of them. She went on a family holiday to Italy and posted pictures on Facebook of her kissing a guy."

"Oh," I said.

"Yes," he said.

"I'm sorry," I said. My experience with a broken heart, of course, was nonexistent. I'd never been on a date or been kissed. I couldn't imagine what it would be like to have a broken heart.

"Not a problem, Alexia. Unless you have lost someone close, it is difficult to imagine how it would affect you, right?"

"Yeah, the world is like an ocean of emotions, and it is hard to deal with it all," I said, based on my own experience of what it was like to grow up without my dad and watch my mother deteriorate mentally.

"Well," he said, "I'm going let Lucky out the back garden then go to sleep. It's two forty."

"Two forty, really?" I was kidding.

"Yeah," he said.

I laughed and said, "Sweet dreams." He laughed the same free-spirited laugh I admired when I watched him kill dragons with his uncle. Then the line went silent but not completely dead. I could sense a presence, like he was there in the same room with me. I closed my eyes, imagining what it would be like to transport to his room, watching Lucky lying in her basket in the corner of his room; or have him transport to my room, where we would be contented with stuffed animals; but that was impossible. Instead, we found togetherness in some magical and peaceful place that I felt safe—that could only be on the phone.

"What are you doing tomorrow?" he asked after forever.

"No plans come to mind."

"Okay, I'll think of something," he said.

A moment later he finally hung up.

Vanessa Helena Amadeo never replied to Justin's e-mail, which probably meant she didn't want to be found, even though her book had given courage to someone like me, who struggled to make sense of my mother's mental-health problems. Justin didn't seem too bothered that Vanessa had not replied; he assured me that we were going to the Lake District anyway.

On Tuesday, exam day, my first paper was for British History. I've never had a problem with exams before, but today it was quite hard. Even though I'd revised for months, my mind was completely blank. I glanced across the classroom to see Mia. She had her head down and was writing speedily. She was smart at everything and the only person I knew who loved exams. Then I looked at the front of the room. Mrs. Pear, the form teacher, glared at me.

I started writing to stop Mrs. Pear watching me over her square glasses. She had a habit of watching you with her glasses on the end of her nose, and then she would walk between the desks and stand next to you. Today was no different. Mrs. Pear walked to the back of the room, and on her way back to her seat, she stopped at my desk just as I put a full stop on the last line. I turned my paper over—exam rules. She continued looking over everyone's shoulders and then went back to the front and sat down on her chair.

She was a great teacher but strict on rules. Rules to smile, rules to look, rules to ask questions—she even had a rule for the way you raised your hand if you needed to use the toilet. No doubt, she had rules for waking and going to bed.

I was on my way to the toilet when I got a text from my mum: "Sophia has had emergency surgery. She is in recovery. It went well. How are you getting on with your exams?"

A second text came a few seconds later, from Justin: "Sorry I didn't wish you good luck with your exams. My gran had surgery, but she is doing fine. I mean, she'd broken her cheek bone. Unfortunately."

That afternoon I biked as fast as I could and stopped by Sam's florist to buy some flowers. She was arranging a bouquet of white lilies—for a funeral, she told me. I was looking at the buckets of roses in a variety of colours, I sniffed the red ones. She noticed me looking at the roses, and, as it was my exams, she gave me twelve pink roses as a treat. They smelled pretty amazing. Then she asked me if I fancied helping her in the shop on Saturdays during my holidays, and I told her yes, I'd like to, as I was looking for a Saturday job, and she told me that she had spoken to my mum and knew that my dad was back.

"How do you feel about seeing your dad after all those years, Alexia?" asked Sam, putting on her sad face.

"I'm not sure how I really feel at the moment with exams. I just want to concentrate on passing, you know?" I said.

"I understand." She explained that she couldn't pay me much, but she would teach me all about flowers and how to make a gorgeous bouquet, and we decided that I should start as soon as my exams were over.

I caught the number fifty-nine bus with my bike; it was too far to bike all the way to Whitley General to visit Sophia. I locked my bike at the area reserved for bikes and found my way to her room on the third floor. I knocked twice on the door. A man's voice I recognised said, "Come in." It was Justin, sitting on a comfy chair next to his gran's bed. Sophia's face was completely covered in bandages, save her eyes.

"Hi," I said. "How are you?"

Sophia grabbed Justin's hand. He nodded.

Justin stood up. "Gran would like you to sit next to her. She can't have a conversation yet, but she is happy that you've come to see her."

"Oh, I have brought you these roses; maybe I should go and find a vase," I said.

"It's okay. You sit down," he said. "A nurse will be in shortly. I'll ask for the flowers to be put in a vase, thank you."

I handed him the bouquet. He showed it to Sophia, who mumbled something I didn't hear. She was clearly still in pain.

"They're beautiful," he said, looking at me with a smile.

I looked away, embarrassed. I took a few steps towards the bed and sat down on the chair. Sophia took my hand. Justin pulled another chair up and sat down next to me. "How are you feeling?" I asked Sophia.

Sophia didn't answer.

"Gran has been suffering with her cheek bone for some time and kept refusing to have surgery," said Justin. "She attended group therapy even when her cheek had swollen. Grandad called my parents this morning from hospital; she just couldn't bear the pain any longer."

Sophia squeezed my hand in response to what her grandson had said. I looked at her hand because I didn't want to look at her face wrapped in bandages, which went right underneath her chin and on top of her head, I assumed to keep her bones together, which was why it was difficult for her to speak. I noticed her well-manicured hands; she had amazing fingernails. Suddenly there was a knock on the door, and Justin said, "Come in."

Two nurses walked in. They were young, pretty, and couldn't help but smile at him flirtatiously. He smiled back politely and asked if they could put his gran's flowers in a vase of water, please.

The nurse with short brown hair and huge hazelnut eyes said, "Of course. They are beautiful."

"Yes, my girlfriend brought them," he said, looking at me with a big grin.

I glanced at him, surprised. He beamed, stood up, and took my hand. Honestly, he's pretty optimistic, but I didn't disagree with the title of girlfriend.

The nurses peeked at me but didn't comment. They were pulling a trolley with medical instruments. I suddenly thought of mum as a pretty young nurse sticking needles into patients like Sophia and wondered what went on between my parents. I wondered if my dad was planning to stay in England, and if so, where would he stay. I had so many questions I wanted to ask my dad, but there was no great hurry.

"Shall we go for a walk while the nurses take care of Gran?" Justin asked.

"Yeah"

"Gran, I'm taking Alexia for a walk. We'll be back soon."

Sophia waved a hand, and I waved back. Once out the door, he took my hand as we strolled along the long, wide corridor with massive windows on both sides. The floor was gleaming; a woman was polishing it with a huge mop. It was a shame that people had to keep walking on her shining floor. We took the stairs instead of the elevator to the ground floor. He stopped at the drinks machines and asked if I would like a cold or hot drink. I said "cold," so he got two cans of Coke from the vending machine, and then we walked out of the big revolving glass door and a short way to the duck pond.

Strangely, there wasn't any snow around the hospital; it was warm with glimmers of sunshine. I sat on a bench, and he sat next to me and handed me a can of Coke. Instead of letting go of the can, he kept hold of my hand. I glanced sideways at him, and he smiled.

"Thank you for taking time to visit my gran. How were your exams?" he asked.

"Okay, I suppose—as far as exams go," I said.

"You've done well, no doubt."

He let go of my hand. I opened the can and took a sip of my drink. It was cold and refreshing.

"Has the doctor said how long your gran will be in hospital?" I asked.

"Not yet. If my gran had her way, she wouldn't be there; she is the worst patient. Since my sister's death. She doesn't want to be in there—too many sad memories—but her consultant is hopeful, so she's bearing up."

"In my view, hospital is a scary place that's only reserved for desperately sick people like your gran at the moment. My mum spent some time in the mental unit after I was born. She told me that it was an extremely frightening experience; she was a trained nurse, but she didn't feel that it lessened her fear."

"Your mum has been through hell, actually. Sometimes I wish that I had a crystal ball or a magic wand."

"Oh, a crystal ball or a magic wand—what would you do with them?"

He beamed, and his eyes narrowed. He took a sip of his Coke and glanced at me. "If I had a crystal ball, I could see who murdered my sister or whether you truly like me, as I truly like you. On the other hand, if I had a magic wand, I could perform magic. I could take you with me to another world—a happier one, away from everything."

"That's crazy," I said. "It's as crazy as me spinning around on a broomstick or belonging to a secret society of witchcraft or something."

"Alexia, that's not a bad idea. Just imagine how powerful we'd be. Broomsticks, witchcraft, magic wand, and crystal ball—we'd be unstoppable. We would be amazing. We could spy on Barratt Joshley and Zac's lab of madness or hover over Vanessa Helena Amadeo's hideaway or whatever."

He was kidding. I laughed, looking at the ducks swimming in the pond, the nurses coming and going and smoking cigarettes on nearby benches, and visitors walking by with flowers and gifts. Justin had a fantastic sense of humour—no one had ever made me laugh like he did.

"One advantage of a crystal ball or a magic wand is that it would give me the power to walk into my exam without revision and know all the answers to the questions," I said.

"Yeah," he said.

"I just wish we had brought some bread," I said, changing the subject.

"You hungry?" he asked.

"No, to feed the ducks."

"I see. Sorry, but we've come unprepared for duck feeding."

"Well I'm sure these ducks are well fed; they don't appear to be starving."

"Point taken. It was so great to see you, I totally forgot that the ducks may like a little grub," he joked.

I laughed. "I'm being serious. I like feeding animals, and ducks are so cute—especially the ducklings." There were six ducklings in the pond, swimming amongst the water lilies, and four ducks—a family.

"I love animals too," he said.

"Yeah," I said, watching a nurse kissing a guy before they got into their separate cars. I glanced at Justin. He was looking at the couple too.

We went back into Sophia's room. She was asleep, and the flowers were in a vase on the table at the foot of her bed. His grandad was there, reading a book by the bed. He shut the book when he saw us. I peeked at the cover; it was about bird watching. Sophia did not strike me as someone who would go bird watching. He pointed to the door, and Justin and I followed him outside.

"You look well, Alexia," said Justin's grandad. "Lovely to see you, and thank you for the flowers. Sophia said you brought them."

I nodded. "It is hard to know what to bring when you're visiting someone in hospital," I mumbled.

"I agree. Roses were an excellent choice. She loves them. Grapes are another option. My wife loves her grapes; red is her favourite, but she can't eat anything at the moment. She's just drifted to sleep; the nurses have given her another injection for the pain."

Justin rubbed his grandad's shoulder.

"Are you staying until Gran wakes?" Justin asked.

"Yes, I don't want to leave her alone. But you go," said his granddad.

"She'll be home soon," said Justin.

When we got to my bike, Justin insisted on taking me home, as it was getting dark. I did not protest. I unlocked it, and he pushed my bike to his truck and lifted it into the back. I waited, watching him carefully ensure that my bike was secured, and then he opened the door for me.

We talked about Vanessa Helena Amadeo on the way home. He told me that he really liked that book and its title, *Seeking Angels*— even with its unusual ending. He said his mum enjoyed reading it too and kept asking him questions about whether he believed in the afterlife. Then he was quiet.

"What was your answer?" I asked.

"To what?"

"The afterlife thing," I said.

He shrugged. "I'm not sure. My gran and my mum have said that they've seen a ghost, or spirit as they called it, and they believe that it's my sister. I'm not that optimistic. People cannot randomly reappear after their death."

"Perhaps seeing the spirit is your mum and gran's way of dealing with their loss," I said.

He peeped at me. "Perhaps, but I wish they would let her rest in peace."

I didn't comment. He turned the engine off when we arrived at my flat and looked out the window to where we had built the snow creatures together. I lived in the coldest part of the North East—snow seemed to stay on the ground forever here. One of my favourite winter pastimes was to count how many months it would take before all our snow eventually melted. Some years it took a whole five months. This year was no different; people walked their dogs past our place, stopping to admire the white stuff.

"I bet once that stuff has melted, we will find the marbles and a lifeless carrot, completely rejected," he said.

"No doubt," I said, opening the door and jumping out.

"Am I that scary?" he asked.

"No, why?" I asked, holding the door open.

"You seem to be in such a hurry to get away," he said.

"It has been a long day with exams, you know, and seeing your gran bandaged up—it was a little overwhelming." I shut the door.

He took my bike out, and pushed it up the path to the door with me walking beside him. When we got to door, he rested my bike against the wall, took my hands into his, and kissed the back of my hands.

"I really like you," he whispered.

I looked at the ground. "I like you too," I said.

He let go of my hands. I took my keys out of my coat pocket, unlocked the door, and Justin wheeled my bike inside.

"Are you revising tonight?"

"No, I'm off tomorrow. Why?"

"Can I call you later?" he asked.

"Sure," I replied.

He blew me a kiss, and I blew him one back. Then I locked the door and watched him walk back to his truck. He looked back before he opened the door, he waved, and I waved back. He started the engine and accelerated down the road. I took the elevator to our flat.

CHAPTER FOURTEEN

D ad was home chatting to Mum while they put the shopping into the cupboards. They both looked at me when I walked into the kitchen.

"How was your exam?" Dad asked.

"Okay," I said.

"I'm sure you've done well," said Mum. "Mia has called twice on the landline looking for you. She said that she tried your mobile, but it went to voice mail. It seems that you left in a hurry; she was worried that something was wrong, and so were we." Dad nodded.

"Nothing is wrong. I went to visit Sophia."

"How was Sophia?" asked Mum.

"Her face was virtually wrapped in bandages. She couldn't speak, but I think she was pleased to see me. I sat next to her. She held my hand."

"Normally the hospital has strict rules and only allows close family visitors on the first day after major surgery. How did you got past the ward staff?" she asked.

I shrugged, "I went right to her door without being challenged, knocked, and Justin was there."

"That explains," she said, shaking her head. "Well, he wouldn't obey hospital rules where you're concerned—you're virtually part of the family."

I smiled. "I'm not part of Justin's family."

Dad looked at me and smiled. He looked different from last night. He had shaved his hairy face and changed his clothes. He looked like he'd been to the barber too—his hair was cut short. He looked more like the dad I remembered. He opened the fridge, put a bottle of milk into the door compartment, and slid the butter he was holding onto a glass shelf. Mum took a few steps forward, holding a box of eggs. Dad stepped aside but kept ahold of the fridge door while Mum bent at the waist to arrange the eggs into the egg holder, and then he closed the door. They looked like a happy couple.

Oh my God. I never, ever imagined seeing my parents talking to each other, let alone sharing domestic tasks. It was very strange seeing my parents together again. Had he moved in? Were my parents getting back together, or was Mum feeling guilty and agreeing to let dad spend time with us?

"I take it that Justin is your boyfriend?" Dad asked.

"He's my friend," I said quietly.

"Oh, and who's Sophia?" Dad asked.

I looked at Mum. She shrugged. Obviously, she had not told Dad about Sophia, but how did Mum know that Sophia had undergone surgery?

"Sophia is Justin's gran," I said.

"She's also our good friend," said Mum. "I bumped into her son Peter in town earlier. He was on his way home from the hospital. He told me about his mother's emergency surgery."

I grabbed an apple from the fruit bowl on the table and was about to go into my room when Dad said, "Your mother and I would like to talk to you."

That stopped me in my tracks. Without turning around, I asked, "Is it urgent?"

"No, it isn't urgent, but it's important," said Dad.

"Can I use the loo first?"

"Of course," said Mum. "Take your time."

I didn't really need the loo—I just wanted a little time to gather my thoughts. I popped my head into Mum's room. The furniture had been moved into the middle of the room. It smelled of plaster, and I noticed that the wall was damp. The builder must have been by to finish plastering the wall. I had a quiet glance around, looking for signs of my dad's belongings, but there wasn't anything noticeable.

I tiptoed into the bathroom, checked the bathroom cabinet, and counted Mum's tablets to make sure she hadn't forgotten to take her medication. It seemed to have the right number of pills. I quickly WhatsApp'd Mia to tell her that I was okay, just anxiety of exams, and I would call her later. She WhatsApp'd me back instantly, "I was worried. You didn't seem your usual self. Are you sure it's only exam nerves? Would you like me to come over to yours? Is your mum okay?"

I WhatsApp'd her back. "Yeah, Mum is fine, and I'm okay. Nothing to worry about, seriously. Talk later." I clicked send and hurried back. Dad was hovering in the sitting-room doorway, waiting for me.

"Your mother and I are in here," he said, as if I'd miss them in our tiny flat.

I looked at my goldfish as I passed—they were looking at each other—then I glanced at Mum sitting on the settee. On the floor next to her were two large boxes.

"Is everything all right?" I didn't think it was my dad's belongings that they were about to show me. Dad sat close to Mum. I wasn't in any great hurry to sit down. I leant on the back of a chair, looking at my parents. Mum nodded.

I remembered asking her if she had loved my dad; she'd never properly answered the question. She'd never dated anyone else either. I'd seen her looking at Todd from group therapy, and he'd stared at her, but it wasn't like Mum had a crush on Todd. Maybe I was reading too much into this weird reappearance of my dad, but seeing my parents together, I was getting the feeling that there was something romantic going on. They kept looking at each other and smiling.

It was obvious that Mum was more in control of her illness and compliant with her medication regime. Maybe she'd had time to reflect and possibly missed Dad in her hours of gloom. Mia often told me that she missed her boyfriend when he went camping. I'd missed dad, and Mum when she'd refused to get out of bed, and I always worried that I would find her dead when I got home from college. It was obviously true that a years-long absence was difficult to come to terms with. His absence had been horrible for me.

"Alexia, I love you, and you know I wouldn't do anything to hurt you, but I've not been totally honest with you. With my depression, I've not focussed on your feelings. Your father has never missed your birthday or Christmas, except for the time while he was in hospital." She took a deep breath. "I knew that too, because I received letters from his friend Mark with news. I kept that from you too, sweetie. It isn't that I wanted to lie. Please forgive me."

"Yes," I said, cutting her off. "I understand. Is that what you both wanted to tell me?"

"Yes and no," said Dad. He glanced at mum, and she nodded. "Your mother and I have been talking about your future. She mentioned that you're planning to find a job and then go to university. If you're worried about your mum's health or money and you didn't want to go far, we understand. We're lucky to have one of the best universities in the North East, Alexia. I've been sensible enough with money that you don't have to put your future education on hold. There's nothing wrong with getting a weekend job, but don't throw your future away."

"Dad, thank you, that's very generous, but all I've ever wanted was to have my dad around—something money can't buy. Now that you're here, let's get to know one another before thinking about my career."

He nodded. I looked at Mum; she looked sad. I wasn't used to having so much attention. Mum was a very affectionate mum; she'd tried to compensate for Dad's absence by giving me extra treats, but she had always been careful with money. We'd never gone without. Her depression had obviously caused her to withdraw and be distant, but hopefully the worst was over. And I was grateful she was still alive.

"Mum, all I've wanted is for you to get better. I wouldn't blame you for being depressed. I love you very much, but Mum, I only wish you'd told me the truth about my dad."

She nodded, still looking sad.

"What's in these boxes? Is dad moving in?" I joked in my attempt to ease the sadness.

"No, these are for you."

"Mine? It's not my birthday yet," I said.

"These are all from your father," said Mum. "One for every year he missed your birthday and Christmas. I'm so sorry, Alexia."

"No, don't be," I said. "It's more special to open them with Dad around." I lied—it would have been more fun to open my presents on the actual days.

He laughed. I sat on the floor like it was Christmas morning or my birthday as they looked at each other with pride. Although it wasn't the same—sitting down to open your presents when you're almost eighteen—it was amazing to watch the look on my parents' faces. Dad especially. He looked sad and happy at the same time. Mum leant with her elbows on her knees, gazing at my reaction. It was a little strange to be unwrapping Barbie doll dresses in princess outfits and size-three trainers with light-up soles, together with a label that says, "happy seven years old, I'm missing you."

I looked away, but my parents had already seen the tears dripping down my cheeks. "Thanks, Dad," I said.

"You're welcome," he replied. "No need to cry. We're lucky to have found each other again—things could have been very different." I noticed the sadness in his voice.

"Why don't I get us a drink?" Mum said. "Alexia, what would you like? We've got your favourite."

"Yes, please Mum. Thank you." What Mum called my favourite was pink lemonade that I used to like when I was eight. She still bought it—sometimes I thought that to my mum, I was still her eight-year-old. She would choose my clothes for school the night before if she was on earlier shifts. Mum never worked on Sunday; we always attended church, and I went to Sunday school no matter what the weather. Mrs. Oliver sang the rhyme "Jesus in Bethlehem" as we carried the donations to the priest, and then we stood at the front, showing everyone our flower drawings. Mine always looked like broken petals on a twig. What would it have been like to have Dad around? The thought made me anxious. I really didn't know much about my dad—his likes, dislikes, habits. Had he ever liked going to church?

Mum put a hand on Dad's shoulder. I noticed him twitch and then quickly put his hand atop Mum's. He said, "A cup of tea, my dear, would be nice, please, and then we should seriously go for dinner. The table is booked for eight."

"Of course," Mum said, pecking Dad on the cheek. He rubbed her cheek, and for a moment, they looked into each other's eyes. I was convinced it was romantic, like they'd never been apart.

"Oh, we're going out for dinner. What's the occasion?" I asked.

Dad twitched again, tipping his head to one side and watching mum walk towards the kitchen. He was obviously in pain.

"Do I need an occasion to take my family out for dinner?" he joked.

"I guess not," I said. Once Mum had disappeared into the kitchen, I asked Dad where was he staying and if he and mum were getting back together. He told me that he was staying in a B&B and that he and Mum were taking things slowly, but he wasn't going anywhere.

"Are you in pain?" I asked.

"A little—nothing for you to worry about. The weather doesn't help a burn victim." He quickly changed the subject. "We're going to view a house this weekend."

"Oh, where?" I asked, trying to suppress my surprise.

"Not far from here. It's a property that your mum and I once looked at, but it was above our price range. It's now back on the market at a reasonable price. She told me about it today, so we've arranged a viewing."

Mum had said that she wouldn't move again. It occurred to me that my parents were making plans. I was worried that it was too soon—Dad just came back; why was Mum telling him about properties? Had she been secretly looking at houses? Did the recent event with the neighbours from hell have something to do with this? I opened another present—a pair of dolphin earrings with matching necklace. The label on the wrapper read Happy Tenth Birthday.

"Dad, thank you. It's great," I said.

"I'm glad you like it, although it was bought for my ten-year-old daughter. Eighteen-carat white gold. You're a little older."

"I love it. I'll wear it for my eighteenth. I don't think gold dates." He laughed.

I stopped opening my presents and started to wonder how Mum had concealed these boxes in our small flat. There were lots of parcels—some small and some large—it would take hours to open them all. It was possible she'd hidden them in our tiny guest room, but she put all the unwanted stuff in there. There wasn't enough room to swing a cat, and I didn't go in there often. I wasn't sure what Mum had told Dad about her mental-health problems, her relapses, and her self-harm. Although I was happy that my parents appeared to be getting on, I was also worried sick that Mum would relapse. Dad had suffered massive burns that must have caused him mental-health distress as well. I'd not witnessed Dad's behaviour, but I'd seen Mum struggling mentally, and that frightened me.

I buried my head in my hands.

"What is the matter, Alexia?" asked Dad.

"Nothing."

"It isn't nothing. Something is troubling you."

I looked towards the kitchen to see that Mum wasn't listening. "Dad, I'm not sure if Mum has had a chance to mention the extent of her depression and how difficult it has been for me with her mental health and my studies. Mum has had continuous illusions of death and hallucinated about creatures like dinosaurs. I love you both very much, I've dreamed of a happy family, but I don't think I could carry on living if things don't work out between you. My life has been pretty depressing."

"I understand. It wasn't what I would have wanted," he said quietly.

Mum walked back into the sitting room with a smile on her face. Dad quickly changed the subject, commenting on the fish tank; he said we used to have a pond with a variety of fishes. I smiled. Mum was carrying a tray, teapot, two cups, and a glass of pink lemonade. She carefully put the tray on the table. I told my parents I wanted to get changed. I took a sip of my drink, and at the same time my phone rang. I glanced at the number; it was Justin. I smiled. Dad noticed.

"Boyfriend," Dad joked. "Young love—what an amazing thing."

Mum shrugged, opened her mouth to say something, but stopped herself. Dad glanced at her with a smile, grabbed the teapot, and poured two cups of tea, handing one to Mum. I pointed to my phone.

"I'll be in my room," I said before answering.

"Alexia, why don't you invite Justin to join us for dinner?" said Dad as I got to the door.

"Dad, are you serious?"

"Never been more serious in my life. A dad has a right to meet the guy who's dating his daughter—am I wrong?"

I took a few steps back, hugged Dad, and kissed his cheeks. "No, you're not wrong." I rushed into my room and shut the door.

"Hi, I thought we agreed that I would call you in a while." I was kidding, of course.

"Alexia," he said. "I've got something to tell you that will surprise you."

"Oh my God, it's your gran. I'm sorry."

"No, it's not Gran, but you cannot mention what I'm about to tell you to anyone—not even your mum—for now."

"Justin, are you okay? You're frightening me. I don't like keeping secrets—especially from my mum."

"I know, but it has to be our secret for now," he insisted.

"If it's important to you, then I agree," I said.

"Yeah, it is," he said. "My dad's friend, who is a police superintendent, has just called to tell my parents about the person they've arrested, who they believe is my sister's killer."

"Who?"

"Todd Walker," he said.

"You're kidding," I said.

"No. We are shocked."

I sighed loudly. "Justin, I'm so sorry," I said.

He said nothing.

"Justin, are you there?" I said. "That's awful. How are your parents?"

"I know. They have taken Lucky for a walk. Rather a nasty shock for my family." His voice was hoarse.

"Totally. Sorry to change the subject. Have you eaten?" I asked.

"No, not yet. You fancy coming round?"

"Yes and no. My dad has invited you to dinner with us. I'll understand if you say no." I wanted to see him, thinking how horrible it is to have met Todd, who possibly killed his sister. I didn't know Todd well, except for seeing him at group therapy, but he didn't strike me as a cold-blooded killer; that was shocking news.

"Oh, yeah, thank your dad. What time?"

"As soon as you can get to my flat," I said. "We're not eating in, but I'm not sure where we're going either."

"Okay. It sounds like your parents are getting on. I take it there wasn't anything serious between Todd and your mum? The way he was looking at your mum at the pizza restaurant suggested otherwise."

"I know what you mean. He might have dreamed of dating my mum, but she wasn't interested in him. I'm sorry, the whole thing sucks."

"Yeah," he answered. "See you soon."

"Okay."

The whole thing sounded mad. I called Mia, putting my phone on speaker while I chose something to wear. "Alexia," she said, answering after two rings, "What's up?"

"I've been opening belated birthday and Christmas presents," I said.

"Was it one of your mum's secrets?" she asked. Mia knew mum's mental problems. She wasn't surprised.

"Yeah, Mum pretended that Dad hadn't sent any presents since I was six, but she'd been secretly hiding them—two full boxes. My dad is back—not had a chance to tell you before, sorry," I said.

"Aunty Sam did mention that your dad was back, and he'd been in an accident. How is he?"

"Yes, he's still in pain. Helicopter blasted into the rig. He suffered first-degree burns. But it's great to see him, and surprisingly, my parents appear to be getting on, like a romantic ghost story in the book of undying love."

She laughed. "I must read that book. You should be happy; it's what you've always talked about—a happy family."

"Yeah, of course. I gotta go—Dad's taking us out for dinner."

"Okay, we must hang out soon. Shopping would be a fun way to take our minds off stuff."

"Okay, that sounds like a plan." I could hear the intercom ring. I quickly yanked a pair of jeans on, put on my blue jumper, ran a comb through my hair and pulled it into a high ponytail, grabbed my phone from my dressing table, and rushed to open the door before Dad answered the intercom.

"Hi!" I said, picking up. "Come on up." I pushed the button to open the door and then opened the flat door and pulled my boots on while I waited for him. I could hear him running up the stairs; Justin never took the elevator. I was concerned that he might be distressed after the news of his sister's killer, but if he was, he was hiding it. He appeared casually relaxed with his usual smile, not even out of breath after rushing up the stairs.

"Hi!" he said, bending to kiss my cheeks. "I'm so glad to be invited. Where's your dad?"

"He's in the sitting room," I answered quietly.

"I wanted to see you," he said.

"Missing me already?" I joked.

"Oh, why would that surprise you? I never stop missing you. You look fabulous." He grinned.

Oh my God, I was flattered. He was flirting and thought I looked fab. He slid a hand over my shoulders, led me into the flat, and closed the door behind. A waft of joyfulness drifted over me. Dad appeared through the sitting-room door.

"You must be Justin. I'm Thomas, Alexia's dad. Pleased to meet you," he said, shaking Justin's hand.

"Delighted to meet you, sir, and thank you for including me in your family dinner party."

"It isn't a party as such—just dinner out rather than eating in," Dad said casually as Mum slipped behind him.

"Justin, I'm glad you could join us," she said with a big grin.

"My pleasure, Mrs. Collins," said Justin, leaning to peck Mum on the cheeks.

"I told you he was a charming young man," said Mum, looking at Dad.

Dad nodded. "I agree. If we're all ready, shall we make a move? Table won't wait forever."

"What's the name of the restaurant, Mr. Collins?" asked Justin.

"Max and Danita," said Dad. "Restaurant and bar. Ten-minute drive away. They're well known for their excellent cuisine. I'm sure there'll be something to everyone's liking." He looked at Mum, no doubt remembering that she used to prefer more traditionally English meat and two vegetables, but she was a little bit more liberal these days; she would try any food.

"I'll drive, if it's okay," offered Justin.

Dad glanced at Mum. She shrugged. "I don't want to deprive you of a drink," Dad replied. "I'm off alcohol, so it makes sense for me to drive."

"I'm driving, and I never drink and drive," Justin insisted.

"Okay then, thanks," said Dad.

I raised an eyebrow.

Dad led the way, Mum locked the door, and my parents stepped towards the elevator. Justin and I headed for the stairs. I heard my dad laugh, but we didn't look back. Justin took my hand and stopped briefly on the way down, looking at me with a smile, I thought he was about to kiss me. I clenched my hands. I'm sure he noticed.

"You surely look amazing." He took a deep breath and then said, "I've got to be in London in the next few days for the launch of my new computer game. I wish you could come."

"You know I can't."

"I understand."

"We better run; my parents will be curious."

He laughed. "Are we waiting till you're eighteen?"

"Waiting for what?" I asked, deliberately sounding surprised, although I obviously knew what he meant.

"First kiss, Alexia."

I wrinkled my nose. "We've not been on a first date yet, and you've just announced that you're off to London. I guess if you like me, then it isn't difficult to wait."

"Alexia, I'll wait however long it takes; you're a special girl." His voice was dead cool, and he was so wow.

I laughed.

Mum and Dad stepped out of the elevator a few seconds after we got downstairs and glanced at us, their expressions speculative. Justin and I pretended that we hadn't noticed, and he rushed to hold the door open while I fidgeted with the zipper of my anorak. My eyes stung as the cold air rushed into them. I was about to rub them when Dad shouted, "What the devil?" His voice echoed in the darkness as a ball of ice smacked into Justin's shoulder. Another one whacked me in the face. We all froze as balls of snow flew past us. Dad tried to pull me back inside, but the door slammed shut. Something flew above Justin's head, showering him with snowflakes that simply melted away.

I twisted around, looking for Mum; she'd bolted against the wall and was pointing to the sky. The wind was howling around us. I stumbled into Dad; he grabbed hold of my anorak. Balls of snow kept on coming at us from every direction. Justin leapt forward and grabbed Dad's wrist. I tried to walk backwards as another ball banged into my face. I slipped and got a glimpse of Mum trembling on her knees before landing on my back. That's when I saw them circle overhead; it was incredible. The wind stopped suddenly. Justin slid onto the snow and lifted me into his arms, and Dad rolled over and covered Mum up.

Justin and I couldn't have imagined our own creations. Up above was the unicorn flying, with the snowman riding on its back and carrying the fish. It flew down just above Justin and me. The unicorn made a horsey noise that sounded like laughter, and the snowman waved. "Something really extraordinary," I heard Dad say.

I shifted, eyes wide, trying to gather my jumbled thoughts. Justin adjusted his grip around my waist.

"You okay?" he asked.

I nodded.

"That wasn't any hallucination!" Mum said loudly.

"No, dear, but what on earth was it?" Dad asked.

"I believe it was a flying unicorn, with friends," said Justin.

We all looked back up. A ball of white stuff landed right in front of us, but the unicorn and friends had vanished. Justin gave me a surprised look, and I suppressed a sigh. It was magical. Nothing had prepared us for that.

"Only witches and wizards could make sense of such creatures," said Dad coldly.

Justin and I glanced at each other, smiling secretly. His idea that we could be witch and wizard may ring true. Justin drove, and everyone was silent on the way to the restaurant. The waitress showed us to a table by a log fire. She asked what we would like to drink and mumbled something about tonight's special. I'd lost my appetite. Mum and Dad ordered pea and ham soup, Justin ordered hot pot, and I had chocolate ice cream with strawberries. The waitress brought our order, and we ate quietly. I kept looking through the window, but the sky was silent as a ghost.

Justin told my parents about his new computer-game venture and his trip to London for the launch.

"Congratulations," said Dad.

"Thank you," said Justin. "It all started at university. At first it was just experimental, but over the years it has become a thriving career—something the public can't get enough of."

"I'm a great believer that everything in life happens for a reason." His voice was deliberately calm.

Mum sat in silence, watching the fire. Around us the room was full of diners chatting, laughing, eating, and drinking. "An eventful night," I heard a man say. "On my way here I stopped by my Uncle Paddy to check on him after his hip replacement. He's not been his old self. We were watching the tele when the windowsill rattled suddenly. I gazed out to see a unicorn flying past and carrying what looked like a snowman and a fish on its back."

There was more laughter, and then someone said, "It must be a full moon, or you had a few on the way."

We glanced at each other, smiling.

CHAPTER FIFTEEN

On Wednesday, I went with Mum to her appointment at the Whitley wing of the local hospital. We arrived thirty minutes early, as recommended on the appointment letter, but waited an hour and a half. In the waiting room, everyone was wearing football shirts and sweatpants, with their mobiles in front of their faces. It was colder than usual in the North East in December. People would glance up periodically when someone walked into the room and look back at their phones, but there wasn't any conversation—not even a nod. It felt like we were all aliens awaiting the mother ship for a zombie mission. The whole place felt uncomfortable. I wrapped my arms over my coat, even though the heating was on and the temperature didn't quite justify it. I was not so keen on going with Mum, but she needed my support during her scheduled review, and she was optimistic about the future.

Mum and I sat next to each other on black plastic chairs across from the water dispenser. Every now and again a person would get up and walk slowly to the dispenser, fill what Mum called a nylon cup of water, and sip while dragging their feet back, making sure that there wasn't any eye contact. The place smelled of disinfectant, and the walls were orange with pockets of leaflets in a metal holder. On the wall, next to the water dispenser was a huge silver-framed picture of a white smiley-faced woman. Her name was Carmen Fairhead, the hospital manager for Mental Health Northeast, all of which was written in gold on a wooden plaque beneath the frame.

I found myself reading the slogan on the board next to the picture. "We're here to support you, assist you, and answer any questions that may be troubling you; but please respect the environment, and we don't tolerate abuse or any sort of violent behaviour towards our staff and consultants. Thank you for your cooperation."

A tall, chocolate-skinned man appeared at the door. He called a person's name, and two people got up and followed him. I presumed one was a relative.

"Who was that?" I asked Mum quietly.

"It must be one of the consultant psychiatrists," Mum whispered.

"Is he your consultant?" I asked.

"No, sweetie, there are a number of consultants. Mine is Dr. Goatbell Vadel, and his trainee is Dr. Zabin, who I've seen on occasion, but today my appointment is with Dr. Goatbell. He reviews all outpatients' progress and discharges them whenever appropriate."

I looked around the room at the other patients. I wondered if they were all mentally unwell and here for their reviews. I'd started reading about mental health to better understand Mum's problems, but it was very complicated. Mum once told me that mental illness was like thieves who distracted their opponents and then stole their minds. Like something you might read in the newspaper or one of those medical magazines in the doctor's waiting room, you never thought that you would fall victim. Mum was a level-headed woman; she went straight from college to nurse training and struck lucky, landing a job in the accident-and-emergency department. Tales of fancying the young doctors and reassuring the hopeless and helpless that walked through the door at A&E was all she used to talk about.

Mum was the kind of person who saw good in everyone. She never had a bad word to say—even when she had to work double shifts due to shortage of staff. She was not the kind of person to be critical—even when someone threw up in the cubicle as she stitched their wounds (that happened too). She would treat everyone with the same dignity. Her life was a fairly flexible and ordinary one by modern standards. She was brought up by a loving aunt after her parents were killed in a road accident, belonged to a walking group to raise money for charity, enjoyed her career, helped out at soup kitchens for the homeless on her days off, and went to yoga and Pilates. She met my dad at a pub on a girls' night out, and they dated for three years before they got married. She had often referred people to mental-health services. She was not the kind of person that sort of thing happened to, or at least she didn't think so.

A short, slim, light-skinned man appeared at the door. "Mrs. Collins," he called with a smile. Mum got up and I followed. He shook Mum's hand and smiled at me, leading us down a narrow corridor with numbered doors on both sides. He stopped at door number seven, opened it for us, and then shut the door and pointed to two chairs. We sat down. It was cosier and the chairs comfier than those in the waiting room.

"My apology for the wait, Mrs. Collins. Busy day." He glanced at me. "Is this your daughter?" he asked.

"No need for apology, Dr. Vadel. Yes, this is my daughter, Alexia," Mum said.

I watched him look at his computer. He nodded a few times, and I started to wonder if Goatbell was his real name, or if he was known in the profession as Goatbell because of his goatee beard. I'd never met a psychiatrist before, but Mia and I had watched *One*

Flew Over the Cuckoo's Nest. I was expecting Dr. Goatbell to be wearing a white coat, but that wasn't the case. He was dressed in a suit and tie and spoke English with a foreign accent.

"How are you feeling, mentally, Mrs. Collins?" he asked.

"I'm more in control of my life and feel that there is light at the end of the tunnel, and I think I'm ready for some normality, like going back to work," Mum said. It sounded more like a convincing statement than an answer to the question.

He ran a hand over his beard and glanced at his computer again. "That's very encouraging, but are you sure you're ready to go back to work in the same department, after what happened? Do you need a few more weeks off to reflect on the future?"

"Dr. Vadel, thank you, I'm confident that I'm ready to resume work—maybe a few days a week to start with."

He looked at Mum for a few seconds. "How is your sleep?" he asked.

"Much better—eight hours most nights, without any sleeping tablets," she said.

He shook his head, "Your medications—any side effects?"

"None."

"Are you still attending group therapy?"

"Yes. Extremely therapeutic."

"What about self-harming? Hallucinations?"

"It happened in those dark and dispirited moments, but it's all behind me."

"Well, you sound determined. I suggest you arrange a meeting with your manager and perhaps move to another department after your experience. Nursing in the same department may cause you to relapse."

Mum nodded. "I understand the danger, but the reality is I enjoy the front line and assisting those who seek my assistance. The skinhead man with a broken nose, the old dears who shut the car door and broke their fingers once or twice, the repeat food and nut allergies, the angry weight-loss victims, the anxious mother whose child has swallowed objects. Caring for them all is rewarding. Gun crimes are not the norm."

"Point taken, Mrs. Collins," said Dr. Goatbell. "I will write to your GP to inform him that I've discharged you. If you do experience any anxiety, contact your GP, who will refer you back to us."

"Thank you," said Mum, pulling to her feet.

"You're welcome," he said, shaking Mum's hand on the way out of the door.

She grabbed my hand the moment Dr. Vadel shut his door. I had never seen my mum walk so fast. She raced down the corridor and out the door, pulling me with her, as if she was frightened that the psychiatrist would send someone after her. She didn't slow down when we got outside. Mum took me around a path to the very back of the building, into a door next to the children's department. She breathed a sigh of joy when we walked into a chapel.

"There," she said. "I wanted to show you this place before Sophia distracted us." She looked around as if to make sure no one was listening. "The night we saw the ghost that Sophia believed was her granddaughter at therapy group."

"Oh, yes, I remember," I said. That was also the first time I met Justin, I thought. He must be on his way to London. It was odd he hadn't texted me yet.

"Alexia, this is the place I used to visit during my break. I find the peace helps me to focus on a stressful day."

"I understand," I said, although I didn't—how could I? I had never worked in a busy hospital. Mum kneeled, closed her eyes, crossed her fingers, and prayed quietly. It was a small chapel—it had a high ceiling with plain glass windows on one side and a solid wall on the other, and hard wooden pews. There weren't any candles or flowers, but it was peaceful. Mum sat up next to me after a while. I could hear footsteps coming from behind. Before I could look back, a man dressed in black wearing a dog collar stopped next to us.

"Mrs. Collins, how are you?" he said. "I'm delighted to see you again."

"I'm much better, Father Cooper, thank you. This is my daughter, Alexia."

"Alexia," he said. "Welcome to our place of worship. Your mother has spent many hours praying here, and I believe your prayers had been answered, Mrs. Collins: your husband is back—wounded but alive. God is great."

I glanced at Mum. She avoided me and continued talking to the priest about dad and his accident. How odd that she had been coming here, praying for Dad's safe return and telling the priest all about it when she had lied to me. Mum stood up and walked with Father Cooper to the front. They were engrossed in conversation about my dad as if I wasn't present. I sat there thinking, how could she do that? All that was before the attack. I wanted to be angry with her, but I just couldn't be.

They say you should really appreciate the time you have, not what you have lost. Mum worked hard, long hours; from the age of five, all I could remember was my mother making sure that I was safe. She had many tasks, but I was the most important. She ensured that I was at school on time and that she was at the gate at the end of the day, or she made sure Sam was there if she was delayed. There was time when it was more difficult. The problem mum had was that the hospital was always short of staff to cover school holidays, and they didn't like to use agency staff to cover the shortfall, so she struggled to get enough holiday.

That was the year that winter caused mayhem throughout England. There was nothing more devastating than to watch the news, which showed floods that had ripped through the riverbanks, washed away trees, and destroyed homes, livelihoods, and in some cases lives.

I counted myself lucky to have my mum. There had been times when I spent endless hours watching her sleep, making sure that she was breathing; times when Mum refused to eat, drink, or open the curtains; and times when I thought she would die of starvation and I would be an orphan. How could you be angry with someone who had been close to death? In nine months, so much had changed: her clothes didn't hang of her shoulders like they used to, she took pride in her appearance, she had found her way back into her kitchen, and she took delight in preparing a meal. She opened the curtains.

She walked back with a satisfied look on her face, smiling at me as if I was supposed to know that she had been praying for my dad and now that he was back, everything was forgiven. I smiled back. I couldn't say anything to her—of course not. Oh God, I loved her. I stood up, we walked out in silence, and Mum lifted her hand onto my arm. It wasn't my place to judge; we all belong to some great cycle of creation—some tapestry that only God understands. I didn't tell mum that, but the future looked bright. I learned the tapestry thing from therapy group; one of Christine's many wise words. Mum took me down a side road to a small café. We had hot chocolate and hazelnut biscuits.

My phone rang as we sat down on an old peach leather sofa with colourful cushions. "Who is it?" Mum asked before I had a chance to check.

"I don't know," I said. It was Justin. I answered.

"What are you doing?" he asked.

"Having hot chocolate with my mum. Are you in London yet?"

"Just arrived at our apartment. Dad's busy phoning for pizzas," he said.

"Can I call you later? Now is not convenient, you know?"

"Okay."

Mum and I enjoyed our drinks and biscuits, and then she called Dad, who picked us up in his Audi SUV. Mum told Dad about her appointment with Dr. Goatbell and that he had discharged her.

"That's good news," Dad said.

Then they asked me if I'd given any thought to what I would like to do for my eighteenth. I told my parents that I didn't want a party, but I would like to invite Mia to a movie—maybe food and a sleepover. They glanced at each other.

"It's your birthday, Alexia. Most eighteen-year-olds dream of a big party with their friends," Dad said.

"I'm not like most eighteen-year-olds. Mia is my only friend besides Justin. I don't think hiring a private club or a DJ would be necessary."

"That can't be true, Alexia; you're a fun-loving girl—you must have lots of friends," Dad said.

"Alexia is very vigilant and shy; she is not as outgoing as most girls her age," Mum said, forgetting to mention that I spent most of my Friday nights and every other night worried about her.

CHAPTER SIXTEEN

W hen I got home, I delayed calling Justin back. I hung out
with my goldfish for a while and fed them, and Dad helped
me clean the tank; Mum went into her room. Dad told me that
when we moved to the new house, I could have a bigger tank and
more fish if I liked. I shook my head. I really would like a dog, but I
didn't tell him that. I still wasn't convinced that things would work
out. Although Mum and Dad were getting on, it wasn't enough to
live together happily ever after. Dad's phone rang, and he went
into the kitchen to answer. I felt duped. An almost eighteen-year-
old dimwit with no mates. It wasn't much fun just looking at fish.
The thing about watching fish swimming around is it makes you
dizzy. So I went into my room, shut the door, dived under the duvet, and read *The Mind of Wizards*. On page 401, Barratt Joshley
rides his horse in his woods when he notices green smoke coming
from Zac's chimney.

"What's that mad scientist up to?" he says aloud.

The horse nods twice and makes horsey sounds as if it understands. Barratt pats its back. Suddenly, two gigantic black birds fly

above and start circling around them. He pulls his revolver from the back of his trousers and aims for the birds, but before he can fire, one of the creatures flies down, snatches the pistol from his hand with its powerful claws, smashes it in two, and flings the pieces into the woods. Barratt howls in outrage. He attempts to ride towards Zac's house, but the birds spatter green liquid stuff into the air, blinding him and turning the whole wood green. It's like pea soup, gathering speed fast. It swallows him and his horse like a massive mammal. When it stops, Barratt is still on the back of his horse, but not where he was previously; he's at the far end of the wood, facing a huge mirror-like castle.

"What the devil is that?" he shouts aggressively.

"No, it's not the devil, my giant friend," booms a voice. "That is VolFail, the home of the great wizard Gingerhook. A castle of hope and happiness for those who seek to be cured of their demons," Barratt looks but can't see anyone.

"Show yourself," he yells with a rather nasty tone.

"I'm down here, and you're up there. If you want to address me, you have to come to my level. I was born small, and you giants eat small people."

Barratt turns his head, looks around and down, but he still can't see anyone. "Who are you? I'm warning you that I'm armed, and my army will kill you and destroy that monstrosity."

Suddenly something pokes Barratt's leg. He jumps, and his horse rears up on its hind legs. Barratt flies into the air and lands on the path to the herb garden. A silver bee buzzes past his nose, and three tiny fairies wiggle into the air. His jaw drops wide as a black swan flies off. He feels weird, facing a tiny woman pointing a stick at him. "Soul," she says quietly. Barratt turns into a dwarf.

"That's much better," she says.

Barratt shouts for his robotic army, but there isn't anyone; he is at the mercy of the stranger who captured him. She tells him that her name is Opel, the oldest fairy of the North, and that she is in charge of changes, happiness, and hopefulness. He looks at her round face and red robe that fit her perfectly. Barratt's coat hangs around his feet. Opel then points to the others that are circling above Barratt. "Oziwell, in the yellow dress, is the fairy that brings sunlight. Next is Helima, in the jade dress—she's a green-fingered fairy. And Delia, dressed in white, is the fairy of peace," Opel tells Barratt. "We have been in these woods for thousands of years before you. We have met many happy people; you are the most grumpy and aggressive we have seen. Zac was powerful—all he did was find a cure for mental illnesses. All you ever did was try to kill him."

I closed the book and called Justin.

He answered on the second ring. "Alexia, how are you?" he asked.

"Okay. Just stuck in my room reading the horror of Barratt Joshley."

"Oh, where are you up to?"

"Page 401. The shocking green smoke and the giant birds."

He laughed. "That's my favourite part. Did you like it?"

"I will be haunted by woodland fairies and mirrors forever."

"It's just a story, Alexia."

"Not a jolly one," I said.

"Point taken. But it unlocked your imagination, right?"

I laughed. "I didn't realise that my imagination was locked, but now that you mention it, I will have to nurture it."

"You're incredible, amazing. I really, really love you," he said.

"Oh. Um, what's London like?" I asked, changing the subject.

"Full of individual characters, magnificent buildings, theatres, art galleries, palaces, tourists, designer shops, museums, lovers holding hands, people out walking with their dogs, others jogging. Interesting place. I take it you have not been?"

"Nah. Not yet, anyway. Sounds great."

"Yeah. Are your ears currently pierced?" he asked.

"Um, yes. Why?""

"No reason."

"Okay. When is your launch?" I asked.

"In the morning. I'm heading home after. My dad is staying in London for another night. He's got a meeting with some business dudes."

A sudden knock on my door interrupted my conversation with Justin.

"Yes? I'm on the phone," I said.

Mum popped her head through the door. "Sorry, Alexia. Have you seen your dad?" she asked.

"I gotta go. My mum needs me."

"Okay, talk later," he said.

"Perhaps." I clicked my phone off. Mum sounded anxious. I rushed out of my room, worried that something was wrong.

"He received a call. He went into the kitchen to answer, and I went into my room," I said.

"I wanted to sort some things out for charity while you two were cleaning the fish tank. I must have dozed off. You know I didn't sleep well last night. Worried about my review. I came out looking for him—he's gone. Alexia, I knew it was far too good to be true." Mum started pacing. "That proves that you can't trust anyone," she kept saying.

"That proves nothing. He probably just popped out for something. He wouldn't just leave without saying bye, Mum." I tried to reassure her or myself, I wasn't sure which.

"Well, he just has," she said.

She walked past me and went into the kitchen. I noticed she was hyperventilating. I followed her, worried she would do something stupid like cut herself. When Mum felt she was losing control, self-harm was the first thing she would do. She would take a knife and go into the bathroom. She didn't want to die. She just felt hopeless after her attack, and that wasn't fair.

She kept opening and closing drawers nervously. "Alexia, I'm not going to, you know, relapse or cut. I just feel he's let us down."

I was so busy watching her that I almost missed the note pinned under the carrot magnet on the fridge.

"Oh, what's that?" I said, stepping forward to read it.

"What?" she asked.

I grabbed the note, handing Mum the magnet. "This," I said, waving the piece of A3 paper. She stared at me while I read it.

"Jessica and Alexia. I received a call from my solicitor; he wants to see me regarding my compensation. I wanted you to come with me, Jessica, but when I popped my head through your door, you were fast asleep, and Alexia was quiet in her room, so I didn't disturb you. I've taken a set of keys. See you soon. All my love, Txx."

"There. He hasn't run away," I said.

She looked at me, breathing a sigh of relief. "I knew that, but you know."

"So have you finished?" I asked.

"Finished what?" she asked.

"Sorting things for charity," I reminded her.

"Oh, that will take a few days, but there's a jumble sale at the church hall next Sunday to raise money for disabled children. I thought I'd help."

"That's wonderful, Mum. If you'd like to help me unwrap the rest of my presents, there's plenty to donate for a good cause."

"Yes, that's a good idea, but you don't have to give away all your gifts," she said with a sad face.

"I'd like to."

Mum and I spent hours unwrapping my presents. She insisted on folding all the wrapping paper, and I read all the notes on the presents. I knew that she was feeling guilty by the curious gaze she gave me, but I didn't say anything about all the lies. God had blessed me in that I still had both my parents; there were so many children without. There were more coats and shoes that wouldn't fit me, and I stopped playing with dolls when I was twelve.

CHAPTER SEVENTEEN

I lay on my bed, beneath the covers. I watched *Emma* and then *Bambi* on my computer and cried myself to sleep when Bambi's mum got killed. It was very hard to wake in the morning. I could hear voices. I argued with the part of me that was sure it was a dream. Logic wasn't part of my common sense. The first thing that came to my mind was that Mum was having one of her delusional episodes and talking to herself. I shifted onto my back. I couldn't have imagined the smell of disinfectant. I was sure I could never have dreamed that up.

It was dark outside my window. I glanced at my phone; it was midday. Mum must be on one of her cleaning madnesses. With one ear to the door, I could hear whispering. I thought that it was Sam, but then realised that it couldn't be her—today was Sam's busiest day. I panicked and hurried out of my bedroom door in my Pooh Bear pyjamas in case Mum was hallucinating, or in case it was her psychiatry caseworker, Clare, who was still keeping her eye on Mum. I stopped dead when I heard a voice saying, "No need to disturb her—I'll come back later."

Oh, crap. Our flat was so small that you could hear any conversation. I heard Mum saying, "She wouldn't want to miss you—I'll go and get her." With that she came rushing to find me standing in the corridor.

"Who is it?" I whispered, although I knew who it was from the voice.

She closed the door behind her, looking at me with a big smile. She grabbed my wrist, and we both dashed back to my room.

"It's Justin. He's suggested taking you out," she said.

I shook my head. "Yes, please."

"Happy birthday. Trust you to get up after noon." We sat on my bed.

God, I'd been looking forward to this day so much that I'd forgotten it.

"Thanks, Mum. Is Dad here?"

"Yes, he and Justin are engrossed in football conversation. I couldn't participate, so I came looking for you."

"You've found me," I joked, kissing her cheeks.

"Cheeky. Would you like to open your presents in your room?" she asked.

"No, later. I need to have a shower and see what Justin has got planned."

"Okay. I'll tell him that you will join us soon."

"Thanks, Mum." I told her not to mention that I'd just gotten out of bed, and that I had forgotten my own birthday. She smiled.

I chose a pair of black skinny jeans and a pink jumper. I carried them into the bathroom, took a shower, dressed, and brushed my hair. Then I reentered my room, put on some lip shine, and dabbed a little perfume on. I kept looking at the pair of dolphin earrings and pendent that my dad had sent for one of my younger belated birthdays. They were pretty and would have looked great on a ten-year-old, as they were meant to.

On approaching the sitting room, I could hear people talking, so I stood with one shoulder to the wall for a while and listened through the open door.

Mum: "So Sophia is out of hospital. I kept putting off visiting—you know, straight after surgery, rehabilitation, and all that. Tell her that I'm thinking of her."

Justin: "Yes, Mrs. Collins, but I'm sure she would like to see you."

Dad: "You're not a college boy?"

Justin: "No, sir, graduated. Few years back."

Dad: "So how did you meet Alexia?"

Justin: "Taking my gran to group therapy."

Mum: "Sophia and I go to the same group therapy. I've told you that, Tom."

Justin: "Gran is looking forward to going back to group therapy. She is missing the interaction and friendship. I like those fish."

Mum: "Thank you, Justin. They are Alexia's. She loves her pets."

Dad: "You design computer games, I understand."

Justin: "Yes, sir. Just got back from London, where I launched my latest game. It has been a great success so far."

Dad: "I've never really played computer games, but it is something that I'm interested in giving a go."

Justin: "I can teach you. It's great fun and a bit addictive."

Dad: "Thank you, Justin, I would appreciate that. You can call me Tom."

Justin: "Thanks. We'll try my latest game. I hope you like monsters."

Mum: "You're very clever to develop something that the public craves. That's wonderful."

Justin: "I know. I'm lucky to have supportive parents."

Dad: "I've never stopped worrying about Alexia, and as parents, it is our duty to be supportive. But I've missed so much of her upbringing with work commitments. She is very shy."

At that point I emerged, standing in the doorway.

"Hi," I said.

Justin beamed, pulled onto his feet from the settee, walked over, and handed me a bunch of roses, a huge card, and a small bag. "Happy birthday!" he said. "Do you fancy going out?" I nodded, taking the gift, card, and flowers.

Mum and Dad walked behind him, holding gift bags and a card.

"A hug for your old dad," he said, holding his arms out.

I smiled and hugged him and then Mum. Mum had the biggest smile on her face.

To please my parents, I opened the gifts. Justin's first—a pair of studs with sparkling stones.

"Silver?" asked Mum, who was watching.

"No, white gold and diamond," said Justin.

"Oh, expensive!" said Mum.

I glanced at him and smiled. I opened his card, which was amazing. On the front was a picture of us with our snow creations on that snowy day. Inside he wrote, "To the most gorgeous girl on her eighteenth. Happy birthday. I hope all your dreams come true. Love Justin."

I count the kisses. There were eighteen little *x*'s. My face felt all hot.

"Thank you," I whispered, looking into his eyes.

He winked, "You're welcome," he said quietly.

Amongst my presents from my parents, there was a baby blue coat, a black pair of knee-high boots, twenty-five paid driving lessons, and cash. Their card was lovely too, with a picture of a puppy sleeping in a box. Oh my God, it was so cute. It read, "We're so proud to be your parents, with kisses." They had both signed it.

It was fantastic to have my parents watching—and a first-time experience. I thanked and kissed my parents, but didn't kiss Justin—not in front of them, anyway. I went back to my room, carrying my card and roses, which were already in a vase of water and wrapped in plastics. I put the vase on my dressing table with my card next to it. Then I put the earrings into my ear piercings, looked in the mirror, pulled my hair into a ponytail for maximum effect, and put on my new coat and boots. I kept looking at the bouquet; it was velvety red roses—pretty and romantic.

I walked back along the corridor. Justin and Dad still stood chatting about football. Newcastle United were playing against Liverpool FC.

"You planning on watching?" asked Dad.

"No, recording on planner to watch later, but my dad will be. Are you?" asked Justin.

"Of course—unless there are other plans," Dad said, looking at Mum.

Mum gazed at him. Dad laughed.

"So where are you going?" asked Mum. Justin looked at me. "It's a surprise," he said.

Mum smiled. "Have fun. It's your special day," she said, as if I didn't know.

We said bye. Justin bustled to hold the door open, and we hurried out. He took my hand as we walked down the stairs.

He drove—not in his usual truck, but in a Mercedes sports car, and he kept glancing at me. The weather had improved, with glimpses of sunshine that were nice but unusual for the time of year. As we cruised towards town, he said, "You look stunning."

"Thanks. It must be the earrings," I said, looking straight ahead through the windscreen.

"Do you like them? They look good on you, but they're a small detail; you are beautiful."

"I like them," I said. "You and my dad seemed to strike common ground, and you've charmed my mum."

"Well, your dad is an NCU fan. That's great. You think they approve of me?"

"No doubt they do. I've never seen my mum laugh like that before. You sure lift her spirit. They just want me to be happy."

"Are you?" he asked, glancing over at me.

"What?"

"Happy."

"Of course. They're just playing overprotective parents."

"Your dad was questioning me on how we met."

"He's just being my dad—making up for lost years."

"It helps when parents like the guy who is dating their daughter."

"Well, you seem to be pressing the right notes. I noticed my parents exchange looks when you hold the door open or lavish me with extravagant gifts."

He laughed, whizzed down a tunnel of an underground parking, and slammed on the brakes. I felt dizzy and bit my lip hard enough that it bled. I thought of a giant spider. Oh my God, I counted down from ten, trying to relax.

We roared between cars before turning right. He located a space next to the exit, killed the engine, but didn't rush to get out. "You okay?" he asked, sounding concerned.

I nodded, busy dabbing my lip on the back of my hand. The only thing I could think of was the salty taste in my mouth. Justin reached underneath his seat, pulled out a first aid kit, and removed an antiseptic pack.

"Allow me," he said.

"I can manage. I'm not sure what happened." I felt embarrassed.

"Trust me, Alexia. I have no doubt that you can, but a swollen lip on your eighteenth wasn't part of the surprise."

I smiled. "Okay, perhaps it's best you do it."

He laughed, pulled a wipe from the pack, and gently pushed it over my lips. He then took a cotton bud, dipped it into a small bottle that smelled weirdly like alcohol, and swabbed it on. It didn't hurt.

"How does that feel?"

"Thanks, a lot better. Is that one of your many talents?" I joked.

"One of the duties of being a first aider is to attend to the wounded," he answered. "Trained with ambulance people at college. I give blood too." His finger continued moving slowly on my lower lip.

I put my hand over his to stop the motion, we looked into each other's eyes, and then it happened. His lips were over mine; we had our first perfect kiss. I closed my eyes and didn't protest. It was fabulous—I felt his soft lips and his tongue probing mine. Delicious.

There was a short pause and then he said, "Shall we? But wait, I'll open your door."

"Um. Okay," I said.

He opened and closed his door and rushed to open mine. He took my hand, "Are we going to the art gallery?" I asked. I remembered reading about an art exhibition taking place.

"We could if you like—later."

I noticed the smile on his lips. "Hold on," I said, "I'm not a footy fan!"

"Away game this weekend."

"Oh, so where are we going?"

"A place that I hope you will like, but if you don't, it doesn't matter; we can go somewhere else."

I smiled, glancing at the university buildings in the distance, thinking of my parents' comment that I should continue in higher education. I'd not made up my mind on the matter. He was still holding my hand. We walked past a group of students, who were laughing, joking, and carrying boxes of beer and pizza. It looked like they were planning a party.

"Student life," Justin sighed.

We turned right down a street and walked towards the river. I glanced up at him. He had a serious look, like a guy on a mission, which he was. Over the water I could see the museum, where I wanted to visit the display of dinosaurs. I was busy analysing

everything: girls in miniskirts, people drinking and smoking outside pubs, lovers kissing, and the sound of a train on the distant
bridge. A white Bentley drove past and stopped at the entrance of
a hotel, and two young men stepped out, followed by two women
in floral dresses, and together they went through the revolving
door of the hotel. Wedding party, I supposed. We walked up a
few narrow steps to a small building with the sign "Welcome to
the oldest family-owned restaurant in the Northeast." I looked
around; it had a yellow door, with tiny windows. It looked like
a little cottage that you imagined should be in the woods, not
in its current location with an amazing view of the Millennium
Bridge. Justin turned and looked at me with wide eyes. "What do
you think?" he asked.

"Of what?"

"This place."

"It is certainly a surprise," I said.

"You like it?"

"Yes, I would have never imagined choosing somewhere like
that."

"The food is really delicious."

"I can't wait." I was hungry.

A man appeared in the doorway. "Justin," he said, holding his
hand out for Justin to shake. He smiled at me but didn't shake my
hand.

"Professor Vaulks," said Justin. "This is Alexia."

He peeked at me. "How is your family?" he asked.

"They are well, thanks," Justin answered.

"I'm glad. Follow me, your table is ready."

Vaulks was short with curly silver hair, slim, and clean shaven.
He was wearing a dark suit and inky shirt. Inside, the place was
bigger than I'd imagined. The walls were forest green, with a huge
broomstick over the fireplace and pictures of elephants and lions
strewn throughout. Vaulks led us to a table by the window with a

view of the museum and pulled out my chair. I sat down, and he dropped a pink linen napkin on my lap. Justin sat opposite.

"Would you like a few moments?" he asked.

"Yes, please," said Justin.

I was busy looking at the balloons, pink with silver number eighteens on. There were four of them. I had not had balloons since I was small. And pink and silver were my favourite colours.

"Thanks," I smiled, attempting to contain my excitement.

He reached over the table, taking my hand. "I want your day to be special—for you to be happy."

"I am. It's not every day you meet a professor with a love of broomsticks and pictures of wildlife. How did you get to know him?"

"A friend of Gran's. They go back a long way. He used to work in the research labs at university. A psychologist. He's been on television, I believe. His work was around personality disorders and psychopaths—best treatments and whatever. After retiring, he opened this restaurant."

"Oh, interesting," I said.

Vaulks came back carrying a bottle of champagne and two flutes. He placed the flutes on the table, popped the cork, and filled the flutes. I gazed at Justin; he smiled back.

"I'll be back with your order," said Vaulks.

"Champagne?" said Justin.

"You never said anything about drinking in the afternoon," I said.

"I don't normally, but it is a special occasion."

"Let me guess—then you're gonna get behind the wheel," I said.

"No, the driver will pick up the car and drive us home when we're ready. Alexia, I would never put you in any danger. I don't take risks."

I laughed and took a sip of champagne. It was a first for me—I had never tasted any alcohol. I couldn't very well admit it to him, so I just took small sips, feeling awkward that he had gone to so much effort.

Through the window I watched a bride and groom pose for their photos, kissing with a view of the bridge in the background. Her dress was beautiful—white like a princess's. Then they walked up the steps of the restaurant. I noticed her bouquet of peach roses. He picked her up, soaking up the magical atmosphere of happiness, and then the bridesmaids joined the couple in a photograph.

"How is the champagne?" Justin asked. He was holding the flute between his fingers, taking small sips.

"Great, but I'm not a drinker, so I'm taking it easy. I like to enjoy such rare and precious moments," I said, looking at the wedding party.

"Yeah, this is a perfect spot, with outstanding views."

Vaulks reappeared with two dishes of lasagne, salad, and plates, and asked if we would like a top up. Justin looked at me, and I nodded. Vaulks poured some more champagne and said if we needed anything, he would be at the bar.

"What do you think of the lasagne?" he asked.

"My favourite—how did you know?"

"Well, I didn't, but I wanted it to be a total surprise, so no menu."

"You've been secretly talking to my mum about my likes and dislikes."

"No, I just used my own intuition."

I laughed, and we ate. The other diners walked past our table, wishing me happy birthday. An elderly couple stopped by and said that we were a delightful couple and that champagne was a symbol of love.

The elderly women asked, "Are you on your first date or just celebrating your eighteenth?"

Justin glanced at me with the biggest beam and said, "Both."

They smiled and said bye. Once they left, Justin said, "They remind me of my gran."

I reached over and patted his arm. Vaulks came back, cleared the dishes, and reappeared with a cake. Oh my God, the workmanship that had gone into making it was impressive. The cake was decorated in pink icing with a silver unicorn, snowman, and fish on top. Although fish and cake wasn't a compelling combination. I was at a loss for words when I read what was written on the cake: "To Alexia, with the greatest affection and thanks for spending your special day with me. Love, Justin."

"It is my pleasure," I said quietly.

He then insisted that I make a wish and blow out all eighteen candles. I did, and I cut the cake, giving him a big piece and myself a smaller one.

It was a real surprise—one that I definitely wouldn't forget. Then, Justin asked me if I would like to take some for my parents. I told him no because I knew Mum would have bought or made one.

"What would you like to do next?" he asked. "We could visit the museum or the art gallery."

"The museum, please," I said.

"Sure," he answered.

We walked over the bridge, his arm over my shoulder. On reaching the museum, we discovered that it was ten to five—ten minutes before closing. Justin led me to the life-size skeleton of a T. rex dinosaur.

Wow, it was amazing to be looking at a creature with razor-sharp teeth and a jaw big enough to chomp me and anything that crossed its path—like the goat in *Jurassic Park*. It sent a little chill down my spine, but I wasn't telling Justin that.

CHAPTER EIGHTEEN

Mum was fast asleep on the settee, and Dad was putting the clean dishes away when I got home. The place smelled of paint. The lights were on, and the peach walls that Mum had disliked for years were now a shade of blue. She'd scrubbed the place, emptied the cupboards, defrosted the freezer, and cleaned the fridge. I went into my room—everything was on top of my bed as part of the process. I wished she would leave my room alone. I glanced at my dressing table; my flowers and card were still where I'd left them.

She used to do this when she wasn't well. She tried to block the voices by cleaning. That was part of her hallucinations: seeing dirt and hearing things. She thought keeping the flat disinfected would drive the voices away from her mind. That was when she missed my company and tried to distract herself by any means she could. With Dad back and her getting better, I was hopeful she would stop.

I didn't understand her behaviour, exactly what it meant, or the way she felt, but I tried to support her as best as I could. I checked on Mum once more to make sure that she was breathing before I rearranged my room. I didn't want to wake her. She looked peaceful with specks of blue paint all over her face. I smiled and kissed her forehead. Dad walked in and whispered, "Would you like a hand tidying your room?"

He switched her light off. I didn't really need his help, but I wanted to talk. I asked Dad if Mum had been stressed about painting the sitting room and cleaning, like she did before Justin came to take me out.

"No," he answered, "she's been fine. She told me that she wanted to change the colour of the walls. We went out, chose the paint, bought it, came back, and painted the walls together. And then she insisted on cleaning while I watched the match."

"Are you sure Mum wasn't acting strange? Like, asking you if you could hear things?"

"No, Alexia. I know you're worried about your mum, but she has been perfectly happy today. She is getting better—I can assure you."

I breathed a sigh of relief. Dad pushed the sofa bed against the wall, taking the stuffed animals off my bed and putting them back on the sofa bed while I rearranged my bed and other things. I was trying to hide both books, *The Mind of Wizards* and *Seeking Angels*, but Dad had seen them.

"What are these?" he asked, grabbing *The Mind of Wizards* and turning the pages without my permission.

Why do parents think that is okay? Now I had to tell him about the books. So I told him about Barratt Joshley and Zac the mad scientist's quest to find a cure for depression while Barratt tries to kill him, and I told him about Vanessa Helena Amadeo searching for the lighthouse man who had kidnapped her mother and about Justin's sister being murdered and Justin's wish to take me to the Lake District.

"You like him?" he asked, looking at me.

"Yes, I do. He's my best friend. My other best friend is Mia. And you and Mum, of course." It was true, but most of all I didn't want him to be left out, and I wanted to go to the Lakes.

"He's your best friend? I was under the impression that he was more your boyfriend," he said, looking amused.

"Um, a bit of both—friend, boyfriend, whatever."

He laughed, pulled the stool from under my dressing table, and sat down. "Take the weight off your feet; we're done here," he said.

I took Winnie-the-Pooh, my soft toy who had only one eye after an accident in the washing machine, hugged it, and sat on the end of my bed, looking serious. He had a smile on his face, and his amused expression caught me by surprise. I wasn't used to pep talks from my dad. I thought he was about to explain the lowdown of the birds and bees. I pressed my lips.

"Alexia," he said, "it's perfectly normal to have a boyfriend. Justin seems a level-headed guy, but he's a little older than you."

I swallowed the lump in my throat—that was why he was questioning Justin earlier. I thought, Yes, he's twenty-one, but he behaves more like my age. I like him, and he likes me. Justin makes me laugh and feel special, in a way that has nothing to do with my dad. "Yes, he is, but it's not unusual for a girl my age to date an older boy," I said, looking at him.

He sighed, his lips pressed together into a caution line.

"All that matters is that my daughter is happy."

"I am."

"Alexia, you're back." Mum appeared in the doorway. "Why didn't you wake me?"

"We didn't want to disturb you. You looked so peaceful." I used "we" deliberately so she didn't think that Dad and I were raving about her obsession with cleanliness.

"Did you have a good time?" Mum asked.

"Yeah, Justin took me to an unusual restaurant owned by a weird professor with a passion for broomsticks," I told her. She exchanged glances with Dad, and they both nodded.

I didn't tell my parents about visiting the museum and seeing the dinosaur skeleton. Dinosaurs were part of Mum's hallucinations. Dad got to his feet and peeked at his watch. "It's time I made a move."

I looked at Mum. They were getting on well, but Dad hadn't moved in with us; he was still staying at the B&B. I understood that Mum wanted to be sure about Dad and whatever.

"Dad must be exhausted after all this painting," I said. "Why doesn't he stay in my room and I sleep on the settee tonight?"

"Yes, that's a good idea. Tom and I haven't had dinner yet. I'll have a shower, and then Tom can have his. Alexia, get your dad a towel."

Once Mum had gone into the bathroom, Dad grinned at me. "Thank you, my darling. Things will improve when we move into the new house."

"Oh, we're still moving?"

"Yes, we're viewing it in the morning."

"You're the best dad in the whole world," I told him.

Suddenly, *boom*—it sounded like someone had crashed. Dad heard it too. I ran to the sitting-room window. Then there was a crack that sounded like a rifle. The street light flickered outside, and we noticed someone or something lying on the pavement and a motorbike speeding away.

"I'll call the cops," said Dad, pulling his mobile out of his pocket.

"Okay. Do you think it's a dead body?" I asked while Dad made the call.

"It looks a possibility."

I looked out again. An old man stood with an owl on his shoulder. He was wearing a long purple coat. Octovia, the giant woman stood next to him. Dad was on the phone with the police, reporting shots fired and what looked like a hit and run. I waved a hand to Dad, who was on the settee. He rushed to the window.

"Officer," said Dad. "I'm afraid I've wasted your time, the person whom I thought was injured is now standing outside, and what's more shocking, it's an unusual old man with a purple coat and an owl on his shoulder, and a very tall woman."

I couldn't hear what the police on the other end of the line told Dad. But I could hear Dad saying, "Yes, a police car patrolling the area is a good idea." He ended the call, and we both looked horrified. The man was still in the same position, looking away from us. We could not close the curtain, as it had been removed for painting. A family of bats flew level with our window, which was a bit strange, as there weren't any fruit trees in the neighbourhood.

"Don't mention this to your mother," said Dad gruffly. "There's something strange going on out there.

We turned to walk away when bright lights flickered through the glass. We both stopped and looked back down the street. Dad and I jumped in horror; the old man had vanished, but there was a huge dog looking in our direction, standing next to a cage with a white owl on top.

"Magic and ghosts are playing tricks tonight," said Dad.

I felt strange—as though I'd watched a horror movie—as dad took my hand, pulling me away from the window. It was all very weird. With the giant woman at the church, the snow creature that came to life, and then the woman dressed in white—now the old man, owl, and dog. I was beginning to believe that Mum wasn't delusional or hallucinating; it was possible she had seen something.

Mum reemerged, looking at Dad and me standing in the doorway of our sitting room. She rolled her eyes. "The bathroom is free, Tom. Has Alexia gotten you a towel?" she asked.

"Oh, sorry, I'll go and get it."

Dad rubbed his left shoulder. He had been doing that quite often; I was sure he was in pain after decorating. When I returned, Mum and Dad were in the kitchen. I heard Dad say, "I don't think

Alexia should sleep on the settee in the sitting room with the smell of fresh paint and no curtains."

"You sleep in my room; Alexia and I will sleep in hers—there's enough space for both of us with the sofa bed," Mum said.

"We'll have a guest room in the new house, and there's nothing wrong with us sharing a bed. You are my wife," Dad said.

"Let's not rush—we'll think about that once we move," Mum said.

Dad laughed. I walked in, killing the conversation, and handed Dad the towel. "Thank you," he said, and he left.

"I don't expect you're hungry?" Mum asked, opening the fridge door and taking carrots, half a squash, and a cabbage out.

"No, I'm still full from lunch. What are you making?"

"Soup. Your dad was talking about soup earlier. It's a bit nippy tonight; that will heat his old bones." She laughed as she said this.

"I think Dad is in agony with his shoulder," I said.

"Yes, I've noticed. I didn't want him to help with the painting, but he insisted. Typical of your dad. He'd never complain."

"He needs to see a doctor for some painkillers," I said.

"He's already on some strong ones; he suffered first-degree burns, and he's lucky to have survived. I'm doing my best to reestablish normality." I noticed the anxiety in her voice.

There was a moment's silence, and then Mum started peeling the carrots.

"I'll help you with that," I said.

"Okay," she said. "So where did you and Justin go, apart from the restaurant?"

Mum passed me the peeler. She took a knife from the drawer, grabbed the onion, and attacked it. I told her about the woman shouting at a man in town and the wedding party. I told her that I drank champagne with Justin, and then we walked over the bridge. She lit the stove, took out a large pot, poured some water in, and dropped in the peeled onion. I chopped the carrots, cabbage, and squash on the chopping board. Mum started filling the pot with the ingredients: vegetables, a little salt, oil, and a cube of garlic. She added more water to the pot, covered it, and turned to look at me.

"Champagne? I must have a word with that boy. Turning my daughter into an alcoholic," she joked.

"He didn't turn me into anything. What did you drink on your eighteenth?" I asked.

"Beer in a grubby pub with a few girlfriends. It sounds like you had a fabulous time. He sure knows how to spoil a girl."

"Yeah, he's okay."

Mum and I set the table in our tiny kitchen. She told me that she was looking forward to seeing the house and moving out of the flat. I asked Mum if I could have a dog in the new house; she said I could, but it would be my responsibility to care for it. I said I would, thinking I could go dog walking with Justin. I hugged Mum once we had finished putting soup bowls and spoons on the table. She hugged me back and then went to turn the heat down under the pot.

"Awesome smell," said Dad. "You've been busy!" He walked over to Mum and pulled her into a hug. She kissed his checks, and he patted her back.

Mum served the soup; I had a little of Mum's to taste.

"Well, that's delicious. We must make soup more often," I said.

Dad smiled, dipping a piece of bread in his soup. I left my parents talking about selling versus renting the flat when we moved; it wasn't the sort of conversation I felt I could contribute to. Besides, I kind of had a headache, so I went to the small cabinet in the bathroom and downed a couple of Anadin. Then I brushed my teeth, went to my room, put my soft stuffed animals on the floor, and curled up under the duvet.

But instead of sleeping, I ended up lying on the sofa bed and replaying the whole kissing thing with Justin. I couldn't switch off thinking about the way his finger had moved on my tender lips, then his lips on mine, and his gentle touch on my hand at the restaurant. I thought about the gifts, card, flowers, the meal, and the champagne; the whole thing had been fantastic. Justin was amazing—everything he did was to make me happy and laugh. It all felt romantic. I'd wanted him to kiss me since we met; I supposed that was normal at my age. I mean, he was handsome, and I was attracted to him. I thought about him nonstop and looked forward to going to the Lakes and having my first sexual intimacy. Justin had not mentioned anything on the subject of sex, but if we were planning to spend a night together, the subject could come up. Oh God, it felt so right but wrong to think about.

Then I started worrying about the owl and dog outside and the possibility that they might come in and kill my parents in their sleep. Suddenly my phone began to buzz. I glanced at the screen; it was Justin.

"Hi," I said.

"Alexia, are you ready for your next surprise?"

"What surprise?" I asked.

"Well, it wouldn't be a surprise if I told you."

I laughed, looking at the time on my phone. "Are you kidding? It's after ten o'clock. What sort of surprise are you planning at this time of the night?"

"When was the last time you went clubbing?"

"Um, like never," I answered. I was a total virgin when it came to nights out with boys, and I only just had my first kiss with him.

"I'll pick you up in forty minutes. Nightclubs don't kick off till eleven."

"You're joking."

"No joke. It's your special party, and I've got the magic wand."

I laughed. "See you soon then."

"That's for sure. Bye for now," he said.

CHAPTER NINETEEN

O h my God, that boy is full of surprises. I threw the duvet
off, streamed out of my room, and rushed down the narrow
corridor to the kitchen. My parents were still in the same position,
with the empty dishes on the table. They both looked at me.

"Are you okay?" they asked.

I couldn't contain my excitement, I told my parents that Justin
had invited me clubbing. They laughed, looking at each other.

"Your dad was just saying that we should have gone to see a
movie to celebrate your birthday, as you did not want any fuss. But
clubbing is certainly more fun," said Mum.

I was about to ask Mum what people wore to nightclubs and
then realised she wouldn't have a clue, so I went back to my room
and decided to WhatsApp Mia and ask for some advice. She called
instantly.

"I have a what-to-wear-on-a-night-out-with-a-boy problem," I
said.

"Exciting," Mia answered. I told her all about it, including bit-
ing my lip, without mentioning the nightclub and Justin's name.
"Do I know him?" she asked when I was finished.

"Not sure," I said.

"College guy?"

"No, he's a graduate designer."

"Wow. How did you meet him?"

"Through my mum's group-therapy connections."

"Hun," Mia said. "You've kept him a secret. Who does this guy work for?"

"Own boss. Shares an office with his dad," I said, smiling. "Computer-games designer famous in England and all over the globe, in magazines all over the world, just launched his latest game in London." Mia was well connected socially.

"Justin Hunter," she said.

"Hmm, maybe?"

"Oh my God. His dad plays golf with mine. His mum is in the same Pilates group as my mum. I've seen him at art galleries with his sister—I mean, before she was killed. He's hot. I'd fancy him like crazy, and you're dating this guy. Have you done it yet?"

"Mia!" I said.

"Hell, Alexia. He's like a sex god, and every girl at college fancies the guy."

"Okay, things to wear on a night out," I reminded her.

"So you're going on a night out with him."

"Yeah," I said, "it's my birthday after all."

"Sorry, hun, to be upfront about the guy; I'm not interested now that you're with him. Is he a good kisser?

"Yes, he's kind of a wonderful kisser." Although I didn't have any previous experiences to compare with.

"Hun," she said.

"Hun," I said.

After a short while, Mia said, "Skinny jeans, T-shirt with a pair of killer heels would be the ticket for a night out."

"Thanks," I said.

"Sorry. I've not forgotten your birthday, you know. I'm down in the dumps at present. It's just that me and him, we shouldn't mention his name, broke up yesterday after two years. He's decided that he needs to focus on his sporting career—how unreasonable is that? He's definitely a loser."

"Sorry," I said.

"Oh, well, at least you're happy," she said. "My dad got me a puppy at long last. It was love at first sight. He's adorable. I'm slowly getting over the boy."

"Oh, well, that sounds like a perfect match, Mia."

"Yeah, you must come round; you'll love him. I've not got you a present yet, so we could go shopping, and you could choose something you like. I expect delicious reports on Justin's other skills."

"Of course," I said.

"Bye, have fun." She hung up.

I knew while talking to Mia that I didn't own any heels. I changed into a pair of inky blue skinny jeans and pulled a white T-shirt on, looking in the mirror. I was about to go hunting in my mum's wardrobe when she knocked on my door.

"Come in," I said.

Mum walked in carrying a shoebox and a biker jacket. She sat on the end of my bed, looking bemused.

"Try these on for size. I bought them years ago but never had the opportunity to wear them."

Mum and I were close in clothing and shoe size; she was a ten in clothes and six in shoes, whereas I was five and a half in shoes and eight in clothes. The box contained a pair of black arch boots with low heels. I fished a pair of socks and tried on the boots and then the jacket. I ran a brush through my hair and rolled it into a bun with a clip to hold it in place. I glanced in the mirror, dabbed a few drops of perfume and a little lipstick, and turned to Mum.

"Oh, sweetie, you look fabulous."

"Thanks, Mum," I said.

The boots and jacket were both vintage leather; I never imagined Mum wearing something like that.

"Alexia," she said, "it has been years since I set foot in nightclubs, but I remember nursing teenagers whose drinks had been spiked with drugs. So be careful not to leave your drinks unattended."

"Okay. I'm not intending to drink anyway."

"You should enjoy yourself, but be aware of the sort of people who go to nightclubs. Not everyone has good intentions."

I shook my head. I was nervous about going out and leaving my parents after what I saw earlier, but I couldn't tell Mum. I heard the intercom ring, and she stood up. I grabbed my phone, keys, and money, and pushed them into my jacket pocket. Mum took my hand to walk me out. Dad was holding the door open. He looked at Mum and me on our approach and smiled.

"You look wonderful, Alexia. Watch out for wizards and witches out there," he said.

Mum raised an eyebrow, but I knew what he was warning me of.
"I will."

Justin emerged looking gorgeous and smelling of expensive aftershave that set my heart racing. Mum was still holding my hand. I looked sideways at her; she nodded and let go of my hand.

"Shall we?" Justin said, holding a hand out. I kissed my parents bye. Dad told Justin that he expected me back safely.

"Definitely," he replied. I took his hand, and we headed for the stairs. I heard Dad say, "She's all grown-up," before closing the door.

"You look amazing," he said, looking at me as we walked down the stairs.

"Um, thanks."

"I love the jacket."

I opened my month to reveal that it was my mum's, in fact so were the boots, and then changed my mind.

"Vintage fashion never dates," I said.

"So true," he answered.

Once outside, I looked around as we walked hand in hand towards the awaiting car. It was not the same one he was driving when he took me for lunch; tonight we were being chauffeured, he told me. The street light was on, and there wasn't any sign of owl, giant dog, or old man. I noticed a police car parked at the other end of the street. That reassured me a little. Frank was holding the back door open.

"Many happy returns, Miss Collins," said Frank.

"Thank you, Frank," I said, diving in the back seat with Justin. We belted up, Frank kicked the engine into life, and we moved slowly along the street. I kept looking out the window, worried that there was something strange in the area—that maybe our flat had been built on a burial ground, and that was why we kept seeing weird things. Justin was looking at me, so I could not hide the anxiety.

"Are you okay?" he asked as Frank took a right turn.

"Um," I said, "Dad and I saw something odd and crazy tonight."

"Oh, like?" he asked.

"An owl, an old man, and a huge dog."

"It's nothing unusual to see an owl at night, and the old man could have been taking his dog for a walk," he said.

I decided not to tell him the gory details because I was so excited to be going to my first-ever nightclub with a boy.

"Yeah, you might be right," I said.

Frank pulled up outside a building and opened the door. Justin slid out and took my hand, helping me out. I looked at the two coffee-skinned guys—tall and muscular with shaved heads—who stood at a closed door in their black suits.

"Mr. Hunter, Miss—welcome to Redquake," one of them said, pushing the door open.

Justin nodded, and we walked through. It was huge inside. We were deafened by loud music and blinded by colourful lights around us. He led me to a booth with a cream leather sofa, and we sat down. It was too big for the two of us; maybe he had invited other people. I was about to ask when a waitress approached, flashing us her perfect smile.

"What can I get you?" she asked.

Justin glanced at me.

"Orange juice, please."

"Are you sure?" he asked.

I nodded. "Yes."

"Two orange juices, please," he said.

The waitress went off. I remembered hearing girls at college chatting about being asked for ID at the door—I was surprised that the bouncers hadn't asked for mine.

Justin put his arm over my shoulder and drew me closer to him. "So your first…"

"Yeah," I said. I tried not to think about Mum's words about drugs in nightclubs. Justin had taken his jacket off the moment we came in, and I was still wearing mine.

"Shall we hit the dance floor?" he whispered.

"Er, okay. Is it safe to leave my jacket?" I asked and instantly felt stupid.

"Yes. Frank is keeping an eye out; since my sister's death, I don't go out without him. He's ex-navy and knows what to watch out for." He waved at Frank, who stood on the stairs. He waved back.

The whole public dancing thing was new to me. I had attempted dancing in my bedroom, but after bumping into furniture and almost breaking my leg, I avoided it. He swept me into his arms; he was a fantastic dancer, of course, and I had two left feet and kept stepping on his. It was embarrassing. The next song was a little faster, but I was so out of time and kept bumping into other people. They scowled at me. I knew I should have taken dancing lessons, but Justin didn't seem to mind that I was possibly the worst dancer on the planet. After a few more crashes into other people, we went back to our private booth.

"Did you enjoy that?" he asked flirtatiously.

I laughed. "I'm sorry."

"What for?" he asked.

"Stepping on your feet. I'm sure you've noticed that I'm the winner of the worst dancer competition."

"I don't know what you're talking about, Alexia Collins."

We both laughed. He took a sip of his drink. I kept looking around the place—high ceiling, red walls, DJ in a high glass room with headphones on, rocking up the dance floor with fabulous music. It was packed with people, young and not so young, enjoying the buzzing atmosphere. It was difficult to have a conversation—the whole place was overpowered by loud music. I should have been having fun, but all I could think about were drug dealers and spiked drinks. Justin kept looking at me, and I pretended not to notice.

"Shall we go somewhere else?" he suggested.

I nodded. He handed me my jacket, and I looked over to where Frank stood. He pointed to a back door—not the same one we came in through. Once outside, waiting for Frank to get the car, he said, "Would you like to come to my house, or would you prefer we tried another nightclub?"

Although I was worried about my parents, I also knew that they were grown-up and could defend themselves. The thought of making another fool of myself washed over me. "Your place sounds good," I said.

"Okay," he answered as Frank stopped next to us. We got into the back of the SUV. When we arrived at his house, his parents and grandparents were still up watching an ancient black and white movie.

"Alexia, how nice to see you," said Sophia.

I smiled and said, "Likewise." I hadn't seen Sophia since visiting her in hospital. I noticed the line on her cheek—a scar from her operation. She seemed to be recovering well.

"Gran is staying with us for a while," Justin said quietly.

His dad pulled to his feet and said, "These nightclubs are closing earlier than in my days."

"No, they're still open," Justin said. "Alexia and I decided to take it easy. We're going to listen to music in my room for a while."

Justin and Alexia exchanged glances. His mum smiled and said, "There has been some strange announcement on the news tonight: flying unicorns with snowmen and fish have been seen in Iceland and America. I don't suppose you've seen such creatures?"

"No," said Justin. He opened the fridge and asked me what I would like to drink.

"Water, please."

He took a bottle of water out of the fridge and two glasses from the cupboard and led the way to his bedroom. He opened and shut the door, laughing. "Remember, I told you they were going to be famous."

I giggled. "Have you told your parents that you're not just a brilliant games designer but also a magician?"

"Correction Miss Collins, actually, *we* created the Ice Pearls, therefore *we're* skilled magicians, but no, I've not told my family."

"But I think they know," I answered.

"Maybe. What sort of music do you like?"

"Um, surprise me," I said.

"Okay, but you would say if you don't like it."

"Promise."

I sat on the settee and watched him. He strolled over to his bedside table, bent at the waist, and grabbed his iPad. He chose the music while walking back. It started playing as he sat next to me.

"Do you like it?" he asked.

"Yeah." It was more bearable than the overwhelming nightclub, although I didn't tell him that. I still had a headache, even though I was overly excited to go out with him. He put an arm around me, I nestled my head on his shoulder. He didn't try to kiss me; we just listened to the music. He took me home about two in the morning, and I went straight to bed.

CHAPTER TWENTY

M y eardrums were still buzzing from the night before; I guessed that's how people felt after clubbing. Then I remembered that Mum was supposed to have slept in my room— that was the sleeping arrangement from last night. I hesitated a moment and looked on the sofa bed; she wasn't there. All the soft stuffed animals were on the floor where I left them. I started to feel anxious that the gigantic man and dog had killed my parents. I flicked the light on the wall to make sure I hadn't mistaken her for my huge bear. I swallowed, fought back the shivers, grabbed my phone from my dressing table, and rushed out of my room. My heart fluttered in my chest, and images of finding my parents' dead bodies overwhelmed me. I didn't quite know what to do.

All I could think about was that I was an orphan. I had just gotten my dad back after his tragic accident only to have him murdered by witches. It was stupid of me to have gone out with Justin, I told myself, but then I was no match for witches and magic. I stopped arguing with myself when I heard a low voice singing "Rule, Britannia!" quietly. I followed the whispering lyric coming from the kitchen. I breathed a sigh of relief when I saw my parents. Mum sat on the chair, and Dad was holding the kettle and pouring boiling water into the teapot.

They both looked as I approached. "Good morning, Alexia. Would you like a cup of tea?" Dad asked.

"No, thank you," I said, trying to smile a smile of relief.

"How was your night out?" asked Mum.

"Fun," I murmured. But my mind was still filled with crazy images that I couldn't merge together. "Are we still viewing that house?"

"Absolutely. We're meeting with the sale agency shortly," Dad said. He handed a cup to Mum before glancing at his wristwatch. Well, we've only got time for a cup of tea. You better get ready."

I nodded, trying to pull myself together. "I love you two so much."

They beamed, looking at each other. "We love you too, sweet pea."

I went into the bathroom, had a quick shower, and returned to my room. I looked at my stuffed animals while getting dressed. Some of them had lost an eye or the stuffing was poking out. It was about time I sorted them out, but I couldn't bring myself to throw them away, and they were not safe to send to a charity shop. I was debating with myself when my phone buzzed. It was Mia.

"Hi," I said.

"Alexia, what are you doing later?" she asked.

"Apart from looking at a house with my parents, I've not got any other plans."

"You moving?"

"My parents' grand plan."

"Oh, a new start is good. How was your night out?"

"Fantastic."

"You're not seeing Justin today?"

"Maybe, but we've not make any arrangements yet."

"Okay. Could your parents drop you at mine to see my puppy? My parents have gone out. We could go shopping when they're back. I can't leave the puppy alone," Mia said.

"That sounds like a plan. I'm sure Dad wouldn't mind dropping me at yours." I said bye and clicked off.

I told my parents about the conversation I had with Mia on the way. Dad was still wearing the same clothes from the day before. He stopped at the B&B to change. Once Dad was out of the way, Mum asked about my clubbing experience. I told her about embarrassing myself on the dance floor. Mum burst out crying. I just stared at her, not sure what to say.

"Sorry, darling," she said between sobs, I should have sent you to dancing classes. It was my mistake. What did Justin say?"

I shrugged. "Nothing. We went to his house after I made a fool of myself by bumping into the other dancers."

Mum took a tissue from her bag, dabbed her cheeks, blew her nose, and then calmed herself before she said, "Your dad is an excellent dancer. He could show you a few moves."

Mum and I exchanged a look. Learning to dance with your dad wasn't what I had in mind, but I was so glad that they were alive— anything was better than making a fool of yourself. Dad walked back carrying a large bag. He was smiling.

"Is Dad moving in with us to teach me how to dance?" I joked.

"Cheeky. Yes, he can't stay in there. The pain is getting worse, and he's had to take his washing to the laundrette, even though there's a washing machine at home."

Mum sounded positively happy. There wasn't the dismissive tone in her voice, like when I last asked her if Dad could move in with us. Dad put the bag in the boot, started the engine, and the Audi SUV sped away. Mum sat in the front seat, and she kept turning her neck to look at me on the back seat. Dad keep peeping at her and smirking. We drove in silence for a while. Mum spoke first.

"Would you teach our Alexia a few dance moves, Tom?"

"Certainly. I take it you didn't shine on the dance floor, then?"

"Two left feet and unimpressive. I don't think Justin was impressed, although he pretended otherwise."

"We'll put that right in no time." Dad was about to say something else when my phone rang; it was Justin.

"Hi," I said cheerfully.

"Alexia, what are you up to?"

"Viewing a house with my parents, then going out with my friend Mia. Why?"

"It's Sunday. Young Carers group day. If you were planning to go, I could take you."

I've not been for a few weeks, but I've been thinking about it. I miss it. "Can I call you back later?"

"Sure."

Dad stopped outside a big Edwardian house with huge wooden gates. There was a white Ford parked in front of us. A man with short salt-and-pepper hair and a grey suit stepped out, waving. Dad waved back as we got out. I presumed that was the sale agent. I followed my parents. We paused while Dad talked to the man.

"Mr. and Mrs. Collins, as I mentioned previously, the house is empty," said the sale agent. "The owners have moved to Australia to be nearer their son and grandchildren." He entered a code and the gates opened. He led the way down a long India-stone drive towards the massive oak door. He pulled a set of keys from his jacket pocket and unlocked the door.

His name was Porter, he told us. I glanced around while he explained that the owners had dropped the price due to the house being on the market for over six months; they didn't want the property to remain empty for too long. If my parents liked the house, he might be able to knock the price down further. Mum and Dad said that they liked the house, having viewed it previously, but that it was out of their price range.

The house was in a quieter, more desirable neighbourhood than the flat, and had a long driveway, flowerbeds, and mature trees. Dad put a hand on my shoulders, guiding me into the hall. Inside it smelled of emptiness, with dust filling the air as Porter opened doors and curtains. Mum was already looking into a cupboard under the stairs. I followed Dad and Porter into the sitting room, and he opened the drapes. The house had a high ceiling and a huge window. Mum walked in behind us, and she paused when Porter suggested that it was a big house, and it was better to work our way through methodically, starting downstairs.

Mum said, "That's a good idea." The house was on three floors. It had a big sitting room, dining room, loo, a massive kitchen and pantry, and a laundry area downstairs. It had a door and stairs leading down to a basement with a study and playroom with a huge LG television on the wall. It had been renovated and redecorated—new kitchen with black-granite worktops, Porter informed us. I was immediately impressed with the grand blue carpeted stairway leading up to the top floor. The light-peach wallpaper looked expensive. Upstairs were five bedrooms—all en suite. It was amazingly spacious in comparison to our tiny flat.

Once Porter finished showing us the layout, he suggested that we have another look around alone while he waited downstairs. My parents said, "Yes." Mum asked me which room I would like as we took another look.

"I really like one of the rooms at the front," I said. It was big, with enough room for my friend Mia to sleep over, plus space for my books and desk.

"That's settled. We'll have one of the back rooms with the view of the river. That leaves three for guests and storage," Dad joked. Mum smiled and grabbed Dad's hand.

I looked at my parents making plans to buy their family home together. Although they didn't need such a big house, it was their dream home. Mum had put on a little weight on her cheeks; she looked healthier, contented. She continued to attend group therapy, but not as often. She and Dad were spending more time together. She remained close friends with Sophia, and together they enjoyed coffee mornings and regular outings into the country.

She no longer mentioned seeing or hearing weird things, like being hunted by dinosaurs, or cutting herself. Mum woke up in the morning and went to bed like normal people. I kept checking the bathroom cabinet; she was still taking her medications, but she was now on fewer tablets and lower doses. She didn't look like a bundle of nerves consumed by depression. Mum was definitely happier since Dad came back.

"This house looks expensive. How could we afford it?" I asked quietly.

Mum looked at Dad. "If we couldn't afford it, we wouldn't be looking," Dad said, smiling.

"Oh," I said.

We walked downstairs. Porter was talking on his mobile. We heard him say, "I'm showing a family around the house—you could view it this afternoon."

Mum and Dad exchanged glances. Porter said to the caller, "Would two forty be okay?" There was a pause, and then he said, "That's fine; I'll call you on Monday," before ending the call.

"My apologies," he said. "Suddenly there's another family interested in seeing this house."

My parents nodded while gazing at each other. "Excuse us for a moment, please," said Dad. He and Mum hurried into the sitting room, closing the door behind them.

I hovered in the hallway, thinking about how my parents were going to afford this house. Had they won the lotto and kept it a secret? All of a sudden, there was money. Mum was planning to go back to work part time; I was not sure about Dad. He didn't look well enough to work again in the same job or anywhere else. Then I remembered Dad mentioning that he had received compensation for his injuries. Mum had also been compensated by the hospital for her assault. I presumed there was enough money between them to finance the house. My parents came back, looking reassured.

"Porter, my wife and I would like to make an offer," Dad said.

"Excellent," said Porter.

Mum and I had another look in the kitchen while Dad and Porter talked figures. She told me that they were making an offer close to the asking price to guarantee that we got the house. She ran a hand over the granite and said it was the most wonderful kitchen she had ever seen. I smiled but didn't comment. All I ever dreamed of was a happy family, and for the first time in forever, it seemed that God had heard my prayer. After a while we heard Porter and Dad laugh. When Mum and I reappeared, Dad informed us that we were waiting to hear from the owners in Australia. With the time difference, it might be later in the afternoon before we heard anything.

We left Porter to lock up. Once in the car, Dad said, "Porter seemed to think that the owners would accept our offer."

Mum shook her head.

I asked Dad to drop me at Mia's. My parents didn't stop talking about the house: the period it was built, its character, craftsmanship, and so on. Mum kept turning to me in the back seat and asking, "What do you think, sweetie?"

"About what?"

"The house, Alexia!"

She sounded cross that I wasn't showing the same enthusiasm, but the reality was I didn't want to be excited about a property that wasn't yet ours.

"The owner hasn't accepted your offer yet; I don't want to raise my hopes."

"You're right. But I'm just excited to have seen the house that your father and I wanted all those years ago, and to eventually able to afford to buy it."

"I understand, Mum," I said. It was amazing to see my mum look forward to something, but I was also frightened that if she didn't get the house she had set her heart on, she could relapse back into the darkness of depression.

I looked out the window of the SUV, trying not to focus on the negativity. Dad laughed as we turned left on the road leading to Mia's house.

"Owners don't like to leave their property empty for long periods; it could attract squatters, who could wreck the place," said Dad. "We've made an offer close to their asking price; I'm ninety per cent sure they will say yes." He was full of enthusiasm.

"I was thinking the same," said Mum.

They were optimistic and supporting each other; however, I was glad when we stopped outside Mia's house. I said bye and buzzed at the gate. Mia opened it. I walked through; she stood on her porch, holding the most beautiful black and white puppy I had ever seen. It had the most astounding brown eyes. She was cuddling it like a tiny baby.

"What have you called him?" I asked.

"Viking," she answered.

"Nice name."

"Yes, he is an adorable boy."

Her parents were still out, she told me. We played with Viking for a while. When her parents got back, they babysat him, and we took the bus into town. We spent an hour and a half going into shops. She bought me a natural colour lipstick and some toiletries, and then we had lunch in a small café as part of my birthday present. We chatted about boys. She asked if Justin was a good dancer. I told her yes, but I didn't mention my two left feet. For once, she didn't have much to bang on about; since she'd broken up with her boyfriend, she didn't even mention his name. That was so unlike Mia. After shopping, she said that she had to go home, as she didn't want to leave her puppy for too long. I waited at the bus stop with her. The bus arrived, and she air-kissed my cheeks and got on.

I didn't wait for my bus. I called Justin, as he had offered to pick me up. He answered on the first ring.

"Alexia," he said.

"Do you still want to pick me up?"

"Of course, where are you?"

"At the bus stop, next to Tesco Express in town," I said.

"Okay, I'm on my way."

While waiting for him, I couldn't help but watch couples kissing and cuddling at the café on the other side of the road. A romantic moment. It was a perfect, warm day, with glimpses of sunshine—fabulous weather for walking in the park. Although I missed the Young Carers group and wanted to continue supporting them, I didn't feel like spending the whole afternoon in a church hall today. I was deep in my own little world when Justin stopped his truck past the bus stop and walked back.

"Hi," he said.

I laughed. "Hi," I said, looking up at him. His lips curled into a smile.

"Shall we take a cake to the group?" he suggested.

"That's an excellent idea," I said, without mentioning that I wasn't intending to go.

"Would you like me to put this in the truck?" he asked, looking at the bag in my hand.

"Yes, please. A belated birthday present from my friend Mia," I explained.

He nodded, and we walked back to his truck and left the bag under the seat. He took my hand, waited for a break in traffic, and crossed the road to Tesco Express. In the shop, he insisted on buying a Victoria sponge, paper plates, napkins, and a pack of plastic knives and forks.

Unfortunately, when we arrived at the church hall, there was a notice on the door: "Closed due to illness." We waited by the door for a while in case the group turned up anyway. He held the cake, and I held the bag of plates and other items. He kept complimenting me, saying that he liked my hair—how my high ponytail showed off my sharp cheekbones. I smiled, aware that he was flirting. I was starting to get used to it. I suggested we go to the park, and he agreed. We walked back down the path between the gravestones to his truck. The weather had turned a little cooler when we arrived at the park, but it was still pleasant. He located a bench next to a big tree, put his jacket down on the seat, and we sat with the cake between us. He cut it with a plastic knife and served us each a big piece of cake with strawberry jam in the centre. I handed him a plastic fork, and we ate while watching children riding their bikes or running past as their parents kept watch. Dog walkers greeted us as they passed. It was our first picnic. Delicious.

CHAPTER TWENTY-ONE

F ive months later spring arrived, and winter vanished like an unwelcome ghost. Everything looked green, birds bickered in the trees, and flowers shot up everywhere. My parents' offer on the house had been accepted; they had bought it and started packing in preparation for the move. Dad was writing notes on an A4 notepad, and Mum was going around with a roll of self-adhesive labels, writing numbers and sticking them on boxes, marking what she wanted to go to charity and what she wanted to keep.

I offered to help, but they declined. I was bored, so I switched the television on and fed my fish while watching the news, but the fish refused to eat; they kept swimming round and round, like two mad pets, as if they knew they would soon be moving to a new home too. I called Dad, who was now sorting things out in the kitchen cupboards, under Mum's instructions. She kept saying, "We are keeping this cup, our wedding present from my friend Holly; or this jug, the first thing we bought together." Dad kept saying, "Of course, darling."

It was amazing to believe that not so long ago, Mum hardly knew the time of day or ate a meal without me kneeling by her bed, forcing her to eat and drink her cup of tea. She would tell me to leave her alone and stop nagging, and I would cry, afraid that she would die. She would force down a few spoonfuls so that I would leave her room, and she'd curl up under the duvet and turn her back like I didn't matter. It was weirdly painful. That was her daily pattern of isolation. I couldn't imagine seeing her and Dad making plans, or her instructing him. She had certainly turned a new leaf, thanks to the realisation that the voices she heard were coming from the neighbours. Yes, she was depressed but not losing her mind. I called Dad.

He poked his head through the door and said, "Yes, sweetie?"

"There's something wrong with my fish. It's unlike them to refuse food."

"Oh," he said, rushing towards me and the fish tank.

"They only eat when they're hungry!" Mum shouted from the kitchen.

Dad and I both looked as one of the fish swam in between the greenery and hid. The other one followed. It was as if they didn't want us to watch them.

"They're suddenly acting very strange," Dad said, glancing across at me.

"I'm wondering whether we should take them to the vet?" I suggested.

He shook his head. "No, let's keep a close eye for a while. It's possible that, like your mother said, they're just not hungry. I would imagine that in the ocean, fish would only eat when they need to—a vet couldn't help with that."

"You might be right," I said.

Mum walked into our small sitting room, carrying two teapots. "Shall we take both to our new house or send one to charity?" she asked Dad and me.

They were two very old-fashioned teapots that she had bought from a charity shop in the first place. Both tall and floral, I'd broken one of the lids when I was trying to make Mum's tea, but she refused to throw it away. She had found a lid from another broken teapot that didn't quite match, but it fitted. Suddenly, before Dad and I had a chance to answer, our attention turned to the TV at the mention of Todd Walker. The newsreader carried on. Todd Walker, an ex-army veteran, had been convicted of the murder of Emily Hunter after being found guilty at Newcastle Crown Court. His solicitor, Jackson Turban, argued that Mr. Walker was not of sound mind when he was assumed to have attacked and murdered Miss Hunter with a hunting knife. He had been under the care of mental-health services and was receiving treatment for posttraumatic stress disorder. His consultant psychiatrist, Goatbell Vadel, gave evidence to support Mr. Walker's struggle with mental illness.

Mum dropped the teapots, and they smashed into pieces. Dad and I jumped up, looking at her. She ignored the broken teapots, rushed across the room, and sat on the settee. Dad and I stared at her, but she totally ignored us. The family heirlooms didn't matter anymore; she was completely engrossed with the news. A picture of Todd Walker flashed on the screen—he had his head down and was being led into a blue van by two prison guards.

"Sweet Jesus. The poor, poor innocent girl," Mum said. "What a psycho to befriend Sophia at group therapy and have pizza in the restaurant, sitting at the same table with her family. Oh my God. He even attempted to seduce me."

Dad looked from Mum to me and asked, "So you know this character?"

"Only from group therapy, but I didn't play any part in his sick game," Mum mumbled.

"I'm glad to hear," Dad said with a serious face.

I didn't mention that Justin had already told me about Todd. The newsreader continued, "The solicitor for the Hunter family spoke on their behalf outside the court. She said it had been a difficult and stressful experience, and now that justice had been done for a much-loved daughter, sister, and granddaughter, the family needed time to grieve their loss." Mum took a deep breath, switched the TV off, stood up, walked back into the kitchen, and came back with a broom and dustpan to sweep up the broken china.

I walked over to help, picking up the bigger pieces that had scattered in all directions on the floor. Dad went back into the kitchen and carried on with packing. After Mum had finished sweeping and throwing the broken pieces in the bin, she grabbed her roll of labels and carried on writing numbers and sticking them on the boxes without mentioning Todd Walker, the Hunter family, or the news again.

I glanced at the fish and breathed a sigh of relief that they were eating and swimming around. I went into my room, shut the door, and sat on the sofa bed with the intention of starting packing, but I couldn't. I kept thinking about the ghost of the girl I'd seen in the room at group therapy that day—the one that Sophia believed was her granddaughter, Emily. I thought about the photograph she showed to the group and the shocked look on Todd Walker's face. He empathised with her as we all did, saying how sad it must be for the family. He didn't appear to be the killer. I felt a sort of numbness as I shivered under my thin vest. I wanted to call Justin but then remembered that their solicitor had mentioned that the family needed time to grieve, so I respected that.

After a while, I went out of my room and into the kitchen. Mum and Dad were debating whether to sell or rent the flat once we moved. Mum was saying that renting would bring long-term income, but she would prefer to sell and invest the money. I stood with my shoulders to the wall, listening to their conversation. I kept thinking of the good memories Mum and I had had in this flat. It was where I grew up, and where we had our movie days of

Absolutely Fabulous, eating popcorn, and laughing together. But I couldn't ignore the gloomy times with Mum's depression.

I'd lost count of the number of times I had explained to the paramedics that my mum didn't mean to die—that those suicide attempts were her cries for help. It was heartbreaking having to watch her be carted away in the ambulance yet again so she could be stitched up for cutting her wrists, praying that she would not die, feeling lonely, helpless, and terrified of losing her. The last straw was the neighbours from hell knocking a hole in her bedroom wall. It made sense that she wanted to sell this flat and leave the bad memories behind. She had stopped wearing long sleeves recently and was confident enough to show her arms and wrists. She was able to look at the marks without getting anxious. I was so glad Dad came back before I lost my mind. No doubt he'd seen the marks too, but I was not sure if they'd talked about it yet. They both looked when I took a step forward.

"You okay?" asked Dad.

I wanted to say yes, it's a good idea to sell the damn flat, but I didn't; instead, I walked over to my parents, kissed them, and give them a big hug.

"What's that for?" asked Mum.

I shrugged. "I love you two so much."

"We love you too."

"I'm going for a bike ride," I said.

"Be careful," Mum said.

I nodded. I carried my bike down the stairs instead of taking the lift, thinking of Justin—he never took the elevator. I kept telling myself that I should do something like send a card to show that I'd heard the news. I rode to the bus stop and waited for the number thirty-six bus to town. When the bus stopped, I carried my bike on, locked it in the bike lockers next to the bus station, and walked five minutes to Hollydale, the biggest card shop in town. The choices were endless. I kept looking at the pictures on the front and reading the messages of condolence inside the cards.

They were sad, and some were too personal. Since I didn't know her personally, I chose one that was a painting of the ocean with a lighthouse and rocks. The message of condolence was simple: "You are gone but not forgotten. Rest in peace." Given her love for art, I thought that was appropriate. I also remembered the messages I had seen at her parents' house.

I bought a pen and a first-class stamp, sat on a bench outside, wrote, "Thinking of you, Love Alexia," then addressed the envelope, stuck the stamp on, walked to the postbox next to Samantha's florist shop, dropped the card in the box, and went to see Sam. She was alone, arranging flowers into pots and pails displayed on the shop floor.

"Hi, is it okay to come in?" I asked.

I stood in the doorway. She looked over to me and said, "Of course, Alexia. What a wonderful surprise. It has been mad busy—my last customer has just left with a bouquet of pink carnations. His wife has given birth to a daughter, he told me. You should have seen the joy on his face—first baby, he mentioned."

"New life, good news," I said, taking my rucksack off my shoulder and putting it on the counter.

"Yes," she said, looking around as if she was expecting to see someone else. "You're alone?" she asked.

"Yeah, Mum and Dad are packing up the flat for the move into the new house."

"Oh yes, of course—your mother has always wanted that house. It was meant to be hers, and after all she's been through, that's just a perfect love nest."

"Have you heard the news?" I asked.

Sam put a pail of red roses on a wooden table by the window and tilted her head a little to the side, as if she was looking past my shoulder towards the door. "No, what news?"

"Todd Walker has been convicted of Emily Hunter's murder."

"Oh my God, no. Wasn't he the guy from group therapy that your mum mentions occasionally?" she asked.

"Yeah, the creepy one that used to look at Mum and supposedly had romantic feelings for her," I said.

"Yes, I remember. Jessica's mentioned him. It took the authorities some time to arrest him."

"Yeah. Do you still want me to help in the florist shop on Saturdays?" I asked, trying to change the subject."

"Yes, if you're still interested in a Saturday job."

"I am."

"Well how about you come in next Saturday for half a day? I'm expecting a large delivery of roses from Kenya. I would appreciate your help."

"Okay, next Saturday it is."

A young couple walked in, looking at the flowers. Sam turned her attention to them. I said bye, left the florist shop, strolled to the bus stop, and unlocked my bike. I got on the number sixty bus that was about to leave; it stopped one stop away from the flat—that would do. I would ride the rest of the way. When I got back, Mum was watching Pilates on Fitness TV. Boxes were stacked against the walls of our sitting room. I laughed. That was my mum's idea of exercise.

"Where's Dad?" I asked.

"Getting takeaway curries for dinner."

"I see. Have you ordered something for me?"

"Sure, your favourite: chicken tikka with plain naan bread."

"Thanks, Mum," I said, sitting next to her on the settee. She reached over and patted the back of my head as if I was a tiny baby.

"Wouldn't it be more fun to actually participate than watch?" I asked, smiling.

She pursed her lips and tipped her head to the side like a puppy waiting to be taken for a walk. "You know how it is with me and physical activities; the satisfaction is in the watching." We laughed.

"I've made a start on your room," she said. I didn't respond.

My mum seemed to have everything under control—a few months ago, that would have been unimaginable.

CHAPTER TWENTY-TWO

On Saturday morning, I woke up at eight, showered, dressed, grabbed my rucksack, and picked up *Seeking Angels* and *The Mind of Wizards* from my dressing table and popped them into my rucksack. Those books were like my world of everything, and I didn't want my parents to pack them. I thought of Zac, the mad scientist character in *The Mind of Wizards*, and smiled.

I rushed out of my room. Mum and Dad were up, dressed, and eating a breakfast of porridge on the settee in the sitting room. Everything was packed and ready for the removal driver. I fished my trainers onto my feet and told my parents that I was going to my first Saturday job ever: working at Samantha's. They already knew; I just wanted to remind them. Mum shook her head, and Dad smiled, saying that he was proud of me and would drive me. I glanced at my bike, which was labelled To Go, along with the fish tank. Our little flat looked like a warehouse with boxes, furniture, and suitcases. Although I had never been in an actual warehouse, I'd seen one on television.

"Have some breakfast before you go," said Dad. "There's some porridge left—apples and banana."

"Not hungry," I said.

Dad opened his mouth to say something. Mum glared at him. "Stop making a fuss, Tom. She won't starve; there's always food at Sam's."

He nodded.

"But I've not packed the rest of my things yet," I said.

"Your mother and I will take care of it," said Dad, "and I'll take you there and pick you up. What time do you finish?"

"At three," I said. Mum smelled of Jasmine, her new perfume Dad gave her as a surprise gift last weekend. I liked the calming aroma. "I'm only working a half day."

"Okay," Dad answered.

"Thank you for packing my stuff," I said.

Dad finished eating his porridge and put the bowl on the table. Mum said she would wash the dishes, Dad kissed her on the lips, and then he said he'd brush his teeth. I kept looking at Mum. She looked a little anxious, and I started to worry that she had overdone it. She was looking at me too for, like, forever after dad left the room. I gave her a hug, and she held on to me as if I was going away to another country. She was warm and loving. But I also knew that my mum was predisposed to stress. That made me uneasy. Dad came back, and Mum kissed my cheeks and stood up from the settee.

"Mum, are you all right?" I asked.

"I'm perfectly fine—I can hardly wait to have the keys to our new house in my hand." Her voice was reassuring; she was probably just excited at the prospect of the new chapter in Jessica Collins's life.

"We better get going, or you'll be late on your first day," Dad joked.

I smiled, taking a last look around, remembering the happy times of playing with my dolls on the floor on Mum's days off. She would ask me which Disney movies I would like to watch while we both knelt on the carpet, looking at our little DVD collection on the floor next to the TV. I would pick one of my favourites, *Cinderella*. Mum would cuddle me and Bounty, my doll with a black face, as we escaped into the enchanting magic of the Fairy Godmother, the mice, the wicked stepmother, the ugly step-sisters, and romance. Those were happier times—before Mum's depression, paranoia, and delusion took over our life. Like in the story of *Cinderella*, Mum had eventually found her glass slippers, beaten depression, and her prince came to rescue her. Meanwhile, I was not sure if I would ever hear from Justin again; it had been five days since we had last spoken—such a lapse in communication was so unlike him. I missed him, but I respected that he and his family were grieving their loss.

"Alexia," Mum said. "Be careful—Samantha's flowers come from somewhere in Africa. She once told me that she found a dead snake in between the roses, from the Kenyan packaging plant, I believe. She researched the species, and apparently it was a poisonous sort."

"Thanks, Mum, I'll bear that in mind."

Dad and I drove in silence. When he dropped me at the kerb outside the florist, he said, "Good luck, sweet pea. Don't forget: we're moving into our new house today. I'll be back at three. Are you excited?"

I shook my head. "Yeah. Thank you for the lift. See you later." My dad still called me "sweet pea," as if I was some sort of flower, even though I was eighteen years old. I wanted to say that Mum looked a little stressed, but then I would have had to explain the change in Mum's personality that I was sure he was already aware of, so I let it drop and waved as he sped away.

I looked through the glass. Samantha was waving at me; I waved back, walking across the pavement towards the door. She had already started displaying flowers in colourful pails outside the door, all arranged in a row of wooden boxes. Inside were bouquets in plastic containers, vases on wooden tables, and lots of flowers and plants in metal pots on the floor, like a beautiful garden. There were rolls of wrapping—plastic and paper with various decorations next to the counter—colourful balloons for every occasion, and ribbons hanging from dispensers. There were dried flowers as well as baskets hanging from the ceiling on wooden beams. Samantha's florist shop was a small building on a busy street corner, across the road from Hunter's Corporation, which was a huge glass building with security at the door. I glanced through the window, thinking of Justin.

Samantha gave me a hug and kissed me on both cheeks. I hugged her back. "The van should be here any minute," she said.

I looked at her blankly. Was this some sort of quiz to test if I was listening? "I'm sorry?"

"The flower delivery van," she said, smiling. "You seem a little distracted, Alexia. Is everything all right?"

"I'm fine, of course. I knew that," I said in an attempt to sound like I was joking. It sounded feeble. My mind and eyes were on the building across the road in the hope of seeing Justin. Samantha shook her head, smiling. I put my rucksack under the counter next to her bag, as I always did when I visited the florist.

"I suggest we have a cup of tea while we wait," she said. "Have you had breakfast?"

"No, not much of an appetite this morning."

She laughed. "No surprise. It's a big day for you, Alexia—a new job and moving out of that flat. I imagine your mother was up at first light?"

"Yes. Mum and Dad were up when I woke up. She is pretty excited about holding the keys to the new house soon."

"I would feel the same if I were Jessica. I'm looking forward to the housewarming."

I looked at her. "Um, honestly, I'm not sure my parents are planning anything special, but you are welcome to see the new house."

She breathed sharply, looking at me. "If anyone deserves happiness, it's your mother, after all she's been through. Alexia, you have been a rock to your mother throughout her illness. My sister Josie had schizophrenia; she used to just sit in her bedroom, looking at the wall and pointing and talking to herself. Mental health is very confusing. I don't think anyone fully understands."

I nodded. "You too, Sam. I couldn't have dealt with Mum's mental-health problems without your support. What happened to your sister?" I asked. Sam had never mentioned Josie before.

"She died of an overdose. I didn't want the same to happen to your mother. We have been friends since we were teenagers; she was there for me when Josie died. We help each other."

I did not want to continue on the subject of mental illness; it was too painful and complicated. I offered to make the tea. Looking at the varieties of flowers, I was under the impression that she had already gotten the delivery. My mobile rang while I was filling the kettle in the tiny kitchenette at the back of the florist shop. I reached into my jeans pocket and glanced at the number. It was Justin. I thought, "Oh my God, he's calling to dump me; he can't face me." I knew that it was too perfect to be true love, I wanted to drop the kettle—my heart racing, my hands trembling. I couldn't make up my mind, and I didn't want to sound desperate to hear his voice. I was, of course. I let it ring five times and switched the kettle on before I answered on the sixth ring. I didn't want to sound dispirited at not hearing from him either. I thought about his lips on mine the last time he kissed me—how wonderful it was. My head started aching.

I remembered him telling me that his last girlfriend Olympia left after the death of his sister. Maybe he dumped her. Let's get it over and done with before Samantha wonders if I've gone to an Amazonian forest to fetch the water.

"Hi," I said.

"Alexia, how are you?" he asked. His voice sounded a little unsure.

"I'm fine. At work. Just started my Saturday job."

"Oh, where are you working?"

"Samantha's florist in Lofty Street."

"Is that the one across the road from my office?" he asked.

I pretended not to have noticed Hunter's Corporation. "Where is your office?" I asked.

"It's on the other side of Lofty Street. If you look through the window, you'll see the building. It's called Hunter's Corporation."

"Oh, I'll have a look when I'm free."

There was silence before he said, "Thank you for the wonderful card. My parents and I appreciate your thoughtful words, and I owe you an apology."

"Apology. What for?" I asked.

"For not calling, or seeing you since the verdict on my sister's murder. It has been difficult for my family and myself to come to terms with the conviction of a man we knew. We had not only met Todd Walker, but he'd befriended my grandmother, and he had dinner in the same restaurant and sat at the same table with my family—and all along he was my sister's killer. He's a psychopath. Only a psychopath would do what he has done."

"I'm sorry, you don't need to apologise. I can't say that I understand, but I'm trying."

There was another silence. I didn't know what else to say, I could only imagine his agony at the loss of a much-loved sister. The kettle boiled. There were two mugs on the little worktop and three red containers without any indication of what they contained. I opened all the lids with one hand, holding my phone to my ear with the other. I found the tea, took two tea bags out, dropped them in the mugs, and poured boiling water over, my phone still stuck to my ear.

I felt weird thinking about Todd Walker and remembering the way he looked at my mum at group therapy. Was he planning to befriend my mum and kill her too? He was a wicked man; my mum had a lucky escape. I could not imagine him as a cold-blooded murderer, but how could anyone know what a murderer looks like?

"I love you. I've missed you," he said eventually.

Oh my God, did he really...love me? He sounded so sure. "Me too," I said.

"What time are you finishing work?" he asked.

"Three o'clock."

"Can I see you? I could pick you up, if it is okay."

"Well, Dad was going to pick me up—we're moving into our new house today. I will call him and let him know that I'm coming home with you."

"Okay, so it is an exciting day—new job and house," he said.

"Yeah." I laughed.

Samantha popped her head through the door while I was still on the phone with him and said, "Are you all right? I was under the impression that you had gone to India to pick the tea leaves."

"Sorry, all done, Sam."

She shook her head and left. I heard her mumbling—I could make out something about romantic.

"See you later. I've got to go before I get the sack on my first day. I would have to blame you."

He laughed. "I take full responsibility, and if your boss sacks you, I promise to find you Alexia Collins's new employment. See you at three, but if Mrs. Florist asks you to leave, we could see each other sooner."

"Don't joke," I said.

"I'm not," he said jokingly.

"Bye," I said.

"I'm counting—can't wait for three. Bye for now." We both laughed and clicked the phone off.

I put my phone back into my jeans pocket, grabbed the two mugs of tea, and rejoined Sam. "Sorry, Sam, I got distracted," I said.

She laughed. "Young love. So is it still hot with Hunter?"
My face heated up. I smiled. "Tea is ready."
"Cold tea is not one of my favourites," Sam joked.
"Not cold—ready to drink, as my mum would say."

CHAPTER TWENTY-THREE

The delivery van had come and gone while I'd been flirting with a boy I thought was about to dump me. Delicious. Making tea, of course, was my first task of the day. I couldn't make a habit of flirting on the job. Samantha was my godmother, but she was also my boss with a thriving business to run. I glanced at the boxes on the wooden table. Suddenly I thought about the conversation I had with my mum earlier—the one about Sam finding a dead snake in a box of flowers that came from Kenya. It was strange, but I started thinking about reptiles and the likelihood of finding one in those boxes.

Sam and I drank our tea while she told me about the art of creating a perfect bouquet of flowers that brought so much pleasure to people's lives. She reached under the counter, producing an album. She turned the pages, showing me the most amazing bouquets she had created. Some were shaped like castles, fishes, and animals. But the most impressive was a dragon-shaped one, with the body in white roses and eyes of red roses. This was for a young man's funeral—he was killed at sixteen by a car speeding through a crossing. His family told Sam that he loved magical creatures, so they chose the dragon. As I looked at the pictures, I thought of Justin and our own magical creatures, the Ice Pearls, and how they had magically been seen in various countries, flying free. I smiled.

"You are passionate about your work, Sam," I said.

She leaned over, kissing my cheeks. "I've never been lucky in love, but I found love and passion in flowers and seeing smiles on people's faces when I present them with their bouquet." She smiled, looking at me. "Well, I can't wait to make your wedding bouquet," she announced.

"I'm not getting married—not yet anyway," I said.

She laughed. "From what I've heard, Justin Hunter is besotted with you."

I stared at her. "Who told you that?"

She was about to say something else when an elderly woman walked in.

"Good morning, Muriel," she said.

"Good morning, Samantha," said Muriel. "We're very lucky with the weather today. I heard on the news that we're expecting sunshine all weekend. I thought I'd go and see Patrick and then have lunch with my daughter, Jacqueline, and granddaughter, Kate."

"Yes, what a good idea, Muriel. I've taken liberty of arranging your usual bouquet of white lilies. I hope you don't mind," Sam said.

"Not at all, Samantha. Thank you—save me waiting," she said, opening her handbag. She took a twenty-pound note and handed it to Sam.

Sam gave her five pounds change and handed her the bouquet of lilies.

"Thank you. I will see you next Saturday," said Muriel.

"Of course," said Sam.

"Muriel is my regular—every Saturday, without fail. Her husband died two years ago after losing a long battle with dementia and lung cancer. She visits his grave every Saturday and insists on taking him lilies as a reminder of her wedding bouquet," Sam said.

"Oh, it's sad but romantic," I said.

"I suppose everyone grieves in his or her own way."

I didn't comment. She asked me to take the boxes into the kitchenette, open them, and put the flowers into containers—vases, plastic pails in water—and bring them back. She would show me where to display them. I peeked at the clock on the wall as I walked past with the first box; it was nine forty-five. Other customers kept coming in, looking at the flowers, ordering bouquets, or buying those that Sam had already made.

I felt a bit odd working in a florist shop. I didn't know much about flowers; roses, lilies, and carnations were as far as my knowledge went, and that from researching on the Internet. Samantha had won gold medals for her skill in flower arranging; she was amazing. Mum told me that Sam could turn dandelions into a fabulous bouquet. It's not hard to believe; judging from her displays all over her shop, Mum was right. Sam's shop was always buzzing with customers.

All these flowers reminded me of Emily Hunter, so young to have died at the hand of a madman like Todd Walker. I wondered if her ghost was still hanging around and if Sophia was still seeing her. Alexia, get on with your job and stop thinking about the ghost of a girl you never met, I told myself.

I opened a drawer, grabbed a small knife, carefully cut the tape atop of the box, and opened the box. I was instantly amazed by the absolutely stunning orange roses facing me—all carefully packed to protect them during transportation. I picked them one by one, putting them in one of the metal pails as I admired how attractive they were—like precious jewels. Roses were so fascinating. I thought of Mum—she liked roses. I would ask Sam if I could buy Mum half a dozen of the orange ones as a housewarming present. She would love them.

In the other boxes were every colour of rose you could imagine: pink, white, red—and some had two colours in one, like pink with a hint of blue. They smelled magical. I imagined myself actually working on the rose farms or gardens in Kenya, where they came from, cutting the roses and packing them into boxes. But I quickly thought of Mum. I would miss her, and she would miss me. I wanted to keep this memory, so I took my phone out of my pocket and took a selfie of me amongst the sea of roses. I WhatsApp'd Justin the picture with the caption "Welcome to my world of dazzling roses with an African safari backdrop."

He answered immediately, "I hope you've not disappeared into another world, like our Pearls; if you have, I will be joining you. They look wonderful—my mum and gran have a passion for roses. I'm taking Lucky to the vet; can I stop and buy a couple of bouquets?" I smiled while reading his WhatsApp message. He was a cool guy, that was for sure, and he still liked me.

"Sure. What is wrong with Lucky? Why are you taking her to the vet?"

"She's okay. Taking her for her yearly jabs. She's missing you."

"She told you that? Dr. Dolittle."

"I can tell by the way she looks at me when I mention your name."

I laughed. "See you both soon, then."

"For sure," he answered.

The kitchenette was narrow, with pails of roses all over the floor; there was hardly any room to move. I started carrying them back into the shop. Sam was serving a customer, so she pointed to various corners to display them.

"They look wonderful, Alexia. As I thought, you will be good at this. You're a natural at flower arrangement," Sam said.

I smiled. Putting flowers into pails and vases could hardly be described as flower arranging. "They are magnificent. Can you keep six of the orange ones for me, please? I would like to surprise Mum—a present for the new house. I will pay for them, of course,"

She smiled. "I will put aside twelve of the orange roses, from both of us. How does that sound?"

"Oh, Sam, thank you. Mum will love them."

"They do look unusual," said a woman in the shop, "I will have a mixture—my husband loves roses. He always says that roses are the most romantic flowers. They bring so much joy into a home."

Sam smiled.

She sounded posh, I thought. I went back to the kitchenette and carried on with bringing the rest of the vases back and displaying them where Sam had said. I'd picked the last pail of red velvet roses when I felt something creeping up my arm. It felt weird and hairy. I instantly thought of Mum saying that Sam had found a dead snake in the boxes. I started to panic and looked at my arm. I shouted, dropped the pail, lost my balance, and fell backwards, landing on the empty boxes. It was a huge, black spider moving up my arm towards my neck. It kept grasping onto my arm as I fell. I was terrified. Sam came running, the only thing I remembered was me shouting, "I've been attacked by a poisonous spider. I'm going to die, get my mum!" Then I lost consciousness.

After that, I felt that I was being pulled through a tunnel by a massive animal, with red eyes glaring at me.

I woke up later that afternoon with a killer headache. I was terrified to open my eyes. I must have moved my arm, because Mum and Dad said at the same time, "Alexia, how are you feeling?"

I opened my eyes a little. "I've got a headache," I answered.

My parents looked at each other. "Thank God you're alive."

I was so glad to see my parents. Looking around, I knew that I was in hospital from the medical trolley at the bottom of the bed. I was wearing a hospital gown, and there was a needle stuck into my right arm. That was another giveaway. Mum leaned in and kissed my cheek. Dad kept hold of my left hand. They both looked exhausted.

I was about to ask if it was a poisonous spider and if I'd been poisoned when Dad said, "No, it has not bitten you, but you have to stay overnight for observation because there is a bump on the back of your head. That must be the reason for the headache." He reached out a hand and rubbed my forehead.

I smiled and attempted to sit up. Dad helped me, arranging the pillow against the bed so that I could sit up. "Why can't I go home if—"

"You'll be out in the morning after ward rounds. Dr. Stefan just wants to keep you overnight. Headaches can mean different things," said Mum.

"Like what?" I asked.

"Head injuries and possibly blood clots," she said.

That was my mum with her nursing hat on. No point arguing. I just stared at her. She gave me a reassuring smile. I was a little concerned that she would be anxious or panicking. At the on-set of her depression, she would have been panicking and pacing around in such situations. But she was calm. I really didn't want to stay in hospital, but I also knew that I didn't have a choice in the matter.

"Is there any food in this place? I'm starving."

Dad laughed. "If you're hungry, Alexia, that is very reassuring," he looked at Mum. "Darling, what time do they serve dinner?"

"Normally between half five and six o'clock," she said.

Dad glanced at his watch, "Not for another two hours. I will go get you something to eat. What would you like?" he asked.

"Sandwich. Chicken, please."

Dad pulled onto his feet and strolled across the room towards the door. He was about to open the door of the single room I was in when he suddenly stopped. Mum and I stared at him. I wasn't sure why I was in a single room—maybe because they suspected that I'd been poisoned, and they had to keep the other patients away.

"I almost forgot—there's a young man in the waiting area who is refusing to leave the hospital until you woken up," said Dad. "What do you think, Jessica? Is our Alexia well enough to receive visitors?"

Mum laughed. "It is visiting time, and it's up to Alexia," Mum said, looking at me.

I knew that it must be Justin but pretended to be surprised and asked, "Who is it?"

"Your boyfriend," said Dad, smiling.

"Um, Mum, have you got a mirror and some makeup? Is my hair okay?"

She gave me a questioning look.

"Alexia," Mum said, staring at me, "I've almost lost you to an aggressive poisonous predator that didn't just want you for its web but to inject you with its poison. You are lucky to be alive. I believe Justin wouldn't mind if your hair was messy or you didn't have any makeup on. Anyhow, you're not one for plastering your face. You are our pretty girl with or without makeup." She looked at Dad, who was still hovering by the door and said, "Why don't you go and call Justin? Then we could go out together while I call Sam. She asked me to call as soon as Alexia came round."

Dad nodded and left without another word.

I quickly used the adjoining bathroom while Mum rearranged the bed linen. The bathroom had a tiny mirror. My hair was messy, and my eye looked puffy. I washed my face, ran my fingers through my hair, used the bathroom, and got back just in time to hear a knock on the door.

Mum looked at me, waiting to ask the person in, so I said, "Please, Mum, can you see who it is? It is a hospital—a knock by my expected visitor is not necessary."

She smiled, opening the door. "Justin, how lovely to see you," she said.

"Mrs. Collins, it is a great pleasure to see you too. I understand it is not too serious, thank God," he said.

Gosh, he was so charming.

"No, the doctor says they would like to keep Alexia overnight for medical reasons, but she'll be home tomorrow."

He walked over to me. I immediately noticed the worried lines on his face. Justin looked at me, like, forever before he smiled. Mum and Dad left us alone. He pulled one of those black plastic chairs closer to my bed and sat down. I was sitting atop of the bed with my legs crossed.

"How did you—?"

"When I arrived at the florist shop to find it closed, I asked the people in the bookshop next door. They said that there had been an accident—someone had been taken away by an ambulance. I instantly thought that something must have happened to you. I dropped Lucky at home and came to the hospital. I was asking at reception when your parents arrived."

I looked at him. He was obviously showing all the signs of a concerned boyfriend. That was good enough for me. I wiggled myself against the pillow, staring at Justin, not knowing what else to say.

"How are you?" he asked, still staring at me.

"Headache, but I'm okay," I said.

He took my hands, "God, I'm so glad it didn't kill you."

"Lucky me," I said.

"Alexia, I couldn't bear the thought of losing you to another guy, let alone a dirty-fanged poison-injecting spider," he said with a sad face.

My stomach rumbled really loud. I laughed.

"That sounded like hunger. Your dad told me that he was going to get you something to eat."

"Yeah," I said.

He reached into his jeans pocket and said, "I've received correspondence from Vanessa Helena Amadeo. Can I read it to you?"
"Really?"
"No joke," he said.

Dear Mr. Hunter,
    Thank you for your interesting letter saying that you and your girlfriend were planning to visit the Lakes in the near future. I understand that you know the Lake District well, Mr. Hunter, from your scouting days. If you happen to be in the area, you are both welcome to pay me a visit. However, do call beforehand, as I have a pet goat that thinks she is a dog and chases anyone who comes close to the gate. I don't have fans. You are the first person to write to me. I'm glad that my little book has brought comfort to those in need. But I'm not famous, nor do I attract busloads of visitors like the World of Beatrix Potter.
Yours sincerely,
Vanessa H. Amadeo

"Oh my God, she has actually replied to you. That is amazing."
    He leaned in, kissed my cheek, and said, "What do you say we take a holiday as soon as you get out of here, before you're tempted to go back to the florist shop."
    "Yes, that is a very good idea."
    A smile curled in the corner of his lips. "I will book us a hotel as soon as the doc gives you the all clear."
    "How exciting," I said.

CHAPTER TWENTY-FOUR

My parents arrived with a chicken sandwich, a pack of cheese crisps, and a bottle of water. The bell rang, and I jumped, thinking that it was a fire, but Mum explained that it was to indicate the end of visiting time. Justin held my hand and said that he would come back at the next visiting time, which was at six o'clock. I was saddened that he had to leave, but I was also starving. Dad left with Justin, saying now that I was fine, he needed to get back to the new house to sort things out. Mum said that the end of visiting time did not apply to a worried mum who needed to make sure that her daughter ate.

While I ate my sandwich, Mum told me that she had spoken to Samantha, who reported that the pest control had spent hours searching for the spider. She was not allowed into her shop till it was found, but the good news was they had found it alive, nestling in between the boxes. They confirmed that it was of a poisonous sort, and it was taken to a safe pace. Mum also said that Sam would come to see me later. She must have lost money with all that distraction, I thought.

I stared at Mum.

"You are my lucky girl," she said.

"I suppose. So I wouldn't dwell on if and maybe," I said.

"That's the spirit," she replied. We both laughed.

When the care assistant knocked with my dinner, mum told him that I'd already eaten. He offered us a cup of tea and asked if I would like some ice cream.

"What sort of ice cream?" I asked.

"The choices are chocolate, vanilla, banana, and strawberry," he answered.

I knew Mum could not resist chocolate; it was our favourite.

"I would say no thank you to tea, but can I say yes to chocolate ice cream? And can my mum have one too, please?"

"Of course," he said, going off to get the ice cream.

Mum glared at me. "Alexia, that was very cheeky."

I laughed. "I knew you wanted one, and I didn't want to share mine."

The care assistant came back with two chocolate ice creams and said, "Enjoy."

"Thank you," said Mum.

We enjoyed our ice cream while I told Mum that Justin had received a letter from a favourite author who lived in the Lakes, and he had invited me on holiday to the Lake District.

"Oh, well, you're over eighteen," she said slowly. "Your father was saying earlier that once we're settled in the new house, we should have a holiday."

"Well, I think that you and Dad deserve it. How is the move and the new house?" I asked.

"We were just about to unpack when Sam called. But there's not a shadow of doubt—that house is the best thing for us all."

"I agree," I said.

"That was delicious ice cream, even for a hospital."

"It made everything better," I said.

"Talking about better; you're looking so much better."

"What a shame that I have to spend the night in here instead of my own bed in our new house."

"I know, but it is for your own good," she reminded me.

Mum left after a while, saying that she had to help dad unpack before he put everything in the wrong places, but they would come back later. I told her that there was no need to come back, that Justin was visiting at six, and if I needed her, I would call.

She kissed my cheeks and said, "Are you sure?"

"Positive."

After Mum left, I curled underneath the duvet on my back, looking around. It was cream but clean, and it did not smell like a hospital. I could hear people chatting outside and laughter. It was reassuring that I was not alone. I thought of Mia. I was sure if she knew I was in hospital she would have called. That reminded me—I had not seen my phone. I was about to get out of bed in search of it when I got distracted by yet another knock on the door. How could anyone sleep with all this knocking?

"Miss Collins," said a woman's voice. "I'm Nadia, one of the nurses, can I come in?"

"Sure," I answered, as if I had a choice.

Nurse Nadia was slim and dark skinned with huge brown eyes. She was pretty, and she held a small silver tray.

"How are you feeling?" she asked with a smile.

"I'm good, thanks. Can I go home?"

"Doctor advises that you stay overnight. Have you had dinner?"

"Yes, thanks. Have you seen my mobile?"

"Oh yes, the ambulance staff gave it to me when you were brought in. I have put it in the locker."

"Can I have it back, please?"

"Of course," she said, looking at my hand, "I will remove this needle. You don't need it anymore."

I nodded, watching Nurse Nadia carefully pull the plaster off, pull the needle out of my hand, drop it on the silver tray, and put a little round plaster back. "Now, before I fetch your phone, can I get you anything else to eat or drink? It is important that you have plenty of fluids."

"No, thank you. Just my phone, please."

As she walked away, I thought of how caring and empathetic she was. Mia might have tried to call me if she knew, but with my phone locked away, she wouldn't be answered. I had best chill and get used to my surroundings. That was when I noticed that the room curtains looked all newly done. The room was modern, with an en suite bathroom and basic furniture, including a tiny wardrobe, one bedside drawer, two black plastic chairs, and a small TV on the wall. There was another knock, followed by Nurse Nadia's voice. She had brought my phone. I asked her for the remote control for the TV, and she said that I had to buy a card to be able to watch the TV.

I did not have any money; that was a nonstarter. She handed me my phone, saying that if I needed anything to ring the nurses' bell, which I noticed was on the wall next to the bed. How crap—a TV that you needed to pay to watch. I was tempted to call my parents to ask them to bring me some money, but I called Mia instead. She picked up on the first ring.

"Alexia, how are you?"

"In hospital after being attacked by a fugitive spider on my first day's work," I said slowly.

"Oh my God, are you okay?" she asked.

"Yeah, doctor insisted I stay overnight. Be home tomorrow. How are you?"

"Time-of-the-month pain," she answered.

"Sorry, how is your dog?"

"Adorable."

Mia told me that her mum was about to serve dinner and that she would call me tomorrow. We said bye. Mia suffered period pains—I knew that if she wasn't in pain, she would not get off the phone that quickly. Samantha came in soon after with the most beautiful bouquet of orange roses I'd admired earlier and my rucksack. I told her that I was sorry for what had happened, and she said all that mattered was that I was all right and that the spider had been found. She brought a vase in which she arranged the roses and put it on my bedside table. She did not stay long; she told me that she had to go home to feed her cats. She hugged me, saying that the flowers should go home with me.

I walked to the small window and looked out at the housing estate beyond and the cars flying past on the street below. Nothing special—not for me, anyway—just an observation. This was not how I was hoping to spend my Saturday evening. I checked my phone; it was six fifteen in the evening. I started to panic that Justin had changed his mind—he did say that he would be back at six; he was late. I decided not to dwell on it and went back onto the bed with my rucksack. I remembered that when I left home this morning, I had put my two books in it: *Seeking Angels* and *The Mind of Wizards*. I did not feel comfortable in that hospital gown, but I couldn't find my clothes to change into; Mum must have taken them home.

I was about to start reading *Seeking Angels* when there was a knock. "Come in," I said, thinking that it would be the nurse checking up on me again.

I quickly put my book under my pillow—I did not want to explain anything to a nurse. *Seeking Angels* was personal to me; I'd only shared it with Justin and his mum. I was glad to see him. Justin walked in with a big smile on his face and his man bag across his shoulder. He was carrying another bag that I recognised as one of my mum's. He walked over to deliver a kiss on my lips.

"Sorry, I'm late. I stopped at your home to pick up this bag; your parents were going to bring it, but they had a busy day. So I offered, as I was coming in. And if there were any concerns, I told them I would ring."

"Thank you for the offer; yes, it has been a busy day for my parents," I said.

He took his bag off his shoulder, put it at the end of the bed, and sat a little closer to me on the bed. He smelled deliciously of a very expensive aftershave.

"I hope Mum has sent me some clothes. Can you pass me the bag, please?" I asked.

"Sure," he said, handing me the bag.

I unzipped it. I was so glad that Mum had sent my favourite pyjamas with Winnie the Pooh on and my Tigger slippers, as well as jeans, a top, and trainers for going home. The bag also contained my toiletries bag, a brush, two cans of Diet Coke, and a small box of chocolates. I laughed.

"Would you mind if I changed into more appropriate pyjamas?"

"Not at all," he said, looking at me with a smile.

I went into the bathroom with the bag, changed into my pyjamas, and splashed a little perfume on. I saw in the tiny mirror that I looked more presentable. When I reentered, he had put the two black chairs together to form a table. There were all sorts of bits of food, and two pieces of red-velvet cake—another of my favourites. I glanced at the bedside table, there were two bottles of green smoothie; I assumed it was apple.

"What is this?" I asked.

"I promised your parents that I would make sure you had some decent food—not that hospital crap. I know you had a sandwich, but that won't last you till morning."

I laughed. "You are so charming. That is why my parents like you."

He beamed. "Well, I was planning to take you out for something to eat. This was not supposed to happen."

You would think he was going to feed a small army. He had brought his iPad. We ate, sitting on the edge of the bed while he showed me hotels at the Lakes. He told me that we would choose a hotel together, so we chose one with a lake view and he booked it. Then we watched *The Princess Diaries 2* on his iPad, sitting next to each other on the duvet on the floor with our backs to the wall. He had one arm around me. I was a little worried that the nurse would come in and ask him to leave, as it was past visiting time, but it did not happen. I shared my chocolates, and we laughed and joked about the movies. He must have gone home after I fell asleep. When I got up the next morning, I was on the bed and my parents in the room. All the food gone, but the apple smoothie was still on my bedside table. The room was tidy, and my parents told me they were waiting for the doctor.

"Did you sleep well?" Mum asked.

"Yes, Justin brought some food; we ate and watched a movie, and then he went home."

I noticed them exchange looks, but they didn't comment.

CHAPTER TWENTY-FIVE

Three weeks later, Justin and I drove to the Lake District. It was an amazing drive, with mountain views and sheep and lambs in the meadows. I was a little nervous at first; I'd never been away without my parents. Then there was sleeping in the same room thing, let alone sharing a bed with him.

Mum had insisted that we go on a girly shopping trip after I came home from hospital. We met up with Sam, who had taken a morning away from her florist shop. She was still feeling responsible for the spider attack, even though it wasn't her fault. She had given me a day's wages and some extra money for me to get something nice to wear for my weekend in the Lake District. We stopped in a little café with an assortment of chairs that did not match, and Mum and Sam ordered black coffees, I had a hot chocolate, and we each had a piece of carrot cake on Sam's recommendation. I discovered that my mum was such a funny one to be out with, cracking naughty jokes.

Sam reached across the tiny wooden table, took my hand, and she looked at me, like, forever before she said, "I supposed it is a romantic weekend away?"

"No, nothing like that," I answered.

Mum put her cup on the table. They both laughed, gazing at me, and then Mum said, "Alexia is over eighteen—there's nothing wrong with a little romance. Justin is a sensible boy, and you're a level-headed girl."

I giggled, eating the last piece of my cake. I looked around the café. It was busy, with young and older people alike enjoying tea, cakes, and laughter—a lively atmosphere. I did not comment on my mum's remarks. I was happy and reassured that she was contented—she was without doubt making fantastic progress in her quest to beat depression.

I was almost nineteen and still a virgin. It was about time I started living my own life, and yes, I was looking forward to whatever happened between Justin and me. But it was not something I wanted to admit to my mum or godmother, Sam.

Sam insisted on paying, saying that it was her treat. Mum and I did not protest—we knew that we would have lost. Onwards to the shops. I bought a few new things for my adventure: two dresses, underwear, a pair of jeans, a T-shirt, and a pair of shoes with a little heel to wear with my dresses. I'm not normally a dress girl, but Mum and Sam said I looked sophisticated in dresses, so I didn't want to disappoint.

Justin had picked me up at three in the afternoon in a white Mercedes SUV. On the way, he let me choose the music, so I played a mixture of songs—Adele and boy-band music. Everything was perfect. He was a careful driver. The magnificent scenery of the countryside made me realise that my mum's illness had deprived us of exploring such beauty. He kept asking me if I was okay.

I nodded. Then I relaxed into the leather seat next to him, reminding myself that I really fancied him. When he pulled up outside a huge Victorian building just after six in the evening, I recognised Belle-Force, the hotel we had chosen together that night in the hospital. He switched off the engine, removed the key from the ignition, and turned his head to look at me.

"That was a great drive," I said.

"I'm glad you enjoyed it," he said.

I laughed. It was obvious that I was nervous; he still looked gorgeous and relaxed after the long drive. He gave me a reassuring smile, but he did not comment.

After gazing into each other's eyes, like, forever without saying anything, he broke the silence and said, "Shall we?" I pushed a button on the key and the boot of the car sprung open. I was looking in the mirror, about to open my door.

"Just a moment, Miss Collins—that is my job."

I pretended not to know what he meant and asked, "What is your job?"

"Opening doors for my girlfriend."

"Oh, be careful, I might get used to that," I joked.

"Your wish is my command," he said with the biggest smile.

He opened his door, rushed to open mine, took my hands, and helped me out. Mum had bought me a small pink fancy case with wheels. Justin had brought a big brown case, also with wheels. Compared to my case, you would think he was going away for a month. He handed me my case, took his, locked the car, and took my hand as we strolled along a stone-paved path leading to the massive, open mahogany door. A young woman with an Eastern European accent and amazing blue eyes greeted us at the reception.

"Good evening—may I take your name?" she asked.

"Justin Hunter," he answered.

She looked down at her computer. "Oh yes. Mr. Hunter, you have booked a suite with a lake view and you are staying with us for three nights—that includes luxury afternoon tea with champagne," she said, looking up from her computer.

"That is correct," Justin said.

"On which day would you like the afternoon tea?" she asked.

Justin looked at me. I did not remember that afternoon tea
with champagne was included in the booking, but then again, I
was suffering from a spider attack.

"When would you like to have the afternoon tea?"

I shrugged my shoulder. "Tomorrow, maybe?" I said.

He smiled, "Tomorrow it is."

"That is fine, when you are ready, let the staff know. The afternoon tea is served in the conservatory or the outdoor terrace if you
prefer. Your table for tonight's dinner is booked for eight thirty in
the west dining room," she said, handing him the key. "Would you
like a hand with your bags?"

"No, thank you,"

"Room 475. It is on the top floor. The elevator is on your right,
next to the stairs. Enjoy your holiday," she said.

"Thanks," said Justin as we moved towards the stairs. I knew
that he wouldn't take the elevator. He preferred the stairs; something I first noticed when he came to my flat. He popped the key
in his pocket and picked up both cases. I followed him up the red-
carpeted stairs that were very elegant.

We stopped at the door of room 475. He unlocked it and
stepped aside, holding the door open to allow me inside. It was a
really spacious, impressive room with a floor-to-ceiling window. I
could not help but leave him to sort the cases on his own; I walked
across the room, opened the door, and stepped onto the balcony
to admire the fabulous view. It was early August, still light, and the
lake was amazing. He followed and stood behind me, wrapping his
arms around me and kissing my neck.

"What do you think?"

"Pretty amazing."

"What would you like to do first?"

"Um, I need to use the bathroom and phone my parents. I
promised to let Mum know that I've arrived safely."

"Okay, after that maybe we could change and head to the bar
for a drink or two before dinner?"

"I'm not a drinker, you know."

"I'm sure you can have a juice, coke, or whatever," he said.

I wiggled out of his arms, went back in, located the bathroom, and shut the door behind me. I looked at myself in the mirror, wondering if he knew that I was a virgin. He had been loving and caring—the question had never arisen. I wasn't so naive to assume that a weekend with my boyfriend would not involve sex, but I wondered when the subject would come up. When I returned, the curtains were still open, the door was closed, and he was bent at the waist, putting his clothes into the drawers. He glanced at me.

"I'm done. I'll go where you have just been, and you can let your parents know that you are safe," he said.

"Sure." I grabbed my phone from where I'd dropped it on the dresser, sat in a chair by the window, and called Mum. She answered on the first ring.

"Alexia, I was just thinking of you."

"I'm fine. We have arrived. Everything is good."

"I'm glad. Enjoy yourself," she said.

"I will. Say hello to Dad." I did not want to start a long conversation. I would tell Mum about the view when I got home.

"Okay," she said.

Justin reentered the room. "Have you spoken to your parents?"

"Yeah, it was just to tell them that I was alive. You know what parents are like—worrying unnecessarily."

He laughed, took my hands, pulled me onto my feet, and sat on the chair with me on his lap. He kissed me, and I returned his kiss. I felt comfortable in his arms, kissing. I wrapped my arms around his neck. I once dreamt about this moment, but I never thought it would happen—not to me anyway. I wasn't pretty enough for any boy to call me their girlfriend. I had seen boys and girls at college kissing, holding hands. I wasn't jealous; it was an observation. My life before my dad came back was loneliness and watching my mum in her own darkness of depression. I never dreamt that someone like Justin would care for me.

"Alexia, have you ever made love before?"

"No, I'm a big V for virgin," I answered self-consciously.

"Oh, do you want to?"

I nodded. "Er, I would like to but not now."

"No, I didn't mean now," he said.

He kissed me and then took my hands together. We stood looking at the view of the lake. It had started to get dark and peaceful. After a while, I took my stuff out of the case and into a drawer. I went into the bathroom to change into a dress and new shoes, and to let my hair loose and draw it behind my ears, showing the earrings he'd given me for my eighteenth.

When I came back into the room, he had changed. He glanced at me with a smile. "You look beautiful," he said quietly.

I smiled. It was romantic, but I wasn't ready to start undressing in front of him—not yet anyway. "What about that drink you promised me earlier?"

He laughed, took my hand, and together we walked along the corridor and down the stairs. We sat on a sofa at the bar next to each other. A young waiter with light skin and dark hair approached and handed us a list of drinks. I noticed the variety of cocktails. I'd never had cocktails before, but I remembered Mia telling me that she had been to parties with her parents and had cocktails. There was always a first time for everything.

"What about a cocktail?" I whispered.

"Yeah, good idea. What about a champagne cocktail?"

I stared at him. "That is expensive, Mr. Hunter."

He beamed. "Only the best for my gorgeous girlfriend. You are a very lucky girl to escape an exotic predator, remember."

I laughed.

The waiter came back, and Justin ordered two glasses of rose champagne. Suddenly, *boom.* Thunder. Lightning forked outside.

"Was that supposed to happen?" I asked.

"It always rains in the lakes," he told me.

We sipped champagne, gazing into each other's eyes, him whispering sweetly into my ear. After two glasses of fizz, we ate a dinner of chicken and chips, washed down with sparkling water, and then went up to our room. He closed the curtains while I brushed my teeth. He then used the bathroom. I took my dress off and dived underneath the duvet in my bra and underwear. When he joined me, my heart was racing. He melted me in his arms, we kissed, and then everything was off; our bodies merged into one. He was a perfect gentleman, and I loved every moment. It could only be described as the most romantic time between lovers.

The next morning, I awoke still in his arms. We showered together. After a continental breakfast, he phoned Vanessa Helena Amadeo from the number on her letter, she answered after six rings.

Justin put his phone on speaker so we could both hear the conversation.

"Hi, Ms Amadeo, it's Justin Hunter. My girlfriend and I would like to visit you, as you suggested in our correspondence," said Justin.

"Mr. Hunter, yes, you and your girlfriend are very welcome. Let's say half past eleven. I will put my goat in her cage, as she would attack you otherwise."

"See you then," said Justin, before clicking his phone off.

The rain stopped, so we agreed on a scenic walk, stopping at The World of Beatrix Potter on the way, and then took a taxi to Vanessa's address. We stumbled across a bunny running from the woods into the road. It almost got flattened by a passing car.

"Oh, Peter Rabbit—running away from Mr. McGregor's garden," Justin joked.

I could not help but laugh. Looking up at him, I saw a twinkle in his eyes.

"I still have the set of books—Peter and Mr. Jeremy Fisher are my favourites—but I've never managed to visit the Lakes with Mum's illness, you know," I said.

He nodded. "My parents took my sister and me when we were young. It is a fascinating place."

He did not let go of my hand and kept asking me if I was all right. We stopped along the way to enjoy the picturesque scenery. We kissed, and he told me that he loved me and that we should go away more often. I told him that I would like that, but I needed a job to pay for things. He laughed.

"It is my pleasure to take you somewhere that you can be free to enjoy. We both have had some distressing times. This is about relaxing and putting the past to sleep."

Justin sure was a caring guy. Like me, he had been through a great deal of stressful events—he with losing his sister, and me with my mum's depression. I understood that I still had my mum, but he had lost his sister forever.

On arrival at The World of Beatrix Potter, I was impressed by the whole attraction, from watching the video of the story illustrations to enjoying the animals, their costumes, and the garden, it was all magical. Beatrix was a wonderful writer who could bring stories to life.

Then we took a taxi to Vanessa's address. It was about a twenty-minute drive. When the taxi stopped at the gate of a stone cottage, an elderly woman was potting in the vegetable garden. We stepped out, and Justin paid the driver. The woman waved.

"Mr. Hunter. You found me. I take it this is your girlfriend. Pretty girl," she said, looking at me with a smile.

"Yes, this is Alexia. She is the reason we're here. Your book has been an inspiration," said Justin.

"I wouldn't have survived without your book. Your story has kept me alive," I said.

"Well, do come in. I'll introduce you to Elma, my goat who thinks she is a dog." Elma the goat was in a big metal cage in the back garden, as if she were a wild animal rather than a little goat. She was making goat sounds, jumping up and down, trying to break free.

"Now behave, and say hello to our visitors, Elma," said Vanessa. Vanessa was a round, silver-haired woman in her seventies, maybe older. She was much older than I'd expected. I imagined she wrote the story when she was a young girl, and having read the book, I still expected to meet a younger woman author whose mother ran off with the lighthouse man. I wanted her to tell me what had happened to the parrot that bit her mother's finger and whether the lighthouse man was a murderer.

Justin kept hold of my hand as Vanessa led us into her cottage. Inside, it was bigger than it looked. She invited us into her sitting room, where a coffee table was set with scones, plates, and rose-decorated napkins.

"Do sit while I make some tea," she said, and she went off to what I assumed was her kitchen.

Justin and I looked at each other. He did not have to spell it out—his face said it all: what the hell. There were stuffed birds and owls everywhere. It was a bit like Beatrix Potter's animals, but on a smaller scale. We both heard her talking to someone or something.

"Shall we leg it before she kills and stuffs us both?" he whispered.

I giggled. There was no sofa, so we sat on old-fashioned chairs that the stuffing was poking out of. That she had used the stuffing to stuff the birds came to mind. Vanessa came back with a tray, a teapot, and china cups.

"I apologise for keeping you waiting, but I had to feed my parrot, or we wouldn't have any rest," she announced.

"Is that the same parrot you talked about in your book—the one who bit your mother's finger?" I asked.

"No, dear, if only," she said with a sad face.

"So what happened to that parrot?" I insisted.

"I suspect it found a home elsewhere, or it started entertaining in a zoo. This one belonged to a friend who has passed away. I promised him I would look after it. Tea, and help yourself to scones," she said.

I don't really like scones, but as she had gone to so much trouble, I ate half with jam and cream. It wasn't bad; my mum always said that if someone offers you something to eat, you should try it even if you don't like it. So I took my mum's advice. Justin was enjoying the scone or pretending to.

She must have noticed us looking at the stuffed animals.

"Those were his too. I can't bring myself to get rid of them. Are you visiting the Lakes for the day?" she asked, changing the subject.

"No, we're spending a few days at Belle-Force hotel," said Justin.

"Oh yes, one of the finest hotels on the lake," she said.

"Vanessa, what happened to your mother and the lighthouse man you talked about in your book—was he really a murderer?" I asked again.

"To be honest, I cannot remember anything of what I wrote, but I'm glad you two seemed to have enjoyed it. Though I'm thrilled that you've come to visit me, I have had enough questions about my past. I don't like to revisit buried wonderland."

Justin and I exchanged looks. It was obvious that the mention of her mother and the parrot were causing her pain. I apologised. We finished our tea and said good-bye to Vanessa Helena Amadeo. We decided to walk back to the lake. Justin insisted we take a boat ride back to the hotel to fully appreciate the tranquillity and continue to enjoy the picturesque scenery. Sitting next to him, watching the birds flying outside the window of the boat, I felt a tiny bit disappointed that I had not learned much about the woman whose book had saved me from losing my mind, but then I looked at it from her point of view. She didn't want to talk about her mother or anything about her book or if she had written other books. Perhaps Vanessa had written the book to prevent herself from losing her own mind.

By the time we got back to the hotel, we were ready for the afternoon tea and a glass of fizz. But we wanted it to be special, so we had a shower and changed. I wore my other dress and shoes. We were the only couple enjoying afternoon tea. I didn't eat the scones but ate cakes and sandwiches. It was delicious and incredibly romantic.

Afterwards when we were truly alone in the bedroom, sitting by the window and watching the ducks on the lake, Justin kissed me and asked if I was disappointed that Vanessa refused to talk about her story.

"A little," I said, "but I also understood that it must be painful for her. Thank you for taking time to come with me."

"Hey, it's not over. That is what a boyfriend does for his special girl. I hope we'll have more time away together."

"Oh yes, this is very special!" I said.

Printed in Great Britain
by Amazon